Frank, he's going

What? What are

The wolfcat—Jeff the wolfcat. He's going to try and kill the apes. For food.

Jeff wouldn't do . . .

Look at the gauges.

We can't allow him to do that! Foy will skin us alive!

But that's what he's going to do.

We've got to stop him!

How?

Break the connection. Get Jeff back here. Wake him up.

Can't do it in time. And it won't help. The wolfcat will attack them anyway, by itself. He must be starving.

We can t let it happen!

We can't stop it.

THE WINDS OF ALTAIR

BEN BOVA
THE WINDS OF

A TOM DOHERTY ASSOCIATES BOOK

THE WINDS OF ALTAIR

Copyright © 1983 by Ben Bova

All rights reserved, including the right to reproduce this book or portions thereof in any form.

First printing: May 1983
First Mass Market Printing: January 1988

A TOR Book

Published by Tom Doherty Associates, Inc.
49 West 24th Street
New York, NY 10010

An earlier, much shorter version of this work was published by E.P. Dutton under the same title, copyright © 1973 by Ben Bova.

ISBN: 0-812-53227-9
Can. No.: 0-812-53228-7

Printed in the United States of America

0 9 8 7 6 5 4 3 2 1

To Michael

CHAPTER 1

He knew that he was going to die.

Jeff Holman lay back on the couch, every nerve in him screaming with tension. He bit his lip to remain silent as the black woman sealed the cuffs that restrained his wrists and ankles, then fitted the gleaming silvered helmet onto his head.

He tried to pray, tried to remember the prayer for martyrs. But he couldn't. Somewhere in the crazy turmoil racing through him, he wondered if being killed by scientists counted as martyrdom. A martyr to secular humanists? He had never heard of that before.

The couch felt warm and soft, almost alive, as it molded itself to the contours of his body. The helmet, though, was cold, hard. It buzzed faintly with an electrical hum that Jeff could hear inside his head. The woman adjusted it carefully. Jeff looked into her face. It was utterly serious, grim.

With the weight of the helmet, Jeff could barely turn his head. Out of the corner of his eye he saw Dr. Carbo standing in the control room on the other side of the heavy plastiglass window.

Why me? Jeff asked himself for the hundredth time. The scientists had needed a student volunteer and their computer had picked Jeff.

He wanted to leap out of the couch and run away, or at least say something to them to show that he was not afraid. But his mouth was dry, his throat raw with fear. Scientific experiment, they had said. Absolutely necessary for the project. For the good of the Village. But Jeff knew better. The rumor among the students was that two of the scientists had already died in this laboratory, and a third was hopelessly insane. That was why they wanted a student "volunteer."

Finally everything was ready. The black woman moved away, out of his field of vision. Jeff heard the heavy padded door to the control room close softly and he realized that she had left him in this death chamber alone.

"All right, Jeff," Dr. Carbo's voice sounded louder inside the helmet than the soft-spoken Italian usually did. The faint trace of his accent came through. "Please try to relax; your blood pressure and other indicators are rather high."

Relax, sure, Jeff thought. Try praying. Try meditating. Nothing. His mind was a terrified blank.

"If there is any trouble," Carbo went on, "I will stop the test at once."

Sure, right away. As soon as I'm dead.

"Are you comfortable, Jeff?"

He started to answer, gagged slightly, then coughed to clear his throat. "Yes," he finally replied, weakly.

"Just close your eyes," Carbo said. "Pretend that you're going to sleep."

Jeff squeezed his eyes shut, knowing that they would never open again. He waited for . . . what? He didn't know what to expect. Pain? The warm glow of drugs? The oblivion that Nirvan promises but never delivers?

He saw little glimmers of light, patterns that drifted across his closed eyelids. The electrical hum of the helmet seemed to shift subtly, changing gradually until it sounded almost like the wind moaning across the desert scrubland of home. The patterns of light and darkness began to dance, vibrate. Starbursts flashed out painfully. His body tensed, jerked against the restraining cuffs, spasmed. Then he felt a cool tingling along his entire body, like a soft breeze.

It *was* a breeze.

He could feel it rippling the fur along his body. He could hear it as it sighed through the forest.

He opened his eyes.

He was sitting on his haunches at the top of a hill, sniffing the breeze for danger and food. Hunger was a deep dull ache within his massive body. But something more than hunger troubled him. Something was wrong, different. He growled, a thunderous rumble that came from deep inside his cavernous chest. Down at the foot of the hill, a malicious-looking snaky thing with feathers looked up sharply, hissed once, then flapped awkwardly into the air and flew into the trees. When a wolfcat growls, all other creatures flee.

He's made contact! Jeff heard somewhere in his brain.

9

But it was a strange, alien voice from far away. It had nothing to do with him. He barely understood the words.

He rose from his sitting position, up onto all six legs, his claws digging into the grassy soil. Down at the bottom of the hill, where the forest began, in there among the trees, there was food. This hilltop was a good place, *his* special place, where he slept and brought his kills to eat. No other beast came to the hilltop when he was on it. And when he left, only the scavengers dared trespass—the lizard-hawks with their ugly crooked beaks and the small, scampering, yellow-eyed jackals whose teeth could crack bones.

He trotted majestically down the hillside, three tons of wolfcat, tall at the shoulder as a young tree, lean with muscle and hunger, moving as swiftly and silently as a gray cloud—a gray cloud armed with dagger-long teeth and claws like scimitars.

He's definitely in contact.

Can he assume control?

Wait . . . give him time. Don't push too hard.

The forest was a darker green than the hillside's open grass. Overhead, up among the swaying, sighing branches, clouds scudded by on the wind, dark against the brightness of the sky. The forest was almost as dark as night, but the whispering breeze brought a symphony of odors from the deep delicious woods: flowers and grasses and mosses and—most important of all—the scents of animals, of food, of the swift-footed antelope that fought with antlers and sharp hooves, the tasty little tree climbers, the shaggy, bristling diggers that stayed in their holes during the daylight hours.

It was early morning and the distant sun was only a bright patch in the sky, low on the horizon, sending long shadows out ahead of him. He saw his own shadow, the hulking immense shadow of a young male wolfcat loping across the meadow grass. Later in the day, he knew, Altair would be too bright to look at directly.

Altair. The word seemed to belong in his mind, yet it felt odd, alien.

Into the forest he stalked, silent as a serpent, claws retracted now and every sense alert for food or danger. The older wolfcats—the fully-grown males who had many females and cubs—could laze during the day and let their females do the hunting for them. They defended their cubs and their hunting territory, and did little more. Young wolfcats had to hunt alone until they were strong enough to challenge an adult for one of his younger females.

He glided through the underbrush silently, his immense bulk slipping through the trees like a wraith. *The stream is where the prey will be.* He was downwind of the stream; already he could smell the antelope drinking there, but they could not catch his scent as he approached. *Good.* His empty stomach drove him forward.

You're not going to let him stay and . . .

I hadn't intended to, but he seems so well-linked with the beast, I'd hate to pull him back now.

But . . .

It's okay. If he's going to work with the animal he's got to allow it to eat.

Strange sounds, he thought. Buzzings, like insects flitting near. But these buzzings were inside his head.

With a shake of his massive mane, he advanced carefully, slowly now, through the underbrush that carpeted the forest floor. He could hear the gurgling of the stream, not far away. He flattened out in the brush, belly to the ground, and inched forward. Then froze. Six of the antlered grass-eaters were standing at the stream's edge, their sharp hooves in the cold racing water. Some of them would bend down to drink while their fellows stayed erect and alert, probing the forest nervously with large wary eyes and erect twitching ears.

Suppressing a growl, he bunched his muscles and got ready to spring. When the nearest one puts down its head to drink . . .

He leaped out of the brush, a gray streak of death aimed at the nearest antelope. His shattering roar froze them all for a split-second, but then they bolted off in all directions, bounding and springing through the underbrush. His intended prey jumped too, but straight ahead, into the middle of the stream. The water was shallow but swift, the footing uneven and slippery. The antelope stumbled. That was all the advantage that a wolfcat needed.

He touched the ground once with his six clawed paws, then leaped again and landed on the antelope's back. A slap of a forepaw broke the creature's neck while his mid- and hindpaws grasped the animal's meaty body firmly. They fell together with a splash.

He scrambled up and dragged his prey to the stream bank, using both forepaws and walking on his hind- and midlegs. The smell of blood, of meat, was overpowering. Raising his great black-muzzled face to the sky, he bellowed out a roar of triumph that shook the ground.

Stop it! Stop it! Get him back!

Yes, of course, you're right. No need to let him take part in the feasting. Terminate.

CHAPTER 2

Jeff opened his eyes and was back aboard the ship.
He knew that his body had never left the couch, and
yet—he shuddered.

They hadn't killed him. They had turned him into . . .
into an *animal*. A powerful, bloodthirsty, hunting beast.
They had taken his mind, his awareness, *himself*, and
turned him into a wolfcat down there on the surface of
this hell-hole planet they were orbiting.

An animal. Jeff felt himself trembling uncontrollably.
He knew they were going to do it. They had explained
it all to him for a week before they tried this test, yet
the shock of its reality made him feel weak. They

turned me into an animal, he repeated to himself.

And it had been exhilarating. The power of that beast! The strength of him. The thrill of hunting down that antelope and *getting* it.

The woman unstrapped his wrists and ankles while Dr. Carbo carefully lifted the helmet off his head. Jeff did not move; he felt exhausted.

The woman looked into his eyes searchingly. "Are you all right?" she asked.

Her name was Amanda Kolwezi, Jeff knew. She was rather good-looking, even though she was black. Not really black, he noticed for the first time. Her skin was more the color of the giant tree boles down on the planet, a rich dark brown. High cheekbones. Eyes that looked almost oriental.

"Jeff," she repeated, "are you okay?"

"Yes." He tried to nod his head. "I'm okay." But his voice was weak, little more than a whisper. He felt drained, almost helpless. Yet terribly excited.

Dr. Carbo came up beside her, smiling at him. "Just take it easy, Jeff. You did a fine job. Very good work."

Jeff started to sit up on the couch but everything seemed to sway around him. The room started to slide off at an angle and he fell back onto the soft padding.

"Jeff!" Amanda grabbed his arm.

"It's all right," Carbo said. "A little disorientation. It's to be expected. He'll be okay in a minute or two."

But he turned and stared worriedly at the monitoring panels against the wall. Jeff knew that they kept track of his body's condition: blood pressure, temperature, pulse, things like that.

For a scientist who was so important to the Village, Dr. Carbo did not look impressive to Jeff. He was short, actually a shade shorter than his assistant,

Amanda; round-shouldered, round-faced, his thinning brown hair always looked like he'd just stepped in from a windstorm. He was soft-looking, even his voice was a soft tenor. His normal posture was a slouch, where Jeff expected the kind of ramrod stiffness that his teachers and Elders inculcated. Instead of the drab gray coveralls that all the students wore, this scientist dressed himself in bright-colored tunics and comfortable slacks that made him look slightly like a round little clown. Dr. Carbo's face had a brownish swarthiness to it, and he was a little jowly, with the darkish shadow of stubble across his chin, like somebody who shaved himself instead of using the treatments that kept a man's beard from growing for months at a time.

Maybe the treatments don't work for everybody, Jeff thought. Or maybe scientists don't believe in them. As a Believer, Jeff followed his Church's rules and kept his face bare. Only the Elders were allowed to grow a beard. Of course, Carbo might be a Catholic. Jeff had no idea what *they* believed.

Amanda came to him with a cup of steaming liquid in her hand. "Here, Pathfinder, drink this."

"Pathfinder?"

She grinned at him. "Look it up in the library. It's a book you ought to read."

A book. He shrugged and accepted the cup from her hand. Strange how the back of her hand was so dark, yet the palm was perfectly pink. The liquid felt warm and good. Jeff wondered how the raw meat of the antelope, still blood-hot, would taste. The thought startled him, jarred him so thoroughly that he almost dropped the cup. Neither Carbo nor Amanda seemed to notice, though.

"How do you feel now?" she asked.

"Okay . . . I guess."

Dr. Carbo nodded and headed back for the control room. Jeff drained his cup and put it down on the couch's headrest.

"Think you can stand up now?" Amanda asked.

"Yeah. Sure."

She slid her arm around his shoulders and helped Jeff to his feet. He stood uncertainly for a moment, finding that he actually was enjoying the nearness of her, the touch of her hands, the scent of her skin. Jeff had never been this close to a black woman before. Back home, in the Church-run housing enclaves with their shrubbery-decorated electrified walls and laser-armed security systems, blacks were the equals of whites — so equal that they lived in their own enclaves, went to their own schools, and even prayed in their own churches.

With Amanda at his side, Jeff walked on spongy legs out of the small laboratory chamber with its stainless-steel walls and plastic-tiled flooring, through the open door to the control room. The walls were soft-textured there, the floor thickly carpeted. Dr. Carbo was sitting at the central console, talking on the picturephone to a narrow-eyed, white-haired, bony death's-head of a man. Jeff recognized him instantly: Bishop Foy, chairman of the Council, the unquestioned leader of the Village.

"He's made solid contact with the animal," Carbo was saying. "If we can establish that good a contact every time, we can use this wolfcat and then go on to adapt other animals."

Bishop Foy's lips pulled back in something approaching a smile. His big uneven teeth made him look even more like a skull. "Do you believe that other . . . " he hesitated, noticing that Jeff had entered the control room, " . . . other students will be able to establish contact with the creatures down there?"

Carbo made a vague gesture with his right hand. "We shall see. If one student has done it, it stands to reason that others should be able to do so."

Jeff felt a pang of anger at that. He didn't know how many of the scientists and Elders of the Village had tried to make contact with the animals down on the surface of the planet. He had been the first to succeed. Instead of congratulating him, they were saying it wasn't anything so special. If he did it, others could. With the anger, though, came an instant reflex of guilt. Pride, Jeff told himself. Sinful pride. He offered a swift, silent prayer to Nirvan. But the prideful anger still simmered inside him.

"So your conclusion is that this test was a complete success," Foy said. His voice was thin and scratchy; it sounded irritable, as though even this good news annoyed him.

Carbo answered, "A success, yes, of course. But we don't know yet if he can control the animal."

"I understand. But he did make firm contact. All the sensory inputs came through? Even visual?"

"Yes," Carbo replied.

"Then the animals aren't blind, after all."

"Those scaly-looking areas across the top of the head are infrared receptors. We knew that. Apparently they have a visual cortex and can see in the infrared wavelengths, where we can't."

Bishop Foy nodded silently.

"Polchek and his zoologists will want to bring a wolfcat up here to dissect," Carbo muttered.

But Foy's thoughts were elsewhere. "The crews

who've been down to the surface reported that vision is nearly useless there, even with infrared sensors. The cloud cover blocks out all the sunlight. You can't see more than five meters ahead. Your sense of distance and direction goes haywire."

"Our sensors must be set at the wrong frequencies," Carbo answered. "Come and look at today's tapes. When we see through the animal's eyes everything is bright and clear."

Foy blinked his narrow, deepset eyes and said nothing.

"If a wolfcat were brought to Earth," Carbo went on, his soft voice picking up speed with enthusiasm, "it would probably be just as blind as we are on Altair VI."

"Perhaps. Perhaps," Bishop Foy replied impatiently. "Bring the tapes to my office as soon as you can. There are many details I must discuss with you, in private."

The picture screen abruptly went blank.

Carbo stared at it for a moment, then made an elaborate shrug that took in his shoulders, arms, hands, and even the expression on his face. He turned to Amanda and said, "Make sure he gets plenty of food and rest. He has a lot of work ahead of him."

Amanda gave a small sigh and motioned Jeff toward the door that led out of the control room. Jeff went with her, feeling more like a laboratory animal than a human being. *I wonder if they're going to dissect my brain when this is all finished?* he asked himself.

The official name of the ship was *Melvin L. Calvin*, but the five hundred students, Elders, and scientists aboard called it simply, the Village.

It did not look like the sleek starships Jeff had seen on video shows, nor like the ungainly rockets that had explored the Moon and the planets of Earth's solar system—all of which were so far away now that the Sun itself was no more than a pinpoint of light, one of the millions of stars that could be seen through the ship's viewports.

The Village was a cluster of globes, bubbles of plastic and metal linked by spidery tubes. It had no front or back in the usual sense, no up or down. Each globe housed a few dozen people, or was a facility of some sort: a library, a meeting hall, a grassy park lined with trees.

In actuality, the Village was like a barge or a houseboat that had no real propulsive power of its own. It had been towed from Earth to Altair VI by a squat, stubby vehicle that was little more than a massive engine with a tiny bubble of living quarters for its crew: Captain Olaf Gunnerson, his son, daughter, and son-in-law—and their computer.

Gunnerson was a professional star-sailor, and his vehicle was nothing more than a tugboat. But it was a tug that could span interstellar distances, for a fee.

His engines were gravity field drives, not rockets. Generating the kind of gravity warps made in nature by Black Holes, the gravity field drive allowed the human race to expand outward among the stars—again, for a fee.

The first to go had been robots, of course. Riding the earliest gravity field ships, they had explored the dead gas giant worlds of Barnard's Star and returned in less time than it took light to span the distance. Physicists argued bitterly over whether or not the gravity drive actually propelled the ships faster than light. One of the rock-bottom principles of the universe was being shaken, and campuses all over Earth trembled with the ferocity of the debate. The younger physicists declared that Einstein had been overthrown. Their elders insisted that this was not possible; even though the ships had *seemed* to go faster than light, what had actually happened was that the gravity warp had bent spacetime so out of shape that the ships left the universe momentarily and then re-entered it elsewhere, lightyears away.

The politicians didn't care which way the physicists decided. They now had a tool in their hands that they could use.

"Colonize the stars!" they cried.

They started to build starships, to be filled with the poorest, most ignorant, least desirable people of Earth. "Export your problems," they whispered to one another. "Send them off to where they'll never bother us again."

But before they could do that, before they could exile the unemployed, the uneducated, the untouchables, they had to send out their best and their brightest—to pave the way.

The least desirable people of Earth could not be launched out into the interstellar void to fend for themselves. Not even the politicians were that insensitive. Robot ships were built to find Earthlike worlds, and then teams of the eager, bright, idealistic young men and women of Earth were sent to prepare these worlds for the colonists to come.

To *these* young men and women, the politicians sang of challenge and commitment. "Tame the new worlds!" they urged. And the eager, bright, idealistic young men and women took up the challenge. Just as the politicians' social technicians had predicted they would.

Jeff made his way back to the dome where he lived. He was twenty-three years old, an undergraduate degree in meteorology freshly awarded him. He had been aiming for a doctorate in weather modification when the call to "Tame the new worlds!" had overtaken him. After six months in the Village, he wondered if he had chosen wisely.

He was slightly taller than average, yet no one thought of him as "big," not even he himself. Jeff had the broad shoulders and strong arms of a farm boy, and a slow, easy smile that often prompted strangers to think he was easy-going, perhaps even lazy. His hair was dark and thick, his eyes the gray of a stormy sea. His psychological profile showed him so close to all the norms that the social technicians thought him dull (only the psychologically weak or unusual interested them). They were quite surprised when their own computers picked him as the student best qualified psychologically to attempt making contact with one of the animals of Altair VI.

He lived in one of the Village's domes with nearly three dozen other students. They were all within a year or two of his own age. Half of them were women. All of them, naturally, were reliable Church members, Believers who had been sent by their Church to tame this new world for all the Believers who were to come as colonists.

All the students had taken vows of celibacy as a matter of course, just as they had while on campus. Sex was a powerful weapon for either good or evil; it had to be channelled properly.

Their vows were duly registered with Bishop Foy, the spiritual and temporal leader of the Village. The vows were also protected by the network of security cameras that watched every dormitory room, every meeting hall, every corridor and chamber of the Village. And the cameras were backed up by dorm mothers in each of the Village's residential domes. The dorm mother in Jeff's dome was a flour-white giantess with the unlikely name of Bettina Brown. The students had quickly dubbed her Brunhilda. She was flaxen haired, fully two meters tall, almost as wide, and strong enough to pick up two students Jeff's size, one in each ham-fisted hand, and shake them until their teeth rattled.

Between Brunhilda and the computer-monitored sensors, Jeff and his dorm mates had little chance for mischief. And little time. Their hours were filled with work, study, and prayer. Even though the gravity field drive made the jump to Altair almost instantaneously, Gunnerson's tug had to tow them for two months out to the edge of the solar system before the jump could be made, and then for two more months they spiralled inward to take up an orbit around the sixth planet of Altair.

The time was spent studying planetology, planetary engineering, and all the other special knowledge they would need to transform Altair VI into a fully Earthlike world, suitable for large-scale colonization. And praying. Prayer was as much a part of their lives as breathing. They prayed when they woke up in the morning. They prayed before each meal and after it. Every task began with a prayer for strength and success. Every night ended with a prayer that their efforts to tame Altair VI might prove fruitful.

But they might as well have saved their energy. Their first few weeks of struggling with the wildly inhospitable environment of Altair VI convinced even the most devout Believers that the planet was beyond redemption, no matter what the robot explorers had reported.

If they could have, they would have returned to Earth.

"It was weird," Jeff was saying to his friends. "It was like—blast, I can't tell you what it was like. There aren't any words for it."

They were sitting around one of the larger tables in the dome's autocafeteria, a dozen students, including Laura, the redhead that Jeff had lusted over so badly that he spent hours in the chapel trying to pray her out of his mind. It did little good.

Most of the students added decorations to their drab coveralls, to put a little color and individuality into their dress: a bright scarf, a medallion or a jewelled pin. Jeff himself clipped the gold symbol of his school's meteorology club to his breast pocket every morning. Laura did not need any decorations; her flame-red hair and jade-green eyes were all the color she needed.

Like all the student domes, theirs was built to remind them of a university campus. The rooms around the periphery of the dome were deliberately decorated in the genteel shabbiness of academia. The center of the dome was a grassy quadrangle edged with scrawny young trees that stretched their branches toward the artificial sun hanging at the dome's zenith.

Every student had an individual dormitory room. Jeff's had seemed spacious to him when the voyage began; now it was starting to feel cramped and tiny. The autocafeteria was a favorite meeting place, with its food dispensers, long straight rows of tables, and general openness. Even the surveillance cameras were tucked away where they wouldn't be too obvious.

Dom Petrocelli was the self-appointed student leader of Jeff's dome, not because he was bigger physically or faster intellectually than the others. Dom was a Convert, and always behaved as though he had to prove to the other Believers that his faith was true. Besides, he seemed to enjoy hurting people with his sarcastic tongue.

He leaned back in the plastic cafeteria chair, making it squeak under him, and eyed Jeff with an amused smile.

"So you got inside the wolfcat's brain, is that it?" he asked.

"Right," Jeff said eagerly. "It was like we shared our minds."

"Must have boosted your IQ a hundred points!" Petrocelli smirked.

The others laughed, and Jeff joined the laughter too, even though he was thinking what a wolfcat could do to Petrocelli's thick skull.

As the giggling died down, Laura—who was sitting next to Jeff—asked, "You really killed one of those deers?"

Jeff replied, "The wolfcat did. I didn't try to stop him."

Laura was very pretty, especially when she smiled. Red hair the color of autumn leaves, deep green eyes, skin like cream. "I don't understand how this mind-sharing business works. It sounds kind of . . . well, psychic, almost."

"No," Jeff said. "It's just electronics. You know the kind of electronic probes they put into criminals' brains, to control their violent behavior?"

Laura and several others nodded.

"Well, that's what we're using. Dr. Peterson and a team of scientists went down to the planet's surface a few weeks ago, stunned some of the animals, and put probes in their brains."

Petrocelli yawned ostentatiously. "We all know that. And they almost killed two men doing it."

Ignoring him, Jeff went on, "Then they hook somebody up to the equipment in Dr. Carbo's lab. It's kind of like a video show, except that you see what the wolfcat is seeing, you feel what he feels. Your mind is linked to the wolfcat's mind."

"I thought they weren't going to try that anymore," one of the other girls said. "Isn't it awfully dangerous? The first two people who tried it both died, didn't they?"

"And Dr. Mannheim is in the cryonics freezer, totally out of it."

"Well, I made contact," Jeff said, trying to keep his pride from showing. "We've made the first step toward taming this planet."

Petrocelli started to make a comment, but the sad-faced little engineer next to him said first, "Well, we'd better tame this planet. They won't let us back home until we do."

Nods of agreement went around the table. They all knew that they would either tame Altair VI or die there.

CHAPTER 3

Dr. Francesco Ignacio Carbo sat in his room, staring at the stars. He knew that Earth was an invisibly tiny speck in the universe gleaming before his eyes. He could not even identify the Sun out of the countless sparks of light that glowed against the infinite darkness.

Darkness and light, he said to himself. The eternal struggle.

Dr. Carbo's quarters were a spacious combination of office and apartment, handsomely furnished with his own possessions. Bishop Foy and the Elders frowned on such luxuries as a waterbed and genuine oil paintings, but Carbo insisted that he was not going to travel almost seventeen lightyears from Earth without some of his own comforts. Still, he missed the cool marble floors of his apartment in Rome, the noise from the streets, the warm night breeze and the splashing of the fountain in the Piazza di Navaronne.

He sighed heavily. Not for these austere Americans, the marble splendor and gaudy crowds of Rome. Here on this ship, this antiseptic womb of metal and plastic, there was no room for the splendors of the pàst, no patience for noise or dirt or people who splashed in fountains and sang late into the night.

You knew what you were getting into when you agreed to go with them, he told himself. But another part of his mind argued, How could you know what they would be like? How could you understand how it would be to live with these puritans day after day, month after month?

He leaned back in his recliner chair and stared at the stars through the plastiglass window set high up along the curving wall of his living room. The stars stared solemnly back, unwinking. They reminded him of Bishop Foy and the Elders. Even their smiles were without joy.

Carbo was the only bachelor among the scientists and social technicians of the Village. There were a dozen single women and unmarried daughters among the staff, and hundreds of nubile maidens among the students. But scientists did not fraternize with the students, who apparently took their vows of celibacy quite seriously, from what Carbo could see. Either that, or they were afraid of getting caught. Even with the staff women, half of them belonged to the Church and the other half seemed to be intent on getting married.

It was an uncomfortable situation for an unmarried Roman of thirty-two.

But face it, Francesco, he told himself, Rome was becoming unbearable.

The Eternal City had endured invasions by the Huns, the Goths, countless mercenary armies, the Nazis, and even swarms of American tourists. But year by year the streets became less and less safe. Starving children begged for pennies, and if you turned your back, they or their older brothers took with violence what they could not earn peacefully. As the ancient buildings and monuments crumbled under the attack of automobile pollution, the very fabric of society was falling apart under the weight of too many hungry, homeless people.

Carbo remembered his own childhood, running through the narrow twisting streets of the city, always in a pack with other boys his own age, always armed with at least a knife. It was a miracle that the Jesuits took him in, a ragged homeless waif, before he either was killed in the streets or killed someone else. The priests were stern and unyielding. They caught him in one of their periodic sweeps of the city, threw him into the terrifying machine that tested his mental abilities, and decided he was going to receive an education. Period. No recourse, no appeal. Little Francesco, who never knew his father and barely remembered the teenaged girl who was his mother, now became a ward of the Jesuit order.

The Jesuits had long boasted, give us the child for its first six years and he will be ours forever. Francesco was too old and too street-wise for such brainwashing. But under the inflexible discipline of the priests he learned to become a clean, polite, soft-spoken young student. And he fell in love — with learning. For the mind-testing machine had been quite accurate: beneath the filth from the streets, Francesco had a first-rate brain. By the time he was fifteen, he had discovered science and plunged into studies that even his Jesuit mentors could not fathom. On his twentieth birthday they reluctantly released him to the University of Pisa, reminding him sternly that he would be in the shadow of Galileo. To their credit, the Jesuits had led the Vatican to exonerate the contentious Renaissance genius some four centuries after he had been condemned by the Inquisition.

Francesco nodded at the priests' mention of Galileo, but in his heart he was more interested in the work of Fermi and the more contemporary Italian scientists.

At the university he found that a special branch of physics intrigued him more than any other: electronics. And this led him into the fascinating world of neuro-electronics, where the transistors and microcircuitry of molecular electronics were being linked to the nerves and brains of human test subjects.

By the time he was twenty-eight, Dr. Francesco Carbo was an international celebrity, and widely touted as a certainty to be awarded the Nobel Prize. His work in neuro-electronics had produced the miniature probes that now could actually control human behavior. Criminal violence was becoming as extinct as the dinosaurs, because every violent offender was fitted out with a neuro-electronic probe that controlled his antisocial behavior.

The streets of Rome were safer, thanks to Dr. Carbo. The streets of every city in the world were safer. And Dr. Carbo could not sleep because of the nightmares his guilt spawned in his own mind.

The world government seized on the neuro-electronic

stimulator as the solution to violent crime. But in reality, the probes merely made such crimes impossible. They did nothing to solve the problems that caused the crimes. The police swept criminal offenders off the streets and into the hospitals for their quick, almost painless brain surgery. But poverty still existed. Hunger still existed. The vast gap between the rich and poor grew wider.

Pacified criminals no longer threatened society. Instead, they tended either to go insane or commit suicide. But crime still existed. The neuro-electronic stimulators themselves became a major source of crime; electronic stimulation of the brain's pleasure centers replaced narcotics and even sex as the world's premier vice. People died smiling with pleasure, starved to death or their brains destroyed by an overload of current.

By the time he passed his thirtieth birthday, Dr. Carbo had himself flirted with the idea of suicide. Even though the world government banned public report of the harmful effects of the neuro-electronic stimulator, he knew what was happening, and the knowledge filled him with remorse. Only his years under the Jesuits stayed his hand. He had never fully accepted their religious teachings, but their moral principles had sunk into the fiber of his being. If it is wrong to kill, then it is equally wrong to kill oneself. Logic was the Jesuits' most effective weapon, especially against a man in love with knowledge.

Still, he turned away the committee from Stockholm when they visited him. Politely, he told them that he could not accept a Nobel if it was offered, because the neuro-electronic probe was as much a curse as a blessing. They tried to argue him out of his remorse, but once they realized it was genuine, they withdrew, telling each other that Carbo is still very young, and the Prize can be granted him ten, twenty, even thirty years later.

It was only by chance that Carbo learned of the starflight missions. He had been seeking solace in the arms of beautiful women, and one night as he and his current *amour* lay side by side on his warm, enveloping waterbed, she said languidly:

"I will have to say farewell to you tomorrow, Francesco."

A pang of alarm tightened his chest. "Farewell? But why?"

"Tomorrow I leave . . . "

"Leave Rome? You?"

He turned to look at her and saw, in the shadows, that she was smiling sadly. "I am leaving Earth. I am going out to a distant star. I will be gone for three years, at the very least. Perhaps I will never return."

She expected him to be shocked, to try to argue her out of it, perhaps even to cry at their separation. Instead, he was silent. She had prepared herself for an angry scene or for the tenderest kind of parting. She was totally unprepared for silence. It infuriated her and she left the next day still seething with resentment.

Carbo flew that same day to the World Capital, in Messina, and ploughed through seven layers of bureaucrats and secretaries before he found the man in charge of the star missions. He was an American, of course, and his assistant was a Russian woman of middle years who sat in a corner of the American's office, stolid as a cow, suspicious as a policeman.

"So you're interested in helping to colonize the stars,

are you?" the American asked jovially. He was a big man, with a loud voice and a wide smile.

Carbo said in English, "I would like to learn more about your plans, yes."

He knew that the American did not recognize his name, but the computer files had produced a complete background of Dr. Carbo, and the American kept glancing at his computer terminal's screen as he harangued his visitor.

Carbo sat patiently through the whole lecture. The American behaved like a low-class real estate salesman trying to palm off some worthless acreage on a gullible foreigner.

"But before we colonize the stars," he finished, "we must tame the planets for the colonists to come."

"I see," Carbo said.

"Now then," the American hunched forward and leaned both arms on his desk, "we have a very interesting videotape presentation that will show you the planets that are going to be targeted . . . "

"That won't be necessary, thank you," Dr. Carbo said. "I think I understand the situation now. You have been most helpful. Thank you."

The American shrugged. "Let me send the tape to your home anyway. Just in case you think of some questions after you leave."

Carbo nodded.

"Are you interested in joining one of the missions?" the Russian woman asked, in a midwestern American accent that exactly mimicked her boss.

"Yes, I am," Carbo heard himself say.

"Which one?"

"The next one to leave."

"No matter where it is going?"

He shook his head. "It doesn't matter."

The American's grin became dazzling. He touched a button on his computer keyboard, and a single sheet of paper slid noiselessly from its printer slot.

"Sign here," he said, pushing the contract across his desk toward this slightly crazy visitor.

On the plane back to Rome, Carbo told himself that it really did not matter where they sent him. The important thing was that colonizing the stars would help to solve the *real* problems of Earth, the problems that his neuro-electronic stimulator had only swept under the rug. The poor would at last get their chance for a new life, on a new world. And he would help them to succeed.

He could not believe the medieval Catholicism of his Jesuit mentors. Or so he thought. But the moral imperatives were ingrained in him nevertheless. He finally felt as if there was something to live for, as the plane carried him back to dirty, teeming Rome.

Now he leaned deep into his relaxer chair and it tilted far back for him, becoming almost a couch. He stared up through the window at the stars that hung like brilliant diamonds in the darkness beyond the ship. The room was softly lit, like the early twilight of a springtime evening back in Rome, An odor of fresh blossoms wafted on gentle currents of air. If he liked, Carbo could change the room's scent to jungle perfume or the tangy snap of the sea, merely by touching a button. Another of the luxuries that Foy and his Elders frowned upon.

With another reluctant sigh he slid his right hand to the control keyboard set into the recliner's armrest. But not to change the room's scent or lighting.

On the far side of the curving wall his desktop view-screen glowed to life and a green light winked on to signify that his computer terminal was waiting for his input.

"Data for the record," he murmured, knowing that even a whisper would be picked up by the microphone built into his chair. "Put in the correct date and time, eh?"

A glance at the screen showed him that the time and date had been entered, in glowing yellow letters.

He hesitated before starting, then said, "Let me see all the physiological data on today's test subject."

He sat up, and the chair moved with him so that its soft fabric never left his back. The computer screen showed a complex graph with intricate curves of various colors to indicate Jeff Holman's heart rate, brain rhythms, breathing, and other vital functions.

"*Bene*. Next."

The screen's picture flicked to show another graph, more curves.

Dr. Carbo studied the information for a long while, going through graph after graph. Then he watched a replay of the tapes that showed what the wolfcat saw when Jeff was in contact with it.

He cleared his throat as the tape ended and the screen went blank.

"Okay, for the record." His voice became louder, firmer, as if he were talking to an auditorium full of students. He had spoken nothing but English for nearly six months now, and even though the computer could automatically translate from Italian, it was English he spoke now.

"Since all our tests with members of the staff resulted in failure, we decided to investigate the use of one or more of the students to make contact with the animals on the surface.

"This decision was not made lightly. Deep hypnotic interrogation of the staff members who failed to establish neuro-electronic contact with the animals revealed that their minds withdrew instinctively from the 'mind-sharing' effect that such contact entails. Psychological analysis indicates that a fully-formed adult personality is too rigid to accept the mindsharing. Adults will not — and probably cannot — allow their *personas* to mingle with that of an alien animal."

Carbo examined his words as they were printed on the computer viewscreen. He made a couple of minor editorial changes, then continued:

"The psychology committee, after lengthy discussion . . . " he grinned, remembering the furious arguments among them, " . . . accepted my suggestion of testing one or more of the students as a contactor. My reasoning was that if an adult personality fails to establish neuro-electronic contact, then perhaps a younger, more malleable personality would be better suited to the task. We have more than four hundred such personalities aboard this ship: the students."

Carbo stopped and peered at the words for several long minutes. That sounds pretty damned supercilious, he said to himself. On the other hand, it is perfectly true. With a barely detectable shrug of his shoulders, he resumed:

"The first two test subjects, one male and one female — computer, fill in their names and ages — were both failures. The reasons are still being studied by the psychologists. The third test subject . . . " he hesitated, then remembered, " . . . Jeffrey Holman, age 23, was an unqualified success."

Carbo paused again. He thought, Now we can start pushing the young man and see how much he can do for us. See the big genius scientist lean on the lowly graduate student.

The robot probes had reported that Altair VI was sufficiently Earthlike for colonization. It was slightly smaller than Earth, and had a slightly lower gravitational pull. Its chemical composition was very Earthlike and there was liquid water on its surface in copious amounts. It was covered with a global, perpetual deck of thick cloud, but that helped to shield the land below from the merciless glare of Altair, a star ten times brighter than the Sun.

What Carbo and his fellow scientists found when they reached Altair VI was a planet whose "Earthlike" air was laced with a lethal level of methane, a world covered by acid clouds that blanketed the land and seas in eternal inky blackness despite the fact that the ground was slightly fluorescent. And the abundant water was frothing with ammonia and other chemicals that made it useless for humans.

Captain Gunnerson laughed bitterly when he realized what the ship's instruments were telling them. "Smog in the air and poison in the water. This planet is naturally polluted. It doesn't need us to foul it up!" Then he bid them good-bye, with a bitterly cheerful prediction: "You'll never tame this planet, no matter how hard you try."

The staff directors and Church Elders met in Bishop Foy's conference room, a narrow, austere chamber bare of decorations.

With all the enthusiasm of a mortician, Foy told them grimly, "We are here. The Church has spent an enormous sum of money to send us here. Even more money and effort is being spent to send shiploads of converts here to colonize this planet. It would be sinful to waste all that money by giving up on Altair VI without even trying to prepare it for colonization."

They all gloomily, reluctantly agreed.

"Very well, then," Bishop Foy said firmly. "Let us begin our task with a prayer."

Martin Foy was the fourth son in a family of eight children, all but the last two being boys. He had grown up on a ranch in the dry scrubland of eastern New Mexico, where it took an acre of semidesert to support a single cow. Despite the laser-drilled deep wells and fusion-powered desalted water pumped all the way from the Gulf of California, Martin watched his father grow poorer and more desperate each year as the price of beef sank in the face of genetically-engineered meat substitutes. Finally, the same day that Martin received his First Communion, the corporation that owned the ranch sent his father written confirmation of his worst fears: the ranch was being converted into a housing development for lower-class city folks who were being resettled by the government.

Martin had always been a good Church member; his parents insisted that all their children be Believers. When he found that he would not be allowed to attend college because his father could not afford it, he enrolled in the nearest Church seminary. While his brothers and two sisters accepted whatever jobs they could find, while his mother wasted away and finally died of cancer and his father withdrew into a private world within his own mind and had to be shipped off to a state hospital, Martin lived the austere but secure life of a novice, then curate, and finally the pastor of a small mission in Bangladesh.

It was there in his sweaty, fetid cubbyhole of an office, behind a ramshackle building that passed for a mission church, that he read about the colonization of the stars. The star missions were enormously expensive, but his Church was going to fund one of the first ones, to a world called Altair VI, and the Church was looking for qualified ministers to lead the way.

Wise in the ways of the world, the Church offered an inducement to volunteers: they would *own* the new world they helped to redeem. Right and title to the land would be given to those who volunteered to prepare the way for colonists.

The temptation overpowered Foy. He left his pitiful mission in Bangladesh with unseemly haste, qualified for leadership of the expedition to Altair VI by sheer tenacity and force of will, and accepted a promotion to Bishop, effective the day the starship left Earth orbit.

So he led the prayer that began the immense task of redeeming Altair VI. Bishop Foy knew well that if the planet was not ready for colonization in three years, he would be replaced. He would lose his share of the wealth that this colony would someday generate. His career would be finished.

The other staff members had no desire to lose their share of the colony's eventual wealth. With the exception of Dr. Carbo, each scientist, social technician, and minister had little on Earth to return to. Yet, strangely, it was Carbo more than any of the others who led the work to tame Altair VI.

They had a huge task facing them, and they knew it. They had to alter an entire planet, almost the size of Earth, enough to make it livable for millions of colonists. If they succeeded, they would become rich. If they failed, they would return to Earth empty-handed, three years older, with nothing to show for their efforts except defeat.

Change the air. Purify the water. Alter the climate. Turn hell into Eden.

They tried.

But they soon found that humans could not work down on the planet's surface. Even in their sturdiest pressure suits, it was too dark and dangerous to remain there for more than a few hours at a time. Robot machinery, controlled from orbit, fared little better. The corrosive air and stubborn plant life knocked the machines out of commission too quickly for them to do any good.

Then Carbo got his chance for personal salvation. There were huge, powerful animals on the planet. Use them. Implant neuro-electronic probes in their brains and control them from the ship. The staff agreed, and excitement ran high. Landing crews of pressure-suited men stunned several animals and implanted the probes in their skulls. Two of the men were seriously injured. All of the animals, with the exception of one wolfcat, died within a few days of the implantations.

Then it turned out that no one on the staff could establish contact with the implanted beast. Carbo's heart sank, and the entire staff turned funereal. Reluctantly, Carbo suggested testing the students. The staff argued against it, but in the end it was either the students or total failure.

Two months almost to the day after they first established orbit around Altair VI, Jeffrey Holman scored their first success by making solid contact with the wolfcat.

CHAPTER 4

The tubes that connected one globe of the Village with another were thickly green with foliage. It was like walking through a miniature forest. The floor was grass, soft underfoot and fragrant. The curving tube walls were lined with shrubs and stunted trees, many of them bearing edible fruit. In addition to providing a share of the Village's food and a large part of its oxygen, the greenpaths provided something even more important to the people who lived inside this artificial world: beauty.

The greenery also helped to camouflage one of the disconcerting things about the Village. The globes were clustered together tinker-toy fashion, with no particular respect to direction, either front-to-back or up-and-down. Since gravity inside the Village was artificially generated and controlled, it always *felt* as if you were walking along a straight and level path under normal Earth gravity. But the tubes actually made strange turns and bends, like the tracks of a roller coaster, plunging sickeningly downward at one point, arrowing up at an impossible angle somewhere else. Even though you could not feel it as you walked along, your visual sense would send up wild alarm signals when it saw your path suddenly veer sharply to the left and drop out of sight. The shrubs and greenery kept you from seeing ahead far enough to frighten your inner mind.

Jeff and Laura were strolling slowly through one of the greenpaths along a trail that wound past a lush garden of flowering shrubs and oriental trees. Neither of them realized that the sounds of an Earthly forest were missing: there were no birds singing, no insects, no water splashing. Only the faint pervasive background hum of the ship's electrical power systems which provided the heat and light necessary for life.

Taking her arm, Jeff led Laura off the trail, pushing through the shrubbery toward the all-but-hidden curving metal wall of the tube. Finally they found what they were seeking, a viewport that looked down on the planet below them.

"It looks so bright," Laura said.

Jeff nodded wordlessly. The planet hung outside, seemingly motionless, enormously massive and brilliant in the harsh light of Altair. Its surface was a featureless disk of white clouds, as smooth and unbroken as a seamless veil. It shone beautifully against the darkness of space.

"That's going to be our home," Laura said.

"When we get it tamed."

She looked up at him. "When *you* get it tamed."

"It's not . . ." He stopped, feeling flustered and flattered at the same time.

Laura smiled at him, as if she knew something that he didn't. Jeff wanted to hold her, to pull her close and lie down with her and forget about those who watched. But he could see, peeking at them from between the gnarled branches of a dwarf tree, the unblinking red eye of a security camera.

Trying to control the urges burning within him, Jeff said, "It's funny, you know. Like, it's not really *me* anymore. When I was with that wolfcat . . . it's . . . I can run as fast as a rocket . . . I'm *strong* . . ."

Laura stepped close and rested her head against his shoulder. He put his arm around her and stroked her flame-red hair.

"You've always been strong, Jeff."

"Not like that!"

"I don't mean muscles," she said, almost in a whisper. "Any gorilla like Petrocelli can have muscles. I mean you're strong where it's important — when you set out to do something, it gets done."

"Yeah . . . well, maybe."

"No maybes. You're the only one who's made this crazy thing work, aren't you? I knew that if anybody could make contact with those animals down there, you could. The scientists couldn't, could they? But you did."

"I'm just lucky."

"No you're not. You're not afraid of it. You like it. You enjoyed being in contact with that animal, didn't you?"

"Wolfcat," Jeff corrected automatically. "Yeah, I think maybe you're right. It's kind of scary, though. I didn't simply make contact . . . *I was him!*"

Laura looked up at him, her green eyes searching. If she was fearful about the future, she did not show it.

Jeff fell silent, his mind filled with the memory of being down in that forest, of having immense strength at his command.

"They're going to need more volunteers," Laura said.

It was an effort to bring himself back to reality. "I suppose they will. Do you want to try it?"

Her eyes went wide. "Me?"

"Sure. Why not?"

She shook her head. "Dr. Carbo won't take women volunteers. He's such a male chauvinist!"

"No," Jeff laughed. "He's just Italian."

"It's more than that," Laura said testily. "Several women have already volunteered, you know. He turned them all down. Said it was too dangerous."

"Well . . . it could be dangerous."

"You're doing it."

"Yes, but . . ." Suddenly Jeff felt confused. He didn't know which side of the argument he wanted to be on.

Less sharply, Laura said, "I'm going to volunteer anyway. And if he turns me down I'll take him before the Council and charge him with prejudice."

"And what'll you do if he accepts you?"

For a moment Laura said nothing. Then, eyes suddenly sparkling, she replied, "Why, then we can be down on the surface of the planet together, Jeff."

"Together," he murmured. Holding her closer, he gazed into her upturned face and kissed her. Laura twined her arms around him. He could feel her heart pounding against him; his own pulse thundered through him. Everything else vanished from his mind: the ship, the planet, the universe disappeared and there was only Laura and himself alone together in an infinite breathless moment.

"UNAUTHORIZED CONDUCT," the Village computer's flat impersonal voice blared through the loudspeakers set into the tube's ceiling. "UNAUTHORIZED CONDUCT. STOP AT ONCE OR BE REPORTED TO THE COUNCIL."

Jeff gazed bleakly up at the loudspeaker's grill as Laura pushed slightly away from him.

The computer was silent for only long enough to scan their faces. "JEFFREY HOLMAN AND LAURA MCGRATH, YOUR CONDUCT IS IN VIOLATION OF YOUR OATHS OF CELIBACY. BE WARNED."

They looked at each other, a mixture of guilt and relief on their faces.

"Maybe I can figure out how to turn off the cameras, someday," Jeff muttered.

Laura giggled. "If you do, the Village will vibrate itself out of orbit inside of ten minutes."

Hand in hand, they made their way back onto the greenpath and headed down the tube back toward their dome.

Halfway home, they saw Brunhilda hurrying toward them, her face florid with unaccustomed exertion as she lumbered along the greenpath.

"There you are!" She pointed a thick, blunt forefinger at them. "You should both know better. I'm ashamed of you! Curfew time is almost here and you're off in the bushes, making the computer sound warning alarms!"

Towering over them, Brunhilda separated Jeff from Laura and walked between the two would-be lovers.

47

They expected a lecture and grim threats of punishment, but instead Brunhilda was almost mild as she told them, "Just because he is such a hero right now, Ms. McGrath, is no reason to succumb to temptation. And you, Mr. Holman, don't think you're too important to be disciplined."

Jeff said nothing, and neither did Laura. They had learned that arguments and protests simply made things worse with Brunhilda.

As they neared the portal to their dome, the giantess said, "If you've got to smooch, at least do it in the privacy of your dorm rooms. If the computer warning had been picked up by one of the Council members instead of just me . . . " She shook her head.

As they entered their own dome, Bishop Foy himself passed by, heading toward the greenpath they had just come in from. He nodded at them unsmilingly, his thoughts obviously elsewhere as he walked past in his lean, loose-jointed amble.

Jeff looked up at Brunhilda as Bishop Foy passed. She caught his stare and slowly closed one eye in a solemn wink. Jeff was so startled that he nearly tripped and fell.

Jeffrey Holman had been born into the Church of Nirvan. His father, director of the leading bank in the Nevada town where they lived, had used the Church as a social and business tool. He Believed, of course; everyone in the town Believed or they moved elsewhere. But Jeff's father expected God to show some faith in Mr. Holman, too. When the town's copper and molybdenum mines closed down in the face of competition from the asteroid mines out in space, Mr. Holman (as everyone in town called him) brought the Church Elders together with the Los Angeles corporation executives who actually owned the bank and arranged a multi-million-dollar deal that turned the town into a "premier residential center" where executives from Los Angeles, Phoenix, and other crime-infested megacities could find a safe home for themselves and their families, far out in the desert.

The town quadrupled in size, the bank prospered, and Mr. Holman was elected mayor—proving that God had faith in him.

It was Jeff's mother who Believed in the Church of Nirvan with the simple abiding faith that demanded nothing in return. She bore eight children, fulfilling the Church's demand for fruitfulness. Jeff was her oldest son; her first three babies had been daughters.

Jeff seemed to slide through life as if God had intended him never to stub a toe. He was a happy, plump baby. He never had a sick day in his life. Once he started school, he charmed his teachers with his quiet, modest behavior and his quick, eager mind. He was always first in class, first in anything he chose to do. The only trouble with Jeff was that he chose to do so little. He liked to read, to sit alone and daydream, to think.

"Somedays, Jeffrey, I worry that you're going to turn into a tree stump," his mother often chided him. Jeff would smile at her and offer to help her with the household chores.

"You've got to show more *drive*, son!" his father would admonish. "Get out of the house and meet people, make friends, *do* things."

Jeff would agree and take a walk down to the town library, to lose himself in books for hours on end.

In high school he steered away from sports. "Too

much work," he said. "And for what? So you can get to date a cheerleader?"

Mr. Holman warned his wife, "If he doesn't show any interest in girls at this age, Martha, I seriously think we should . . ."

"Be patient, Mr. Holman," his wife said. "You just be patient with the boy."

Jeff easily won a full scholarship to the state university, but asked his father to pay tuition for a friend of his who had barely failed to qualify and couldn't afford college. Mr. Holman, like most bankers, did not like to spend money on people who actually needed it. But between Jeff and his wife—and their use of Church pressure—he became magnanimous. The local TV station was apprised of his open-hearted gesture and did a four-minute feature on the subject as a sidebar to its coverage of the high school graduation.

The weather fascinated Jeff, and after his first two years at the university, he decided to specialize in meteorology.

"We know so much about science," he explained eagerly to his father, one weekend when he had driven home for some solid cooking, "yet we still haven't been able to figure out how to make the weather behave the way we want it to."

"Perhaps God doesn't want us to tinker with the weather?" his mother suggested.

Jeff smiled at her. "If He doesn't, then He'd better let me know pretty soon. I'm going to study weather modification."

It was in his senior year that Jeff heard the call to colonize the stars. The campus was abuzz with the excitement: the Church had taken a contract with the world government to tame one of the outer worlds and make it ready for colonization. Students were being allowed to volunteer for the grandest adventure of all time.

When Jeff went home for Christmas vacation that year, he found his father adamantly opposed to sending students off to strange worlds beyond the solar system.

"I've let the Elders know how I feel about this," Mr. Holman said firmly. "Cannon fodder! That's what they're after. Those old men want to send kids your age out to the stars—they'll never come back. Mark my words. They'll all get themselves killed out there."

"But the Church would never deliberately send young Believers into mortal danger," Jeff's mother protested mildly.

"Oh wouldn't they? There's money involved, Martha. Billions of dollars. Trillions! And the chance to proselytize millions of poor people from all over the world. Do you think the Church is going to pass up such an opportunity just because a few thousand youngsters will get killed?"

Jeff listened intently, saying nothing.

"And those old men get an extra bonus out of it, too. They get rid of the next generation of natural leaders. They ensure their own hold on the Church by sending off all the idealistic youngsters to the stars."

"You're probably right, Dad," Jeff said at last. "But I'm going to volunteer anyway."

And nothing his parents could say or do would deter him. For easy-going, quiet, studious Jeffrey Holman had learned one basic lesson from his hard-driving father and his steadfast faithful mother: once you've made up your mind to do something, *do it*.

By the fourth time Amanda strapped him down in the couch, Jeff was completely at ease. Dr. Carbo hovered over him, one eye on the monitor gauges, as Amanda fitted the helmet onto Jeff's head.

"Today is going to be different, Jeff," Dr. Carbo said, his round dark face totally serious, unsmiling. "You have made contact with this wolfcat three times now . . ."

"Crown," Jeff heard himself say. "His name is Crown."

Carbo glanced at Amanda, then looked back at Jeff, an odd expression on his face. "You've given the animal a name?"

"That *is* his name. I didn't give it to him."

Carbo fell silent.

"Crown," Amanda said, smiling. "That's a good name."

Jeff tried to nod but the helmet was too heavy and fitted so snugly he could barely move his head. He hadn't realized that the wolfcat had a name until the word popped out of his mouth. Did I make it up, he wondered, or did Crown really have that name before I linked up with him?

"Okay," Dr. Carbo said finally, "his name is Crown. Today we want to see if you can get Crown to do some scouting for us. We're going to head off toward the east . . ."

He droned on, his voice very serious, his face grim. Amanda fussed around Jeff, checking all the connections, telling him without words that if he ran into any trouble they would be here to pull him out of it. Jeff gave her a fleeting grin, and she arched an eyebrow to show him that she had caught it.

Jeff found himself drumming his fingertips on the cushioned fabric of the armrests, impatient to get

Carbo's briefing over with. He felt eager to be back on the world below them, to get back to being Crown.

At last Dr. Carbo finished. He and Amanda left the chamber and went into the control room. Jeff could feel the surge of electrical excitement that rushed through him as they turned up the power on the equipment. He closed his eyes and forced himself to relax on the couch.

Carbo stood beside Amanda and watched the young student seemingly fall into an instant sleep. Easily. Too easily. He had seen people embrace drugs and the direct cortical stimulation that his neuro-electronic probe could provide with the same happy, beatific smile on their lips. He tried to put that worry behind him. This is something very different, he told himself. The boy shows no evidence of addiction. Not yet, at least.

Jeff seemed to be in a deep slumber, totally relaxed, every muscle slack. Then the closeup monitoring viewscreen showed that his eyes began to move rapidly behind his closed eyelids. His fingers clutched at empty air. His head jerked and twisted. On the main control panel the data monitors whined to life. The central viewscreen glowed and formed the scene from the hilltop that was becoming familiar to them.

"He's done it again," Amanda whispered.

With a curt nod, Carbo replied, "It gets easier for him each time."

She made a small movement that might have been a shake of her head. "It looks as if it puts him in pain."

"There's no trace of pain on the monitors."

"I know," Amanda said. "But . . . "

"He's enjoying the experience. He's a hero. Every young man wants to be a hero."

"Maybe so. But he's losing weight. Have you noticed that?"

"A kilo or so. Nothing to worry about."

"I worry," Amanda said.

Crown awoke instantly. Not that he was ever deeply asleep. A wolfcat has no natural enemies, but still there are dangers: a brainless serpent, a hungry pack of scavengers, another wolfcat challenging him for his hilltop.

He got up on all sixes and stretched, catlike, before trotting out from under the rock ledge where he had slept the night. In the gentle, diffuse light of early morning he gazed out from the top of his hill. The forest beckoned, with its scents of food.

No, not the forest. Eastward, across the grasslands, toward the rising sun.

Crown grunted. Food was in the forest, but there would be food in the grassland, too. He had eaten well the day before. Hunger could wait. For a while.

Still, it felt strange to turn his back on his own hunting territory, to leave his hill and the forest. With a final glance over his shoulder, he lumbered down the hillside and turned off toward the grassy open land that stretched out to the horizon and the morning sun.

He's doing it! He's controlling the beast.

There were new odors in the grassland. Strange scents. The area was fairly flat, with nothing more than a gentle roll here and there to break the monotony. No trees at all, although there were some clumps of shoulder-high brush, and the grass itself came up to Crown's knees. The wind was strong. With nothing to get in its way, the wind no longer sighed; it gusted and shouted as it whipped Crown's fur and made the grass

54

bow down in waves that he could follow from the horizon right up to where he was walking.

By midmorning Crown's innards were a massive empty cry of hunger. But there seemed to be no prey in sight. There were scents aplenty, but he could not see any animals.

He stopped and turned to face the wind. The food smells were strong, fresh. Not the same scents as those back in the forest, though. Different odors. Different animals.

Crown crouched down on the grass, flat on his empty belly, low enough so that his huge bulk was almost entirely hidden by the grass. Nothing but the gray unmoving curve of his back showed above the tops of the waving fronds. Unmoving, unblinking, hardly breathing, he watched and waited.

Gray clouds were building up overhead, lower than the perpetual deck of smooth pearly cloud that Crown knew as the sky. These were like angry fists of darkness, and they dotted the plain with scurrying shadows as they blew past on the urgent wind. Crown watched the grass, now bright in daylight, now dark in shadow.

Something moved! A small, brown, furry thing, only about as big as one paw. But food.

More than one! A brown furry head poked up over the tops of the grass, looking around nervously, nose twitching as it sniffed for danger. Crown was downwind, it couldn't catch his scent. The head went down and another one popped up, off to the right.

Not much food, but better than none at all. Crown waited, not moving a muscle, a gray silent hill hidden by the grass. The little things were scampering through the waving fronds, coming closer, closer. Crown tensed. Closer . . .

He leaped, roaring, landed on one animal, killing it instantly, then leaped again and caught another. The grass was suddenly alive with them, jumping and scattering in all directions, chittering, screaming shrilly as they raced to escape the huge roaring death that had pounced into their midst.

Crown dashed this way and that, trying to catch a few more of them, but they easily eluded him. Some of them skittered right under his belly and out of reach before he could swat them. For several foolish minutes he thrashed through the grass, roaring, twisting, jumping, and got nothing. It was like trying to pick up water with your fingers.

With a final growl of exasperation, Crown returned to the two creatures he had killed. Not much food for a morning.

A ground-shaking roar made him look up.

A huge wolfcat stood several leaps away, staring at him with huge, dagger filled jaws. His muzzle was white with age, but the strength of his roar and his massive size showed that he was still powerful, more powerful than Crown.

Crown had no intention of giving up his kill, small though it was. He growled back at the intruder.

Another wolfcat rose out of the grass beside the first one. A female. She growled too. And a third, on the other side of the old male. Then behind him, Crown heard more warning growls. He turned to see two more males, smaller and younger than he. That made five against him.

Crown understood their growls and roars. It wasn't the food they were after. Crown was in their territory. *He* was the intruder, and this family of wolfcats was going to get rid of him.

They were circling around him, eyeing him warily and snuffling, grunting. But the circle was drawing tighter, closer, with every step they took.

Crown stood over his two tiny kills, a rumbling growl filling his throat. The elder male halted his pacing and roared his full fury. From a scant ten meters away, his bellow was shattering.

Crown snatched at one of the furry things and scampered away, dashing between the two younger males, clutching his tiny kill in his right forepaw and running crookedly on his other five legs.

They chased him for a few minutes, roaring after him. Then, satisfied that Crown was leaving their territory, they let him go with nothing more than a few more warning roars.

Crown dashed over the grassland, loped up a slight rise, then stopped to look back at the wolfcat family. The old male was still standing stiffly, fur bristling, facing directly toward Crown. But the others had already started back toward wherever they had come from. Crown snarled his anger and frustration, then resumed his pace across the grass, away from the other wolfcats.

They're territorial animals. He won't be able to hunt for food wherever there are other wolfcats.

Then he'll have to find a territory where there are no other wolfcats. Or establish himself as the head of a family.

That's easier said than done. A lot easier.

There wasn't much meat on the little furry thing. Crown was still ravenous when he resumed his march across the rolling grassland.

A storm began to darken the sky as he paced onward. The sky became black with low clouds, the wind began shrieking in earnest, bringing scents of other wolfcat families to Crown's sensitive nostrils.

On his hill, when it rained Crown would slink under a rock outcropping or into a cave. In his forest there were plenty of trees and thick bushes to keep off the worst of the storm. But here in the open grasslands there was no shelter. Nothing except a sea of grass, whipped into a frenzy now by the furious wind.

A streak of lightning broke the sky in half and as its thunderclap exploded overhead the rain began to pour down so thick and heavy that Crown could barely see past his muzzle.

Lightning again! He had never seen the jagged tongue of lightning so close, so blindingly bright. *Down! Lie down or you'll draw the lightning onto yourself.* With a muttered snarl of sheer misery, Crown hunkered down into the wet clinging matted grass and mud. The rain pelted him mercilessly.

It wasn't merely rain. Stinging stones of ice peppered him, rattled off the thick bone of his skull armor, even cut him through his heavy fur. Crown winced and growled as the hailstones stung him like ten thousand needles. He dug his muzzle deeper into the grass, into the ground-turned-mud, trying to get away from the hail.

It may have been only minutes, but it seemed like hours. At last the hail stopped, and then gradually the rain tapered off and finally ceased altogether. The clouds lingered, though, scudding along dark and menacing, hurrying as if they had somewhere important to go.

Through the long gray afternoon Crown trekked across the endless grassland, staying out of sight of other wolfcat families, avoiding every other animal, choking down the gnawing hunger that echoed in his stomach. By nightfall he was wearily climbing a range of low, rolling hills. Water gurgled nearby. He scented a good-sized antelope and then saw it—brown and white, with wicked-looking horns and fleet, slim legs—as it edged toward the splashing brook for a drink. Crown dashed at it, chased it when it sprang away, caught it and killed it in one blindingly fast motion.

He had eaten only a small portion of his kill when the other wolfcats showed up. In the swiftly gathering darkness of twilight he could make out their menacing shapes and heard their growls of warning.

Crown growled back. *I'm hungry! This is my kill.*

They paced slowly toward him. Crown quickly crammed as much of the kill into his craw as he could manage, then splashed across the brook and slinked farther up into the wooded hillside's slopes.

Still achingly hungry, he slept at the base of a tree. He dreamed of his hilltop, his forest, as soon as he fell asleep.

"He's really sleeping," Amanda said in a surprised whisper.

"He's had a very long day," Carbo said. "But we can't leave the animal in those hills for too long. We've got too much invested in him to lose him now."

Amanda peered through the control room window at Jeff's slumbering body. "You can't expect him to . . ."

Carbo waved her silent. "We have to do it. We can keep him asleep as long as the animal sleeps. Use the electronic tranquilizer. He'll get more actual rest than he would in his mother's arms. You can feed him intravenously and use the massage units to keep up his muscle tone. He must be here and alert when the animal wakes up." The urgency in his normally soft voice made it sound almost like an angry hissing.

Amanda made a sour face. "That's no way to treat him!"

"There's no other way!" Carbo snapped.

"What if you make him sick? Or kill him? What then?"

"But we'll take good care of him. For god's sake, Amanda, don't make things more difficult than they already are! There's too much at stake."

"That's exactly my point," she said.

For an instant the two of them stood facing each other, the slim black woman and the jowly stubble-bearded man, electricity crackling between them.

Despite herself, Amanda smiled. "Now don't go getting yourself into a sweat, *dottore*. I'm on your side. I just don't want us to get so excited about this that we hurt the . . . test subject."

Carbo broke into a relieved grin. "Okay. Okay. I understand. I knew I could count on you."

With a shake of her head, Amanda replied, "What you *don't* know could fill libraries."

"Eh? What do you mean by that?"

"Forget it," she said airily. "I was just thinking out loud."

With a puzzled frown, Carbo said, "Sometimes, Amanda, you worry me."

"Sometimes I worry myself."

Carbo stared at her for a long moment. Then, as if shaking himself free from a trance, he said abruptly, "Okay. You make certain that he is well-exercised and well-fed while he sleeps. Another big day coming up tomorrow. The animal ought to get to the camp by midday if nothing goes wrong."

He headed for the door and Amanda asked, "Where are you going?"

"For food. We camp here tonight," Carbo pointed toward the window and Jeff, "with him."

"Oh. Sure."

"I'll bring you dinner on a tray. What would you like to eat?"

"Steak," said Amanda, "blood rare."

She laughed when he grimaced.

CHAPTER 5

Crown awoke when the sun came up, brilliant Altair, a sullen smudge of light penetrating the unbroken gray clouds of morning.

These hills were good, almost like home. He could smell food in among the trees. And the shade from their high leafy branches would ease the heat of midday.

No. He can't stay. Must get to the camp.

Slowly, stiffly, Crown got to his feet. His nose twitched and he stared into the still-dark shadowed woods. He rumbled with hunger. But he turned away and started up toward the crest of the hills and then down the other slope, heading out toward the broad rocky desert that stretched as far as the eye could see.

Overhead a great winged beast soared among the scattered low clouds. Crown watched it as he trotted out from the shelter of the last trees and onto the sparse grass that edged the stones of the desert. He had never seen anything like this flying beast before.

It was much bigger than the birds of the hills and forest that he had known. It seemed to have only a few feathers, out at the tips of its wings. Its beak was short and powerful, and flashed with teeth. It flew with hardly a flap of its leathery wings, soaring easily on the heat currents that were already rising from the desert wasteland facing Crown.

Crown stopped at the bottom of the hill, where the grass thinned away and finally ended altogether. There was nothing but bare rock and heat ahead of him. He turned and looked back toward the woods that covered the upper slopes of the hills. The wind that was blowing down from there felt cool and told him of water and food animals living among the shady trees. He growled, tossed his mane—and headed grudgingly out into the desert.

His control's fantastic! That poor animal must be starving.

It's more important to get to the camp than to feed it. The animal can go hungry for a day or two.

And if it dies of hunger?

It won't.

Yes, but if it does?

We'll have to find another one.

And what happens to Jeff?

We'll cross that bridge when we come to it.

It was brutally hot. The rocks were broiling, and as Altair climbed higher into the clouded sky the heat from the rocks scorched Crown's paws.

A lizard-hawk soared high overhead, as if it was waiting with all the calm patience of inevitable death. Crown pressed on, driven by a force he could not understand. Fear was unknown to him, but the hungry wolfcat realized fully that this desert offered no food, no water, only danger and death. Still he padded onward, his six powerful legs working like the pistons of an engine.

Rocks. Nothing but rocks. Huge boulders, taller than some trees. Tiny pebbles that stuck sharply into Crown's paws. Heat currents danced up from the rocky desert floor, making the whole world swim dizzily. Crown trudged on, slower and slower, forgetting everything, even his hunger, as the fearsome sun climbed higher and higher to blast him with unending pitiless heat.

The lizard-hawk still circled over him, high above, watching and waiting. Then, in the shimmering heat haze, Crown saw more of them. Four lizard-hawks. A dozen. Many, many more. Circling, circling, off on the far horizon.

Suddenly he understood what that meant. Crown stopped and watched as the hawks began to descend, swooping down and landing with wide outstretched wings. They were far away, off on the horizon, and he could not see where they were actually touching the ground. But he knew why they were landing. Something in his brain told him what they were doing.

He turned away from his original path and started toward the congregation of hawks.

No! He's supposed to go straight to the camp.

Jeff's still in control, look at the monitors. But he's allowing the animal to turn off.

Something's gone wrong. We'll have to terminate . . .

Wait. Wait. Let's see what Jeff wants to do.

Wearily, baking under the merciless sun, Crown pushed himself toward the place where the hawks were coming down. Something inside his mind told him that, in a desert like this, the hawks could be nothing but scavengers. They landed where there was meat. And since they had started landing only a few minutes ago, the meat must be fresh.

Boulders bigger than Crown himself shielded the hawks' landing place from his view. He clawed his way across their scorching heat and squeezed between those he could not get around.

Finally he stood atop a huge, weathered flat rock, blazingly hot, cracked and bleached white by the sun. He no longer noticed the heat or the pain in his paws. He stared hungrily at the scene below.

Nearly a hundred of the lizard-hawks had gathered around an animal. It was a giant beast, as big as Crown himself. But very different. Its fur was mottled green and brown, and covered with dry, whitish dust. Its head was rather small, but its face showed two good-sized eyeplates mounted side-by-side, for looking straight ahead. Its mouth was armed with strong, sharp teeth, but they were small—not fangs. It had only four legs, and it looked as if only the hind legs were meant to carry the beast. The forelegs were longer, thinner, and ended in paws that had six rudimentary fingers.

It looks like a bear, an ancient Kodiak bear.

But those forepaws look more like an ape's than a bear's.

It was not dead yet. It was down on its back, its hind legs moving feebly on the dusty ground. Its eyeplates looked dull, but it snarled with pain and fear at the hissing, flapping hawks as they awkwardly hopped closer to it. It thrashed its arms whenever a hawk came close. Its stubby fingers ended in sharp hooked claws.

The hawks circled the dying animal; their toothy beaks seemed to be smiling.

This is fantastico! Cut in the extra data tapes. No one has seen an animal like this before.

It hasn't been in any of the reports?

None that I've seen. We've discovered a new . . . what's he doing now?

Oh no!

Crown bunched his muscles and roared out a challenge to the hawks. Startled, they flapped into the air, making the world crackle with their shrieks and the leathery beating of their wings. Crown roared at them once more as they sped high into the sky.

Then he turned and leaped for the downed ape's throat.

Jesu Christo!

Jeff . . . how could you?

The ape was too weak to fight and Crown gorged himself while the hawks hovered overhead, complaining noisily. But they waited for him to leave before they dared to descend and start to fight over the remains.

With a final roar of triumph, Crown left the bloody carcass behind and resumed his trek across the rocky wasteland.

It was late in the day when he came to another range of hills. They were steeper and rougher than any hills he had ever seen before. Their bases were solid rock, slashed with narrow ravines cut through them by ages of rain erosion. About halfway up their rugged slopes, grass and brush clung precariously to the rock. Farther up, near the top, there were trees. A thick, beautiful forest hid the top of the ridge line; the branches swayed rhythmically in the breeze and sang sweetly to Crown.

Crown climbed catlike, more in leaps from rock to rock than step-by-step. As he neared the top of the ridge, his ears perked up. Something strange up there. A dull, booming sound, over and over again. He had never heard anything like it. His fur bristled, his lips pulled back to bare his teeth. A low growl rumbled from the cavern of his chest.

The slope was gentler up near the top of the ridge. The grass felt deliciously cool to his singed paws. But the strange sound was louder up here, drowning out the gentle voices of the wind and sighing trees. *Sss-vroom . . . sss-vrrooommm!* And now a strange new scent came to him, wafting in on the steady breeze, a scent Crown had never known before.

Slinking through the grass and brush, belly almost touching the ground, ears flattened back and teeth showing, Crown crawled through the woody under-brush as silently as a gray shadow and suddenly found himself facing . . .

Something in his brain broke into laughter. Crown's tensed muscles relaxed. He sat down on his haunches and stared out at the beach that stretched below the crest of the hills and watched the waves build up on the ocean, steepening and steepening until they crashed over on themselves with a long, foaming, mighty *sss-vrrroooommm!* of surf.

Crown had never seen an ocean before. Neither had Jeff. He simply sat there next to a thick, gnarled tree trunk and watched the blue-gray water gather its strength and rush in toward the land, a white curl of foam flecking the crest of each wave. *Vrrooomm!* The waves broke with a thundering, shuddery roar and slid up onto the sandy beach as nothing more dangerous than froth, while the next wave was coming in.

Finally Crown got up and trotted down the easy slope of the hill and out onto the beach. His paws left deep prints in the sand as he went straight out toward the water. He bent his massive head and lapped at the little slitherings of water that edged up and swirled around his six legs. It tasted much too salty to drink, but now he knew what the strange new scent was.

The breeze was cool and tangy with the new odor, but there was no food on that wind. Up in the hills, among the trees, Crown knew, was where the food existed. But probably there were other wolfcats up there, too. That could wait. At least, for a while.

The camp's on this beach, about four kilometers north.

Crown headed north, loping easily along the sand. Every once in a while he would veer out to splash into the surf, romping playfully like a cub, pawing at the water and sending up huge sheets of spray.

He's playing!

It's the first time he's been at the beach.

Madonna! We have serious work to do and he's playing!

Don't be a sourpuss.

Crown finally arrived at the camp. Long before he could see it, he smelled it. Rancid, oily smells. Strange new odors that made him wrinkle his muzzle with distaste.

It looked even worse. Scattered across a long curving section of beach were hundreds of blocky metal

69

machines. Some had treads and bulldozer scrapers on them, some were wheeled. Others were simply standing there, bulky square shapes that tilted oddly where the sand beneath their dense weight had shifted. Farther up the beach was a huge plastic dome, big enough to house dozens of people. Jagged holes had been smashed through it, and long streaks of soot smeared its once-white flanks.

Crown padded closer to the machines and sniffed at them. Dead. No food here. The metal was dull and rust-stained.

That stuff was supposed to be impervious to rust. Not in the air down there.

There was no danger here, Crown decided. He did not realize that the stench from the machines could hide the scent of a snake or even another wolfcat, perhaps. But there was no food here, either, and Crown gazed up toward the trees at the top of the ridge line above the beach. The sun was going down and the shadows of the forest looked dark and inviting.

He won't be straying very far. Let's terminate. Break contact.

Amanda Kolwezi stared at the screens and instruments on the control panel before her. Frowning slightly, she touched a series of buttons on the keyboard.

She swivelled her chair to look out through the control room window at Jeff, who lay quietly on the couch, the silver helmet on his head and the sensor contacts on his wrist and ankle cuffs.

"What's the matter?" Dr. Carbo asked. He was standing at the far end of the wall-long control board.

Amanda made a clicking sound with her tongue. "He's not coming out of it. It's almost . . . almost . . . "

"What?" Carbo made it to her chair in three quick, nervous strides.

"As if he doesn't *want* to come out of it." Amanda was watching Jeff's body as she spoke. A smile flickered across his sleeping face.

"Just disconnect," Carbo snapped. "Power down and go through the regular termination cycle."

"I know, but he's not helping. The other times he withdrew before we powered down."

Carbo glanced at the couch. "It won't hurt him. Take the power down slowly. He's been in contact with the animal for more than thirty hours now; withdrawal is bound to be slower."

"Are you sure . . . ?"

"It won't hurt him, even if he doesn't cooperate."

Amanda shook her head, but so slightly that only someone who knew her as well as Carbo did would have caught the gesture at all. "I hope you're right."

She made the necessary adjustments on the keyboard instruments, then fixed her eyes on the couch. Jeff's body stirred slightly. He let out a long sigh, almost a moan, and Amanda realized that she was holding her own breath.

Jeff opened his eyes. He saw the curving metal ceiling of the laboratory. No sky. No breeze. No ocean and throbbing surf. Only the hum of electrical equipment and the flat metallic tang of the ship, with the faint odor of clinical antiseptics laid over his own body scent.

Dr. Carbo's face slid into his view. "Are you okay?"

Jeff blinked. His eyes felt gummy. "Sure . . ."

Amanda came up, smiling, and started to unbuckle his cuffs. "You must be tired. You've had a couple of big days."

"A couple? Oh, yeah, of course." Jeff felt somebody—Dr. Carbo, of course—lifting the helmet off his head. His scalp itched . . . no, tingled.

"Wait a minute," Amanda said softly. "Don't try to sit up yet."

She disappeared from his view for a moment. *I wonder what Crown's doing without me?*

Amanda came back with a plastic cup filled with an orange-colored liquid. "Here, drink this," she said. "It'll bring your strength back. Hard work, lying on that couch for two days."

"Two days . . . right." Jeff sipped at the drink. It tasted cold and sweet.

"Go on, finish it. Won't spoil your dinner."

Jeff sat up and swung his legs over the side of the couch. Amanda stood right beside him, smiling, her hand on his shoulder.

"What time is it?" he asked.

Amanda glanced at her wrist. "Five after six."

Nearly sundown.

"I'll walk you back to your dorm," Amanda said.

"I can make it myself," Jeff replied, but not very strongly.

"You've been flat on your back for more than thirty hours. We've had the vibrators stimulating your muscles, but you might still be a little woozy."

Jeff tried standing up and was glad that she was there to lean on. "Yeah," he admitted. "I see what you mean."

"Come on, I'll make dinner for you. You've had enough liquid nourishment. How about some real food?"

With a grin, Jeff nodded. "I'm starving," he realized.

Amanda laughed. "Next stop, Amanda's gourmet kitchen."

Carbo stood by the instrument panel, watching them wordlessly as Amanda walked Jeff out of the laboratory, her arm around his shoulders.

For long moments he stared at the door after it closed behind them. Then with a tight-lipped scowl on his swarthy face, he went back to reviewing the data from the day's work.

CHAPTER 6

Jeff had never seen the quarters of a member of the technical staff. They were all housed in a dome on the opposite side of the Village from the domes of the students.

Amanda's apartment started with a spacious living room, furnished with big viewscreens and comfortable sofas, carpets scattered across the plastic flooring and tapestries hung on the walls, all in the slashing bold yellows and ochres and rich browns of her native Congo.

Then there was the kitchen, not much bigger than a short, wide aisle crammed with gadgetry on either side. But it was all for her and her alone. No one shared it. And just the dining area between the kitchen and the living room was almost as big as Jeff's dorm room.

"Bathroom's down the hall," Amanda said with a wave of her hand.

Jeff took the hint and went off to wash up. He passed the open door of her bedroom and saw that it was dominated by a large bed, rumpled and unmade, a zebra patterned coverlet lying carelessly halfway over a corner of it, halfway on the floor.

Jeff hesitated a moment at the bedroom doorway, his mind suddenly filled with pictures of Amanda on that bed, her dark skin shining against the white sheets.

He shook his head to drive such thoughts from his mind and stepped resolutely into the bathroom. He splashed plenty of cold water on his face before returning to the kitchen.

"The place is in a mess, I'm sorry," Amanda was saying as she pulled foil-covered trays from racks built into the kitchen wall and popped them into the microwave oven. "You've been keeping us pretty busy, you know."

Jeff did not answer. He watched her, noticing for the first time how her white medical uniform both concealed and revealed her trim feminine figure.

The wall phone buzzed.

"Answer phone," Amanda sang out.

The ten-centimeter picture screen above the phone's speaker grill fluttered momentarily, then formed an image of Bishop Foy. He looked even grimmer than usual.

"Dr. Kolwezi, is Jeffrey Holman there with you?"

Amanda's eyes darted toward Jeff, then back to the screen. "Yes, he is," she answered. A little guiltily, Jeff thought.

"I want to see you both in my office," Foy said, in his scratchy thin voice. "At once!"

"But Bishop Foy . . ."

"At once!" The screen went blank.

Amanda carefully pressed the phone's OFF button, making certain that neither sound nor picture could be transmitted, before she muttered, "Someday I'm going to spit in that man's face."

Jeff felt shocked. Foy was a pain, of course, but he was a *Bishop*. He wielded authority, and a Believer never argued against authority, no matter how he felt inwardly.

Still muttering angrily to herself, Amanda flicked the switch that turned off the oven and headed for the door, not even glancing behind her to see if Jeff was following.

Amanda Kolwezi was the only black woman in the class of one hundred fifty-four at the University of London. She was the only black and the only woman to receive both an M.D. and Ph.D. simultaneously. But the day of her graduation was not a happy one. She had received an official telegram the evening before, from the government in Congo, that her brother had been killed by government troops in an anti-guerrilla battle in some obscure dusty little town in the nation's southernmost, poorest province.

Amanda went through the long, tedious graduation ceremony alone. Her fellow students, many of them the closest friends she had in the world, thought that she looked very haughty and aloof on graduation day.

"Has it finally gone to Amanda's head?" they wondered. "Has she finally realized that she's the most brilliant one of us all?"

After the long speeches, and the awarding of diplomas, after the processional march and the hymns and the congratulations, Amanda left the others to celebrate with their families. She raced back to her tiny flat, hiking up the skirts of her maroon graduation gown in both hands as her long legs carried her down the shower-glistening narrow streets of London.

Keno Jumyata was already in her flat when she got there.

Amanda felt no surprise. She hadn't expected Keno consciously, but now that she saw him lolling on her shabby, sagging bed, she realized that she had been waiting for him to show up for the past several days.

She closed her door and heard its lock click. No need to ask Keno how he got into her room; he could charm, bully, or infiltrate his way anywhere, she knew.

He was handsome, with the strong graceful body of a black lion and a disarming smile that made Amanda's heart flutter even now, even though she knew that he used it as deliberately as a soldier uses a gun.

"I heard about your brother," Keno said, without preamble.

"Were you there with him?" she asked, her voice flat and hard. She knew he hadn't been.

"No. I was in the capital. I flew here to you at once."

Amanda pulled the graduation gown over her head and let it drop to the floor, alongside the pile of books she no longer needed.

"You flew to me at once," she said. "To console me?"

"To bring you back to your people."

She looked at Keno for a long, desperate moment

and almost, in her weakness, flew to him to bury herself in his strong arms and cry out her grief and anger and despair.

But instead she stood where she was, tall and proud, and said simply, "I'm not going back."

That made his eyes go wide. "What do you mean?"

"I'm not going back to Congo," Amanda repeated. "Not now. Not ever."

He swung his long, lithe legs off the bed and sat up. "Of course you are. You're going back with me. Tonight. I have the tickets in my valise."

"I am not going," she said, folding her arms stubbornly across her chest.

Keno gave a heavy, grunting sigh, then slowly got to his feet. He must have flown all night without any sleep, Amanda realized. He stood, tall and massive, dominating the tiny, shabby room.

"You are a princess of the Kolwezi," he said, in a deep, strong voice that resonated with authority. "Your people call out to you. They need you. It is your duty to return to your homeland and help to lead your people against the tyranny that rules the land."

"My duty?" Amanda asked. "As it was my brother's duty?"

"Yes," Keno said.

"And what did his duty gain him? Was he killed by bullets or a grenade? Or did they use gas this time? Or fire bombs from their airplanes?"

Keno's head sank down on his chest.

Advancing a step toward him, Amanda asked, "What good did your revolution do for my brother? Will you build a statue to him once you have won? Have you collected a few cells from his dead body so that you can clone him and make him over again in twenty years?"

"It is not my revolution," Keno said. "It is the people's revolution."

"Really? The people?"

"All the people of our land . . . including the Kolwezi."

She nodded bitterly. "Which is why you needed my brother, to make the Kolwezi follow you. Which is why you need me now."

Keno reached out and took her shoulders in his strong hands. "I have always needed you, Amanda. Come with me now, return to your people. Help me to fight the tyrants . . . "

"So that you can take their place," she said.

"I will lead our nation to greatness! With you at my side."

"As your queen?"

He shook his head vehemently. "We will have no royal titles. I will be President, you will be the First Lady of the land."

Wordlessly, Amanda pulled away from him and went to the closet next to her empty dresser. She slid the screen back and took up the travel bag that she had packed the night before.

Keno's eyes lit up. "You're coming with me!"

"No," Amanda said, tossing the bag on the bed and heading for the alcove where the sink and shower stood. "I am going to St. Louis, in America."

"What?"

"I have signed up for a star mission. I am leaving this Earth far behind me."

"You can't be serious!"

"I have signed the contract. My plane leaves in three hours."

"You're upset. Your brother's death . . . "

"Had nothing to do with it!" she snapped. Tossing

her few toiletry articles onto the bed beside the travel bag, Amanda said, "I signed up for the star mission a month ago. I want nothing of your revolution."

"But you must!" Keno insisted, his voice suddenly going high, pleading. "It is your duty."

"No. Not my duty. My brother saw it as his duty and what did it earn him? Martyrdom. He'll be more useful to you dead than alive, won't he, Keno?"

The tall black man said nothing.

"Someday you will be President of Congo. I fully believe it. You will be President whether I am with you or not, because being President is all you want out of life. You don't need me to help you."

"I will be President because the people need me!"

"You will be a tyrant, just like the tyrants you seek to overthrow."

"No! Never!"

Amanda almost smiled at him. "Keno, you are so naive about yourself. You truly believe that you will lead our people to greatness. How? With what? The few natural resources we possess are almost worthless, now that the world gets its raw materials from the asteroids. The land is poor. The people are ignorant, hungry, and diseased. What greatness can they achieve? Only the building of more splendid palaces for their leaders. You will make a great president for them; you will have the most splendid palace of them all. Be sure to put my brother's statue out front, where the village farmers can see it when they come to visit their President."

He scowled in anger for a moment, but fought to control himself.

"You are running away," he said.

"Yes. I admit it."

"And you call me naive."

"I am running away to a new world, a clean world, where we can start afresh, where ignorance and poverty will never exist because we will build this world *right*, from the beginning."

Keno shook his head. "You are a fool."

"Am I? Millions of people will be settled on this new world, once we have prepared it for colonization. And those of us who go there first, who do the work of preparing it, will *own* that world. We will be landlords of whole continents, Keno. Not the princess of a few thousand fly-infested villagers—I will be the queen of a new land."

"The world government would never . . ."

Amanda stuffed her last remaining items into the bag's side zipper pocket. "Not a queen literally, of course. I will not rule the people. I will merely lease them the land they farm. I will become very, very rich. I will be free to do as I choose, without even the obligations of a queen to tie me down."

"So you think."

"So I know!" she flashed.

Grasping her wrist to force her to look at him, Keno said, "Don't you understand what the world government is doing?"

"Colonizing the stars," she said.

"Yes, but how? By enticing the strongest and brightest men and women of our generation to leave Earth and go out into space."

"What's wrong with that?"

"They are getting rid of our generation's natural leaders," he bellowed. "They are *buying* you, and all the others like you, with promises of doing good for the poor while at the same time stuffing your own pockets with gold."

"No . . ."

"Yes!" Keno insisted. "Don't you think that the tyrants your brother and I struggled against are not part of this monstrous scheme? They *want* strong young leaders such as you to leave the Earth . . . leave it to them, the old, corrupt tyranny of the old, corrupt generation."

For half a minute Amanda stared into Keno's blazing eyes. Finally she disengaged her wrist from his hand, bent down and zippered the travel bag shut.

"Even if what you say is true, I am still going to the stars. I never want to see Congo again. I never want to see the land, the people, who have killed my father, my mother, and my only brother."

"You don't want to avenge their deaths?"

She shook her head. "I leave vengeance to you, Keno. I only hope that you will not be as unforgiving a ruler as I think you will be."

She left him in the shabby little flat, standing there beside the unmade bed with his fists clenched at his sides. She did not even bother shutting the door behind her. She went to Gatwick Airport, boarded the hypersonic rocketplane and arrived in steaming, muggy St. Louis half an hour later. She was met at the plane by a representative of the Church of Nirvan, a smiling, well-scrubbed young American woman. That was Amanda's first inkling that the star mission she had been assigned to was to be run by the international Church.

When Amanda and Jeff got to Bishop Foy's office, he was sitting hunched behind his long black desk like a troll glowering from beneath his bridge. Seated in front of the desk, looking uncomfortable, were Dr. Carbo and two other scientists: Harvey Peterson, chief of the anthropology group, and Louisa Ferris, the Village's ethicist.

Foy did not bother with introductions. He gestured Jeff and Amanda to the two vacant chairs before him.

"You let that animal kill a creature we have never observed before," the Bishop said to Jeff as he sat down.

Jeff almost laughed, he felt so relieved. All through their hurried walk from Amanda's apartment to the administration dome, he had been terrified that he was in trouble with the Church for allowing himself to be in Amanda's apartment with her without even a security camera to watch him.

"Well?" Foy demanded.

"He had to eat, sir," Jeff said simply.

Looking over at Carbo, Foy snapped, "Wasn't he given orders not to harm the ape?"

Before Dr. Carbo could answer, Jeff replied, "The ape was almost dead anyway. The scavengers would have been tearing it to pieces in another few minutes."

Dr. Peterson, the anthropologist, was gray-haired, lean, tall, with kindly blue eyes and a wrinkled, sun-browned face that looked as craggy as a weathered rock. He said softly to Jeff, "But it's a new species, you see. It might be the Altair equivalent of a pre-hominid ape."

"There must be others," Jeff said.

Bishop Foy shook his head angrily. "That's not the point! What I want to know, Dr. Carbo, is whether you gave this student an order or not, and if you did, why he disobeyed that order."

For the first time, Jeff noticed that Dr. Carbo looked very tired. There were pouches under his eyes. His round shoulders slumped even more than usual.

"There was no time to give an order," Carbo said.

"No time? How can that be?" Foy demanded.

"Sir, have you ever seen a hungry wolfcat?" Jeff asked.

"Certainly not!"

"Well, when you starve a wolfcat for two days and then put him in front of a few tons of meat . . ." Jeff was slightly shocked to hear himself speaking so informally to a Bishop, but he went on, "well, just don't get in his way."

Bishop Foy glared at him. The others in the office stirred uncomfortably.

"Dr. Carbo told the truth," Jeff went on. "There was no time to give an order, and Crown wouldn't have obeyed an order to ignore that food."

"Food?" shrilled the ethicist. "That was a primate ape! It might even have been intelligent!"

Dr. Louisa Ferris was round-faced, round-bodied, a ruddy-cheeked gray-haired lady who reminded Jeff of his favorite aunt. She was the only person in the entire Village who was not responsible to Bishop Foy. Dr. Ferris represented the world government, and reported directly to the Bureau of Colonization, at the world capital in Messina. Her assignment was to make certain that Bishop Foy and his staff followed the laws laid down by the world government. If she found those laws were not being obeyed, her reports could terminate the work at Altair VI, dissolve the contract between the world government and the Church of Nirvan, and send Foy and the entire staff of scientists and students back to Earth in penniless disgrace.

"Intelligent or not," Jeff insisted, "the animal was dead meat."

She recoiled in horror.

"It could not have been intelligent," Bishop Foy said, suddenly on Jeff's side. "We've scanned the planet thoroughly. There is no sign of artificial habitats, no villages, no artifacts of any sort."

"It's a big world down there," Dr. Peterson murmured. "Plenty of room for surprises."

Foy shook his head stubbornly.

"I wonder," Peterson added, "if a ship like this had orbited Earth a hundred thousand years ago, if it would have detected any sign at all of the human race. Yet human beings lived on Earth then—without villages or artificial habitats."

The Bishop grimaced at him, then turned back to Jeff. "Don't you fall into the error, young man, of thinking that you are indispensable to this project."

The thought had never occurred to Jeff. But now that Bishop Foy mentioned it, Jeff realized that no one else had been able to establish contact with any of the animals down there and perhaps he *was* important.

"Jeff may not be indispensable," Dr. Carbo said, his voice even softer than normal with weariness, "but that wolfcat is."

"Eh? What?"

"It's the only living animal we have with a probe in its skull. If we lose it, we have to start all over again from the beginning."

"Or give up," Amanda whispered.

Foy ignored her.

Dr. Ferris, somewhat more calmly, leaned forward slightly in her chair and said in an almost pleading tone, "Now, I know it must be very difficult to handle this wolfcat . . . "

Jeff was tempted to tell her, No it isn't; it's fun. But he held his tongue as the ethicist continued.

"If there is an intelligent species on Altair VI, we must know about it as soon as possible. It would mean that we are not allowed to colonize the planet. It would be a violation of one of the Bureau's most fundamental laws if we despoiled such a world and extinguished an intelligent species."

"They are not intelligent!" Bishop Foy repeated, his voice harsh with impatience.

"But they might be trainable," said Dr. Peterson, with an easy smile on his weather-beaten face. "They might be more valuable to us as . . . " he hesitated, glancing at the ethicist, " . . . as helpers, than the wolfcats. We've got to find out more about them."

Carbo, Amanda, and Dr. Ferris nodded as one.

"We will," Foy snapped. To Jeff, he said, "And I want you to remember, young man, that you are a member of this Village—not a wild beast of prey. You are valuable to this community only insofar as you can control that animal and make it do as we wish. If you cannot control it, or if you refuse to control it, we will find someone else who can and will. Is that clear?"

"Yessir," Jeff said, suddenly afraid that they would take Crown away from him.

"Very well then," Foy sank back in his chair. Its high back dwarfed his tiny form. "Continue your work. And may God grant you success."

Jeff murmured an Amen, and he thought he saw Dr. Ferris' lips move also. If she's a Believer, Jeff wondered, would she ever be able to take the government's side against the Church?

Once they were back in the curving corridor outside Bishop Foy's office, Jeff stammered to Amanda, "It's, uh, kind of late. I . . . I guess I'd better get back to my dorm."

She looked relieved. "Okay, Jeff. I understand. Make sure you get a good meal into you, though."

"The best the cafeteria can whip up," he promised.

Dr. Carbo came up beside her and said to Jeff, "I want you at the lab a half-hour before local dawn, down there on the beach. Check the central computer and set your alarm accordingly."

"Right," said Jeff.

As he started off toward the students' cluster of domes, reluctantly leaving Amanda behind, he heard her say to Carbo, "I've got a couple of real steaks in the cooker. You hungry?"

Jeff hurried away before he could hear Dr. Carbo's answer.

CHAPTER 7

Pain!

Pain so strong, so shocking, like hot knives in his guts, that Jeff almost wrenched himself free of the cuffs that restrained him and threw himself off the couch.

Amanda saw all the gauges on the control board flash into red overload signals. Carbo froze stockstill and stared through the control room window to where Jeff lay writhing and moaning aloud. But he grasped Amanda's wrist firmly when she reached for the emergency cutoff button.

"Not yet," he muttered through gritted teeth.

Crown was lying on his side, bleeding.

His right foreleg was soaked with blood, throbbing with red-hot pain. Other gashes raked his body, mostly his back. The pain was so screamingly intense it almost made him black out.

Up on the ridge line above the camp, in the trees, an old wolfcat bellowed his warning. Crown had tried to hunt in his territory in the misty hours before dawn, hoping that the wolfcat families in the woods would be asleep. But the old leader and four of his males had attacked Crown mercilessly. Crown had fought back, out of hunger and desperation. But the odds were much too great. They didn't want to kill him, merely drive him away from their own food supply. Crown didn't drive away easily. When he finally did admit defeat he was half dead.

Now he lay panting beside a crumbling piece of machinery on the beach, his blood soaking into the sand.

Pull him free, Frank! We can't let him take this overload.

Don't panic. He's handling it. The gauges are going into the green again . . . see?

Block off the pain, then. Lower the intensity match.

No. Only if we absolutely have to.

Crown growled weakly and got stiffly to his feet. Limping, aching, still oozing blood, he made his way through the strange machines and boxlike buildings of the abandoned camp. The odors here were strange, evil. Dead things. Things that were never alive. But not like rock or sand. These shapes were completely alien to Crown. Yet . . . yet . . . there was the faintest trace of something. Something else, a live scent, but very faint and very different.

Crown staggered along the sand and collapsed next to a huge rusting tractor. His head was spinning, the world was going blurry. But through it all he sensed the odor of food. It was a question of time. Food had been here once. It would come back again. But would it come before Crown starved or died of exhaustion and loss of blood?

Dr. Carbo studied all the gauges and sensor readings, pressing his lips into a thin bloodless line, then told Amanda, "Okay . . . pull him out of it."

With an audible sigh of relief, she began tapping on keyboard buttons.

Carbo muttered, "We can't let the animal die, but it's no damned good to us if it's too weak to move."

Amanda was frowning. On the couch in the lab chamber, Jeff's body lay still—either asleep or unconscious.

"I said pull him out of it," Carbo repeated.

She looked up at him. "He's not responding."

Carbo went to her and gripped the back of her chair in both fists. "Try it again. Slowly."

Amanda went through the disconnect sequence again. Then they both gazed through the thick window at Jeff, who was writhing on the couch, his body twisting slowly, restlessly. "No . . . no," he breathed.

"He wants to stay linked," Amanda said, her voice shaking with fear.

Carbo could feel sweat beading on his forehead and upper lip. "Damn! His willpower might be the only thing keeping that animal alive."

"Or the animal's pain could be killing Jeff."

"No . . . I don't think . . . "

"Look!" Amanda shouted.

All the gauges on the control panel were climbing upward again: heartbeat, breathing rate, electrical brain activity, all of them.

"Something's stimulating the animal."

"But Jeff . . . "

"Look at the screen," Carbo said.

Crown focused his vision on the beach and the camp, forcing the pain to the back of his mind.

The scent was stronger now, and getting even stronger by the minute. Something alive was making its way toward him. Food.

Crown didn't move. He tested his muscles by tensing them. They felt stiff, dull with pain. His foreleg was still bleeding, but it had clotted well by now and the blood flow was down to a trickle. Worse than the pain was the hunger inside him. It made him weak and slow.

The wind was coming off the sea, but at an angle that brought odors from up the beach, above the alien camp. A chill mixture of snow and rain was sifting down on the beach, so lightly that the snow evaporated as soon as it touched the sand. Crown had never seen snow before, but he ignored it for the time being. It was still early morning; the ocean was muffled in fog that would burn away as Altair rose higher in the sky.

And then Crown saw them. They seemed to take shape out of the mists that drifted across the beach. Apes, like the one he had found in the desert with the hawks. But these apes were strong, healthy. There were three of them prowling cautiously on all fours through the far end of the camp.

Family group: father, mother, cub.

Some cub. He's the size of a football player.

Call Dr. Peterson; he'll want to see this firsthand.

Already did it; automatic paging.

Down on all fours like that, they look more like bears than apes, don't they?

We'll let Peterson decide.

Crown didn't move. Hardly breathed. He waited for them to get closer, close enough to spring. The biggest one. Get the biggest one first, with one fast pounce. The others will run away. Or if they don't, at least they'll be easier to fight with the big one out of the way.

Frank, he's going to try to kill them.

What? What are you talking about?

The wolfcat — Jeff. He's going to try to kill the apes. For food.

Jeff wouldn't do . . .

Look at the gauges.

We can't allow him to do that! Foy will skin us alive!

But that's what he's going to do.

We've got to stop him!

How?

Break the connection. Get Jeff back here. Wake him up.

Can't do it in time. And it won't help. The wolfcat will attack them anyway, by itself. He must be starving.

We can't let it happen!

We can't stop it.

The apes were coming closer. Somewhere far back in his mind, Crown wondered why they were here on this beach, going through the camp. Did they come this way often? Was this a trail for them, or part of their territory?

The male was huge, much bigger than Crown himself,

a massive mountain of sandy fur topped by a heavy domed head with crests of solid bone above the eyeplates. But he didn't seem to be alert for danger. The wind kept Crown's scent away, and the odors of the dead machinery overwhelmed the area anyway. The apes seemed more intent on getting past the alien camp than anything else.

Through the misty rain and snow Crown saw that the male had thick curving claws on his hindpaws, but not on the forepaws. His teeth looked strong, but no match for Crown's own.

Tensing himself, quivering with anticipation, hunger and smoldering pain, Crown waited as they approached, waited, waited . . . and then sprang.

He leaped roaring right onto the surprised male's chest and tore out his throat before they both tumbled onto the sand. The ape made a gurgling sound, spurting thick red blood, then went silent and limp. Crown scrambled to his feet, wincing as he thoughtlessly tried to put some weight on his injured foreleg.

The female was about ten meters away, snarling, her cub cowering behind her. She reared up on her hindlegs, and with a forepaw she grabbed at a piece of pipe that had fallen off a nearby machine. Maintaining her distance from Crown, she brandished the pipe over her head.

Look at that!

Their forepaws are grasping hands.

And she knows how to use a weapon! Wait 'til Peterson sees this!

The cub was still on all fours behind its mother. Crown stood over the dead male and roared at its mate. The female did not attack, merely stood her ground and surveyed the scene, growling, holding the metal pipe threateningly over her head.

For long moments neither animal moved. Crown had his kill and wanted no more trouble. The female ape could see that her mate was dead, but her cub still lived. Slowly she backed away, edging farther from Crown, shambling awkwardly on her hind legs. The cub scuttled along behind her, always keeping its mother between itself and Crown.

Finally the ape let the metal pipe fall, dropped down to all fours, and trotted off into the mist, her cub following alongside her. Crown watched them as they headed away from the camp in the same direction they had originally been following: southward.

Crown roared once more, then settled down to eat.

Get Jeff back here. Now!

Jeff opened his eyes. The lids felt gummy, as if he'd been asleep for a long time. He blinked at the ceiling panels overhead, with their squares of soft lighting. For a moment he didn't know where he was. Then he realized he was back on the ship.

"Crown," he started to say, but his voice came out as a misty croak.

Dr. Carbo leaned over him. He stared at Jeff intently, his swarthy face tense with concern. "You're all right, Jeff," he said softly. "You're safe."

"But Crown . . . he's alone down there . . . "

"He'll be all right. Don't worry."

Amanda came into view, her eyes showing worry too. "How do you feel, Jeff?"

"Okay."

"You gave us a scare, you know."

Jeff wanted to nod, but the helmet was too heavy for him. "He was hurt."

"We know."

Amanda started to disconnect the cuffs while Carbo slowly lifted the helmet from Jeff's head.

"He's all alone down there," Jeff repeated.

Amanda made a smile and said, "What's the matter? Scared that your little old pussycat can't get along by himself for another few hours?"

"He's so badly hurt . . . "

"Never mind about him," Carbo growled. "He killed another ape. We're going to be in worse trouble than the wolfcat is, as soon as Foy finds out."

Jeff felt anger surging up in him. "Do you expect Crown to eat sand? He *tried* hunting in the hills and the other wolfcats nearly killed him."

"I know, but Foy . . . "

Jeff sat up and swung his legs over the couch's edge. "Let Bishop Foy try making contact with one of the animals down there," he said defiantly.

"We're getting pretty antsy," Amanda said, laughing.

"Never mind that," Carbo said. "Take Jeff across to the infirmary. I want a full medical checkup. Now."

"Right."

Amanda led Jeff to the corridor door, but before she could open it, the door slid back to reveal Dr. Peterson, the gray-haired anthropologist.

"You called for me?" Peterson said to Amanda.

"Come on in, Harvey," Carbo said. "I have some tapes to show you."

Amanda nudged Jeff out into the corridor. Once the door had slid shut behind them, she said, "You don't want to be in there while they review this morning's tapes. Let's get to the infirmary and turn off the phone."

The infirmary was in the same dome as Dr. Carbo's

laboratory, only a few minutes' walk along the central corridor. It was completely automated. The diagnostic system was an archway of gleaming metal studded with sensors that were connected to the medical computer. Jeff stood under the metal arch for a few seconds, and the viewscreen on the wall showed a complete physical profile.

"You're disgustingly healthy," Amanda said, touching the keyboard button that would store the data in the computer's memory bank.

"I feel okay," Jeff replied as he stepped out of the archway.

"When you first made contact with Crown this morning . . ."

He sucked in his breath. "Yeah. That was a shock."

"But you bounced back within minutes." Amanda made a clicking sound with her tongue. "The resiliance of youth."

Jeff grinned at her. "Like you're old and gray."

"I'm getting there," Amanda said. With a sidelong look at Jeff she added, "Too bad you're so healthy. Why couldn't you have a broken leg or a bad tooth? Even acid indigestion would do."

"Why . . . ?"

"Then we could pop you into an infirmary bed and say you weren't allowed to see any visitors."

Jeff's puzzled face showed he still did not understand.

"Now we have to go back and face Dr. Peterson," Amanda explained, her voice becoming heavy with worry. "And, sooner or later, you know who."

"Bishop Foy."

"Old death-warmed-over himself."

Jeff took a deep breath. "Well . . . if we've got to face them, let's do it and get it over with."

"More guts than brains," Amanda muttered. "Okay, into the valley of death rode the six hundred."

"Six hundred what?"

As they pushed through the infirmary doors and back out to the corridor, Amanda said, " 'The Charge of the Light Brigade.' "

"Light brigade? What's that?"

She gave him a stern look. "Jeff, you really ought to read more books. That's a very famous poem, about a battle that took place hundreds of years ago."

"I've read poetry," Jeff said defensively. "But we weren't allowed to read about war. Too sinful."

Dr. Harvey Peterson leaned back in the little plastic chair in front of Dr. Carbo's main viewing screen, his lanky arms and legs dangling, his weathered, craggy face somber with deep thought. Carbo sat beside him, hunched over into a nervous round ball.

Jeff could feel the tension in the lab as he and Amanda stepped back into the control room. Peterson turned and fixed Jeff with his Arctic blue eyes.

"You're doing quite a job with that wolfcat," he said, honest admiration in his voice.

Surprised at the compliment and slightly embarrassed, Jeff muttered, "Uh, thank you, sir."

"He really didn't have a choice," Carbo blurted. "It was either kill one of the apes or starve to death. You can see that, can't you?"

"Oh, I see it, all right," Peterson said easily. "But our good Bishop—he's not very flexible about these things, you know."

"I know," Carbo said, looking miserable.

Peterson ran a hand through his gray hair. "This is going to drive Foy right up the walls. A tool-wielding animal. The Altair VI version of a primate ape. Brother, does that present us with a problem."

Jeff stood by the door, unmoving, every sense alert to catch Peterson's meaning.

Carbo was nodding unhappily. "You mean, they might be intelligent."

"Yes. And if they're intelligent, we're not allowed to colonize."

"But if we're not allowed to colonize . . . " Amanda started, then hesitated.

Peterson turned his ice-blue gaze to her. "Then we have to go back to Earth. We've failed."

CHAPTER 8

The next morning Jeff sat alone at a table in the dining area, slowly picking his way through soy meat and fruit concentrate. It was late in the morning. Most of the other students were already at their assigned tasks. The dining area was almost empty.

"Jeff! Why aren't you at the lab?"

Laura McGrath put down a tray full of eggs, fruit, cereal and milk on the table and slid into the chair beside him. Jeff waited until she said a swift, silent grace before answering.

"They're having a big meeting in Bishop Foy's office," he said when she looked up again.

Laura caught the tone of his voice. "What's the matter? Has something gone wrong?"

Slamming his fork down on the dish with sudden anger, Jeff burst out, "They just don't understand! They want Crown to work for them like a machine. Well, even a machine needs energy, needs fuel, doesn't it?"

"Yes, of course." Laura's green eyes were wide at the vehemence of Jeff's outburst.

"They made me take Crown away from his natural habitat, and now they're pissed off because the only thing he can kill and eat are the apes."

Laura's face reddened slightly at his profanity, but she said nothing.

"Look," he went on, intently, "is it Crown's fault that they want him to stay in a place where there's nothing else to eat? Is it my fault?"

"No," Laura murmured. "How could it be?"

"But I'm the one in trouble . . . or, that is, Crown's in trouble. They're going to kill me. Him, I mean."

Laura put a hand on Jeff's wrist. Her fingers felt cool on his skin. Calming. "Jeff, slow down. Take it easy. Don't get so excited. You know how harmful that can be. Excitement leads to sin."

"Yeah, yeah, I know."

"Have you meditated on this problem?"

"I didn't sleep all last night, thinking about it."

"Would you like me to pray with you over it?"

Jeff hesitated. For the first time in his life, he heard himself say, "What good will prayer do? This is a *real* problem, Laura. It's life or death."

Her mouth fell open. "What are you saying, Jeff? Of course prayer will do good. More problems are solved through prayer than through cursing."

Jeff leaned back in his chair slightly, retreating in the face of her glowing certainty.

Her grip on his wrist tightened. "You come with me, Jeffrey Holman. It's time you came to chapel."

He let Laura pull him to his feet and reluctantly went with her to the Chapel of Nirvan.

It was empty, and dimly lit. Around the chapel's circular walls were all the symbols of the early religions, the precursors of Nirvan: cross and crescent, star and sunburst. A Buddha smiled serenely at them from a three-dimensional picture cube. Christ the Pancreator gazed solemnly into their eyes. A dazzling, shifting geometric display represented the unrealizable form of Allah. The stern Yahweh of the Old Testament, a thoughtful Confucious, a beatific Moroni. And in the center of the circular chapel, hanging in midair suspended only by an invisible vortex of energy, shone the eternal Globe of Nirvan. It glowed feebly, almost as dull as pewter, but Jeff and Laura both knew that at times it could blaze brighter than the Sun.

Silently they pressed their palms to the identification plate that connected to the chapel's computer. The empty circular pews rotated until the chapel's one aisle swung to their location. The nearly-soundless mechanism stopped, leaving only the faintest trace of a chorus singing a hymn of praise in the background of their awareness.

The cool air of the chapel was tinged with incense, a fragrance that instantly recalled to Jeff's mind the church back home on Earth, his parents, the world he had left far behind. He allowed Laura to lead him to the frontmost pew. They slid into it and sat on the cushioned bench. She gripped his hand tightly.

"Pray, Jeff. Pray for guidance and help. Nirvan will hear you, you'll see."

Jeff bowed his head and closed his eyes. He knew that Laura was doing the same, praying with an earnestness that shamed him. He tried to form words in his mind, but all he could see was Crown — not from inside the beast's mind, but Crown as an outsider would see him: a huge, powerful, six-legged, sleekly maned wolfcat, majestic and magnificent.

But Crown was hurt, he knew. Far from his own territory, alone in a strange place, in danger from his own kind, forced to do things no wolfcat would naturally do, controlled by an alien presence in his brain.

Jeff opened his eyes and looked up. The Globe of Nirvan glowed more brightly, a pale yellow light suffused it.

"You see?" Laura said, smiling excitedly. "Nirvan hears our prayers."

Jeff knew that the light was simply due to their presence in the chapel. Everyone knew how it worked. The Globe was connected to a heat sensor. The more people there were in the chapel, the brighter it glowed. The same sensor controlled the level of the air conditioning. But to Laura and the truly Faithful, the mechanism for accomplishing the phenomenon was simply a mechanism. It had nothing to do with the religious meaning of the phenomenon.

Nodding, Jeff whispered back, "Well, let's hope Nirvan does something about them."

"JEFFREY HOLMAN," a soft female voice spoke from the loudspeakers in the ceiling. "JEFFREY HOLMAN, WANTED IN BISHOP FOY'S CONFERENCE ROOM IMMEDIATELY."

"There's your answer," Laura said.

Jeff stared up at the ceiling, at the speaker grills and the Globe. He realized that Nirvan's answer to a prayer did not necessarily have to be an answer that the supplicant *liked*.

Even though the table in Bishop Foy's conference room was circular, so that no one could sit at its "head," Foy was clearly in charge of the meeting. He sat facing the door that Jeff came through, ushered into the austere little conference room by the Bishop's secretary—a student from Jeff's own dome.

Like his office, Bishop Foy's conference room was a monastic little cell, bare of all decorations except a representation of the Globe woven into an otherwise blank tapestry that hung on one wall. A door connected to the anteroom where his secretary worked, another went into his private office.

No one sat next to Bishop Foy, so that even though the conference table was circular, to Jeff it looked as though the Bishop was on one side of it, and Dr. Carbo, Dr. Peterson, and plump Dr. Ferris sat bunched together across from him, as far away as they could get. Like students who are afraid of the professor, Jeff thought. But he took the chair next to Dr. Carbo, and wished that Amanda was here to help protect him.

"We have a serious problem on our hands," said Bishop Foy, staring straight at Jeff with his narrow bloodshot eyes. "Dr. Carbo's work has progressed to the point where we must make some hard decisions."

Jeff felt instantly annoyed. Dr. Carbo's work? I had something to do with it, too!

"Let's examine what we've actually accomplished to date," Carbo said, shifting nervously in his chair.

Foy made a sour face, but did not object.

Hunching over the table's edge, Carbo said, "Our young friend here has made consistent contact with the experimental animal, and has shown a degree of control over the beast that we would all have considered phenomenal, only a few days ago."

Peterson nodded. Jeff noticed that Dr. Ferris had a finger-sized tape recorder sitting on the table in front of her. Even though Bishop Foy's computer recorded all meetings, she apparently wanted to keep a record of her own.

"We should now be proceeding along two lines," Carbo continued. "One, getting more students to work as contactors with the experimental animal . . ."

Let other students contact Crown? Jeff's pulse leaped.

" . . . And second, we must send a team down to the surface to implant more animals with probes, so that we can control them."

"Especially the apes," Peterson said. "That's got to be our highest priority. Those creatures may have the beginnings of intelligence . . ."

"If they do," Dr. Ferris interrupted, "we will be forced to close down all attempts to colonize Altair VI."

"If they are intelligent," Bishop Foy said, stressing the *if*.

"I would say they have already shown prime indications of intelligence," answered Dr. Ferris. Turning to Peterson, she asked, "Wouldn't you agree, Harvey?"

Peterson glanced at Foy before responding. With a hike of his shaggy white eyebrows, he said slowly, "We have one instance of an adult female picking up a length of pipe and making a threatening gesture with it."

"That's tool-using," Dr. Ferris said, "and tool use is *prima facie* evidence of intelligence."

"Is it?" Foy snapped. "Are you certain of that, Dr. Ferris?"

"Chimpanzees use tools, on Earth," Peterson said, "and they are considered proto-intelligent."

"But not intelligent. Not like human beings," said Foy.

"Chimps have also been trained to use language," Dr. Ferris pointed out. "That is *certainly* a sign of intelligence."

Foy shook his head from side to side, his deep-sunk eyes glaring at her. "A dog can be trained to walk on its hind legs, too. Does that make it an Olympic sprinter?"

Peterson put up both his hands. They were surprisingly big, long-fingered.

He said, "Before we stumble into a very old and very deep argument, let me tell you what official anthropological dogma is: the chimpanzees of Earth are regarded as *proto*-intelligent. That does not put them in the same class as human beings."

Foy seized on his statement. "Then if we found a planet that was inhabited by chimpanzees just like those on Earth, but nothing higher—the government could not object to our colonizing it."

Peterson leaned back in his chair and considered the question for a moment. "I honestly don't know what the government would do in a case like that. I think they'd be split right down the middle."

Bishop Foy waggled a bony finger at him. "The law is quite specific. It says that the presence of an *intelligent* species is the important factor. We are not allowed to colonize a planet already inhabited by an *intelligent* species."

"Wait a minute," Carbo said. "Let me ask this: Suppose the human race disappeared from Earth.

107

Simply vanished, overnight. Everything else is left exactly the same, no ecological changes. The Earth as it is today, except that there are no more human beings on it. Would the chimps evolve into a truly intelligent species?"

"Evolve?" Foy bristled.

"Develop, change, learn more," Carbo corrected himself.

"That would be impossible," the Bishop snapped.

With a trace of a smile at the corners of his lips, Peterson said, "I'm not so sure. In your terms, Bishop Foy, the question is, would God bring about another race of intelligent creatures on Earth . . . perhaps altering the chimpanzees until they are as intelligent as we?"

Carbo nodded.

"I know that you secular humanists still believe in heresies such as Darwinian Evolution," Foy said slowly, his voice lowered to a menacing hiss. "But we Believers know that one kind of animal can never change into another kind. Chimpanzees were created chimpanzees and they can never change into anything else."

"Then the chimps could never become fully intelligent?" Carbo asked, looking skeptical.

"Never!" Foy answered before Peterson could. "And I don't want to hear anything more on that subject."

"But wait just a minute," Carbo insisted. "That means that if the apes are not fully intelligent now, today, they never will be. Is that what you believe?"

"Yes."

"Then, as far as you're concerned, if we don't have to worry about them becoming more intelligent, more human, then all we have to find out is whether or not they are intelligent right now."

Foy saw the point he was driving at. "Why, yes . . .

that's correct," he said, smiling his ghastly smile.

"Now wait a minute," Peterson said. "The world government isn't going to stand for that approach. Messina doesn't make scientific judgments on the basis of the Church of Nirvan."

Carbo turned to Dr. Ferris. "Louisa, do you have a set of criteria that can tell us what we should look for? You've already mentioned tool use and language. Are there more?"

She looked alarmed. "Why, I suppose there are. There should be. I'll have to scan the references."

"You represent the world government here," Carbo said. "You'll have to tell us what the guidelines are."

Dr. Ferris glanced at Bishop Foy, a flash of guilt in her eyes.

"Whatever the rules tell us," Peterson said, "we should be examining those apes very closely."

"I agree," Carbo said. "We must send a team down to the surface and implant a few of them with probes."

Foy's bony face curdled again. "That is extremely dangerous."

"There's no way around it," Peterson said. "We must have more of the animals to work with."

"H'mm." Foy drummed his lean fingers on the tabletop, then turned toward Jeff, as if suddenly discovering him.

"Ah, young Mr. Holman," he said. "You seem to value that wolfcat of yours more highly than my instructions."

Carbo jumped in, "That wolfcat is the only experimental animal we have, remember."

"I'm quite aware of that," Foy answered, without taking his smoldering eyes from Jeff. "And you seem to be well aware of it too, Holman. You think you're indispensable, don't you?"

"No sir," Jeff said. "But Crown is."

"Crown?"

"The wolfcat," Carbo explained.

Foy snorted contemptuously. "Indispensable, eh? Well, he won't be for long. Peterson! Start preparations for landing another team on the surface. We'll implant enough animals to make both that wolfcat and this unruly young man superfluous to our needs."

CHAPTER 9

The following morning at the contact lab Jeff arrived before Dr. Carbo. Amanda sat alone in the control room, in front of the blank viewscreens and silent console panels, munching on a muffin. A mug of steaming coffee sat on the console desktop at her elbow.

"Another day, eh, Jeff?" she said brightly. "Frank's going to be late; big conference with Peterson and Polchek. They're organizing the landing teams."

Jeff took the chair beside her and nodded glumly.

"Want some breakfast?"

"I had mine already, thank you."

She peered at him. "You look like you lost your best friend."

"Maybe I have."

"What do you mean?"

Fidgeting in the chair, fumbling in his mind to find the right words, Jeff stammered, "Crown . . . they're going to take him away from me. They're going to implant other animals . . . then they won't care what happens to him."

Amanda's dark eyes showed that she understood. "Then Crown won't be so important, huh?"

"Right," Jeff agreed. "Then they won't care what happens to him . . . whether he starves or gets killed by other wolfcats or what."

"Maybe you won't be so important either."

Jeff looked up sharply at her.

"Is that what's bothering you, Jeff? You're the most important man in the Village right now, whether Foy admits it or not. But once other animals are implanted and other students are working with them, your importance will diminish."

"No," he insisted. "I'm worried about Crown."

"And yourself?" Amanda smiled gently.

Jeff frowned and looked away from her. But he had to admit it. She was right. He turned his eyes back to her. Amanda was still smiling patiently at him. She knew. And she *cared*. And she was beautiful.

"Yes, you're right," he finally confessed. "I am worried about myself."

"There's nothing wrong with that, Jeff. You'd be a little crazy if you weren't."

"But—well, look, I know that it's important to implant more animals and get more students to make contact with them. It's vital! I *know* that. But I don't like it. It's wrong of me; it's sinful. But I still feel this way."

Amanda rolled her chair to Jeff's, until they were almost touching. She took both his hands in hers and leaned her face so close to his that he thought she was going to kiss him.

"Jeff, you know that I'm not of your faith. I can't tell you anything about sin, or at least, about the way your church deals with sin. But one of my degrees is in psychology, and I know that the emotions you're feeling are completely normal. Anyone in your situation would feel the same way."

He shook his head, suddenly overcome with sheer misery. "But that doesn't make it right."

"It's not so terribly wrong, either," she said. "You're not harming anyone."

"Maybe if I prayed more . . . "

"Work is a form of prayer, and you're going to have plenty of work to do. No matter how many students we use, you're still the only one we have right now."

He tried to smile.

Squeezing his hands tightly, Amanda said, "And you're still a very important man to me."

Jeff felt his heart stop. For an instant the entire world seemed to halt in its tracks. There was nothing in the whole universe except this beautiful black woman who smiled at him so lovingly.

I'm in love with her! he realized. I love her more than anyone in the world has ever loved a woman before! But before the first wild shock of joy finished reverberating through his nervous system, Jeff realized that this, too, was wrong and sinful. Not only had he taken the vow of celibacy, but Amanda was not even a member of the Church. It wasn't that she was black; the Church preached racial tolerance. But she wasn't a Believer. He didn't know any blacks who were.

113

Jeff's mind spun giddily. Love and the fires of passion battled within him against guilt and strange, cold, sullen fingers of anger that clutched at his heart. Can't I do anything right anymore? he wondered. Why am I feeling so many sinful thoughts?

"What's going on in here?"

Jeff jerked around in his chair to see Dr. Carbo striding into the control room, scowling.

"Dammit, Amanda, I expected you to have him hooked up and ready to go. We don't have any time to lose. Let's get to work."

Rising to his feet, Jeff noticed for the first time that he was several centimeters taller than Carbo.

"Just a minute," he said, surprising himself with the steel in his voice. "I want to ask you something."

"What?" Carbo asked as he went to his chair in front of the control panel's main viewscreen.

"Yesterday, in Bishop Foy's office, you seemed to agree with him about . . . "

Carbo flung his head back and said to the ceiling, "*Madonna mia*, not you too! Peterson raked me over the coals for half an hour this morning."

"But you said . . . "

"I gave Foy an excuse to send a team down to the surface to implant more animals," Carbo said, heatedly. "He believes evolution is a false doctrine, and that's fine by me, as long as it helps us to do our work."

Jeff felt himself frown. "But you seemed to agree with him . . . "

"That if the apes are not fully intelligent now, they never will be. Yes, I allowed him to think I agree. So now *he* allows *us* to implant more animals, to study them more thoroughly, to get enough information about life down there so that we can make an intelligent decision about whether or not we should try to alter the planet enough to allow colonization to begin."

"Then you don't agree with Bishop Foy?"

"No. And I don't agree with Peterson, either. I think it's too early to make up our minds, one way or the other. We need to know much more, first. And we'll never learn more if we stand here all day *talking*!"

Jeff grinned with relief and headed for the door to the contact room. It was so much easier being Crown than being Jeffrey Holman.

The days stretched into weeks, and the weeks began to mount up toward a month. Jeff spent almost every waking moment in the contact lab, on the couch, in Crown's mind, his body. From sunrise to nightfall every day, he was Crown. He was in the wolfcat's brain when Crown woke each morning; he was there when the great beast hunkered down his huge body for sleep.

Jeff's routine became almost as instinctive as an animal's. He got up long before the rest of the Village was awake. He ate, exercized, and then went to the lab. Amanda was there waiting for him, always. Most of the time Dr. Carbo did not show up until much later, after Jeff was already on the couch, in contact with Crown.

Jeff treasured those few moments each morning with Amanda. He lived for them. He never dared to tell her that he loved her. He never dared to hope that she loved him. But just being close to her, near enough to hear her voice, to smell her perfume, kept him going from day to day.

Often at the end of a grueling day-long session Jeff would eat dinner at the autocafeteria in his own dome.

At first Laura managed to be there every evening, but Jeff found himself too tired, and too involved with thoughts of Amanda, to pay much attention to her.

"I'm trying out for a contact mission," Laura told him one evening, her green eyes shining with excitement.

"You?" Jeff asked.

"Yes, me. What's wrong with that?"

He pushed the last remaining morsel of stewed rabbit around the rim of his plate. Far in the back of his mind he thought of how small rabbits are, how paltry they would seem to Crown.

"Well?" Laura demanded. "What's wrong with me making contact with one of the animals down there?"

"Nothing," he said.

"You don't seem very happy about it."

"I'm pretty tired, Laura. It's hard work, you know."

"Meaning that you think I can't do it?"

For the first time that evening, he really looked at her. She had a redhead's temper, all right.

"No, not at all. I'm sure you can do it. It's just . . . well, it's not easy, that's all."

Laura pushed her chair away from the table and grabbed the tray containing her half-finished meal. "I thought you'd be excited about it! I thought you'd be *happy* for me! But what everyone's saying is true, isn't it? You don't *want* anyone else to make contact with those animals. You want to be the only one!"

Before he could reply, she turned and stamped away from him, leaving him totally alone in the cafeteria.

Jeff ate alone from then on. And as his life in the Village became more and more routine, automated, it became less and less real to him. What was real was Crown's life on the surface of the world called Windsong.

Jeff could not figure out when the name came to him. Perhaps it was late one afternoon as Crown stood on the crest of one of the hills that overlooked the beach. From this particular spot, as he looked out toward the sea, he could not see the humans' camp. There was only the curving line of the hills, with their wind-bent trees, green and full of life, and the bright sand and the ocean. Waves marched up to the beach, driven by a wind that made the twisted trees bow low and sing.

Windsong.

Dark clouds hurried across the sky, changing, boiling, floating high in the air as they wafted by.

Windsong.

Over the days and weeks, Crown solved the problem of hunting in these rich wooded hills without running afoul of the wolfcat families that claimed the territory for themselves. He joined one of the families.

The wounds from his first encounter healed within a few days, and the ape he had killed kept him well fed for that long and more. The only scavengers he saw along the beach were the circling, gliding lizard-hawks, and these he kept off merely by staying close to his kill during the daylight hours. At night, when Crown slept, the birds slept too. But finally even the great bulk of the ape dwindled and began to smell foul with decay. Crown moved away, and in less than a day the lizard-hawks picked the carcass clean to the bone.

Crown headed up into the woods the next day, and Jeff tensed mentally, knowing that when Crown tried to hunt down a meal in those woods, the nearest wolfcat family would attack him.

To Jeff's surprise, though, Crown did not go hunting. He padded through the wooded underbrush until he found a small wolfcat family, lolling in the spotty sunlight that filtered through the trees. A grizzled old male, three females, and a pair of cubs less than one year old. The cubs were barely two meters long, muzzle to tail.

Crown watched them from a distance for the better part of the day, staying well screened in the leafy foliage that grew among the trees. He saw the females hunt down a snorting, tusked, tough-hided creature, a kind that Crown had never seen before. After they had killed it, they dragged it back to the shaded hollow where the male lay at his ease, allowing the cubs to tussle playfully under his watchful eye.

As the family settled down to its meal, Crown stood up at his full height and slowly approached them, silently, his head held low. The male looked up from his gorging and uttered a warning growl from deep in his chest. Crown stopped at the edge of the hollow and lifted his face to the sky.

Why is he doing that?

I don't know. Maybe we should call Peterson, or one of the others.

No need for that. We're getting it all down on tape. We can . . . look at that!

The old male walked slowly, menacingly, toward Crown, his growl like the rumble of distant thunder. The females stood by their kill, watching. Crown stood unmoving, his head lifted high, his throat exposed to a sudden, life-taking slash.

The elder sniffed at Crown for long moments, then turned his head back toward the females. The smallest of them tore a piece of bleeding meat from the dead boar and, holding it in both forepaws, walked up beside the old male and laid the food on the ground in front of Crown.

Jesu Christo! They're offering him food!

It . . . it's like a ritual.

Amanda, we'd better not let Ferris see this until Foy does. She'll go hysterical.

We can't keep this from her.

I know. I know. But we certainly don't have to go out of our way to tell her about it!

Crown accepted the meat and ate it. The elder male was big, powerful, in his prime. He had no fear of Crown, once Crown showed him that he would be submissive. The females were his, but in a few years the cubs would be old enough to start mating. A wolfcat family with only one male was a rarity; if this wolfcat family had included a male cub instead of two females, Crown might not have been accepted so easily.

Jeff understood that, and wondered if Crown had known it instinctively or if the wolfcat had reasoned it out for himself. The idea troubled Jeff for many days afterward. He was glad that Crown now had a family and could hunt without danger. But something about the way Crown had gone about solving his problem kept Jeff awake night after night until he finally realized what it was. He sat bolt upright in his bed after hours of thrashing about fitfully. The shattering truth of it hit him with the clarity of a religious revelation.

"The wolfcats are intelligent!" he said aloud, into the empty darkness of his dorm room. "Not the apes. The wolfcats!"

CHAPTER 10

"Intelligent?" Dr. Carbo looked at Jeff skeptically.

"The wolfcats are intelligent," Jeff repeated. "I know they are."

Carbo and Amanda were strapping Jeff into the contact couch, to begin the morning's work. It was still dark down on the hills overlooking Crown's beach. The wolfcats were still sleeping.

Amanda said, "Maybe we'd better call Peterson."

"He's busy getting the landing team ready," Carbo replied. "I don't think we ought to bother him with this."

"But we've got to!" Jeff insisted. "It's important."

Carbo lowered the gleaming metal helmet onto Jeff's head. "What makes you think that they're intelligent?"

"The way Crown behaves. And the way the wolfcat family took him in. It was a kind of ritual. That wasn't the way dumb animals act."

"Chimpanzees behave that way," Amanda said. "They use gestures and have pretty intricate family relationships."

"See?"

"But chimps aren't intelligent," Carbo said.

"Aren't they?"

"Not officially. Not as far as Bishop Foy is concerned."

"What about the world government?" Amanda asked. "Chimpanzees are on the officially protected list. Chimps, dolphins, whales and androids—killing them is punishable just as though you killed a human being."

"But the Church doesn't accept that," Jeff said, feeling the weight of the helmet on his head.

"And Foy runs this mission," Carbo muttered.

"But he doesn't run Louisa Ferris," Amanda said sharply. "She represents the world government."

Jeff glanced at Carbo, then at Amanda, and then back to Carbo again. The two of them were facing each other, electricity sparking between them.

"Now wait a minute," Carbo said. "I don't want us to get into the middle of a battle between Foy and Ferris . . ."

"Church and state," Amanda murmured, almost smiling at the irony of it.

"We have our jobs to do," Carbo insisted quietly. "Let's do them."

Jeff struggled to sit up but the cuffs and the helmet held him on the couch. "But what about Crown?" he demanded. "What about the wolfcats down there?"

Carbo closed his eyes, as if in great pain. "I'll speak to Peterson about it. Tonight. I'll arrange to have dinner with him and ask his opinion. Now let's get to work."

Jeff could see that there was little more he could accomplish. He willed his tensed body to relax on the couch, thinking to himself, But there's a lot that Crown can do. Crown can *prove* that the wolfcats are intelligent.

He closed his eyes and waited for the neuroelectronic probe to establish contact with the wolfcat. As he felt the now-familiar sensations of sinking, plummeting into an inky oblivion, a new thought assailed his consciousness:

If the wolfcats are intelligent, and we have to stop trying to colonize the planet, I'll have to stop making contact with Crown!

Crown awoke from his night's sleep and shook his maned head, as if trying to clear away a bad dream. He got to his six paws and stretched languidly. The cubs were already awake, lying still between the two slumbering females, watching Crown carefully. They were too young to understand what had happened; they still regarded Crown as a stranger, an intruder. The old male, Thunder, seemed to be asleep also, but he lay facing Crown and it was impossible to tell from a wolfcat's lidless eyeplates whether it was awake or not.

Crown snuffled at the cubs, then padded off into the woods. As a family member, he had to show that he could help to provide food. Jeff did not even try to control him as Crown tracked down one of the canny, sharp-tusked boars. It was a large one, and it showed absolutely no fear of the wolfcat as Crown backed it against a rock outcropping where it could not run away from him. The boar charged at Crown, head low, seeking to get under the wolfcat's jaws and thrust upward with its projecting tusks against Crown's throat or belly. But Crown was too fast for that; he sidestepped the lunging boar and broke its back with single powerful blow of his forepaw. The animal screamed once, then Crown ripped its throat out and it died, quivering as its blood gushed onto the grass.

Crown carried his kill back to the glade where Thunder and the family still lay resting. The cubs raced up to him, circling him and his kill as he approached the older male. The females stayed respectfully beside Thunder, who stood on all sixes and purred happily as Crown deposited the kill at his feet. The head of the family tore off a haunch for himself and carried it a few steps away, then settled down to eat. The females stood by the kill expectantly. Crown took a chunk of meat for himself, then they each took theirs, leaving the remainder for the cubs to gnaw on.

His belly full, Crown felt an urge to see the beach once again, even though he disliked and distrusted the ugly alien machines that lay strewn along the sand. But he got up anyway and headed out toward the top of the ridge line, where he could see the beach and the ocean. Thunder and the rest of the family stayed behind, sated and content for the time being.

It was only a few minutes' walk to the top of the ridge line. Crown surveyed the littered beach, watched the waves rolling in from the far horizon, and thought of his own hill, so far away now that it seemed like another world, a long-distant past that could never be recaptured. He raised his muzzle toward the pearly gray sky, where Altair was a vague glowing blur climbing toward zenith. Strangers would soon be dropping out of that sky, strangers who would change this world of Windsong. And Crown knew that he would be expected to help those strangers.

He growled. Not in anger, for wolfcats know nothing of such a human emotion. Crown growled in pain, in understanding of the pain that was to come.

And on his couch thousands of kilometers above the cloud-shrouded surface of the planet, Jeff Holman writhed and moaned with the same realization, the same pain.

Harvey Peterson ate slowly, chewed his food carefully, and listened attentively to what Frank Carbo was telling him.

"I'll have to look at your tapes," he said, putting his fork down on his emptied plate.

Peterson, Carbo, and Amanda Kolwezi were eating dinner together in Amanda's apartment. She had volunteered to cook for them, an inducement that Peterson could not resist, no matter how busy he was preparing for the expedition to the planet's surface. His wife, one of the Village's medics, had evening-shift duty.

"Where is Holman now? Can I talk with him about this?" Peterson asked.

Carbo, pushing his chair back away from the table slightly, answered, "Jeff's sleeping. At least, he ought to be. He's been working long days, and I want him to get as much rest as he possibly can."

"He's been working very hard," Amanda said. She sat between the two men, her back to the wicker screen that covered the doorway to the kitchen.

125

"And he has much harder work coming up," Carbo went on. "He'll be using that wolfcat to help you and your landing team, Harvey, when you go down there."

"But if the wolfcats really are intelligent . . . " Peterson mused, stroking his chin.

"Then we're wasting our time here," Amanda said.

"And the Church's money," Peterson added.

Carbo picked up a crust of bread that remained on his plate, brought it to his mouth, then thought better of it and returned it to the plate.

"Do you think for one minute," he asked them, "that Foy would admit that any animal down there is intelligent?"

"It's not Foy's decision to make," Amanda said.

Peterson agreed. "Dr. Ferris is the one to say yes or no, not Bishop Foy."

"She's a member of the Church, isn't she?"

"What's that got to do with . . . " Understanding dawned on Peterson's face. "You don't think that she'd let Foy influence her decision, do you?"

Carbo shrugged elaborately. "We're a long way from home. And Foy doesn't want to be a failure. His Church has sunk tons of money into this colony."

"It's not a colony yet," Amanda corrected.

Peterson hunched forward in his chair and leaned his long, sinewy arms on the table. The sparse hair on his arms was almost white from years of exposure to the sun; the skin was deeply tanned, leathery.

"Now, I know Bishop Foy pretty well, I think. He's no fool; he won't ram through a colonization effort over our protests, I'm sure."

"I am *not* sure," Carbo said.

"He's a man of God," Peterson insisted. "He has a conscience, just the same as you do."

"So did Machiavelli," Carbo replied. "And the Borgias were such good members of the Roman Catholic Church that several of them became Popes."

Peterson laughed. "But that was centuries ago."

"Your own playwright, George Bernard Shaw . . . "

"I'm Norwegian, not English!"

"Shaw was Irish," Amanda said.

"Whatever he was," Carbo answered irritatedly. "He once said that a religious fanatic, who is willing to die for his faith, is just as willing to let *you* die for that same faith."

"What do you mean?" Peterson asked. "I don't see the connection."

Carbo pressed his hands together, almost as if in prayer. "Bishop Foy *believes* in his religion. His religion tells him that 'lower animals' cannot be intelligent. His religion tells him that evolution is nonsense. His religion tells him that Man . . . " he turned to Amanda and made an apologetic dip of his head . . . "Man was created by God to rule the world. No other creature matters."

"I wouldn't state it that way . . . "

"But he would. Foy would."

Amanda said, "Frank, aren't you overstating things?"

"Am I?" Carbo got up from his chair and went to the computer terminal screen on the desk in Amanda's living room. He punched a few buttons as Amanda and Peterson, exchanging puzzled looks, left the dining table and crossed the room to join him.

"Take a look," Carbo said, jabbing a stubby thumb at the screen. "From the Church of Nirvan's own Bible. The Book of Genesis . . . which *they* prefer to Darwin's 'Origin of the Species.' "

Peterson bent his lanky frame to stare at the computer screen. Amanda took the desk chair and sat in it. The screen read:

'So God created man in his *own* image, in the image of God created he him; male and female he created them.

'And God blessed them, and God said unto them, Be fruitful and multiply, and replenish the earth, and subdue it; and have dominion over the fish of the sea, and over the fowl of the air, and over every living thing that moveth upon the earth.'

Peterson's craggy face, illuminated by the glow from the screen, went somber. "Be fruitful and multiply. What a mess that's gotten us into. Seventeen billion people on Earth . . . "

"That's not the point," Carbo said, his soft voice almost a whisper.

"Then what is the point?" Amanda asked.

"According to the Church of Nirvan, according to the guiding principles of this colonization effort, God has given Man a blank check to subdue and dominate all the other creatures of the world."

"Of Earth, you mean," Peterson corrected.

Carbo shook his head. "No, of whatever part of the world we happen to be in. The Church is sophisticated enough to allow for the fact that the human race is no longer confined to one planet."

"Subdue and dominate," Amanda echoed.

"That's right," Carbo said. "God isn't interested in ecology. Man was told by God—they believe—that he can do whatever he feels necessary to any other creature in the world. And even if we come across an intelligent species, if it doesn't look human then it doesn't matter. Only we were created in God's image; the rest are nothing more than beasts."

Amanda swivelled her chair around to look up at Carbo. "But you don't think that Foy . . . "

"I think that Foy will follow the dictates of his religion, especially when they reinforce his own personal self-interest."

Peterson walked slowly to the recliner chair next to the sofa and sank into it. "Then . . . even if the wolfcats *are* intelligent, Foy's attitude would be unchanged."

"That's right."

"But it's up to Dr. Ferris to stop any action that would harm an intelligent species," Amanda said.

Carbo nodded glumly. "Do you honestly think that Louisa Ferris can stand up to Bishop Foy? I don't."

CHAPTER 11

Peterson left shortly afterward, looking very unhappy.

Amanda, sitting beside Carbo on the sofa in her living room, said, "You've dropped a ton of bricks onto his shoulders."

"I didn't mean to," he replied. "You think I should have stayed silent?"

"No. I don't see how you could."

"I had to tell him."

"Yes," Amanda agreed. "It's just that he's already got so much responsibility, what with heading the landing team and all . . ."

"I know."

"So you think that Jeff's right? The wolfcats are intelligent?"

Carbo threw up his hands. "How can I say? I'm not an anthropologist. I'm not even a psychologist! It's not my field."

"But it's your responsibility. *Our* responsibility, I mean."

"Yes," he admitted. "My responsibility. I can stop this whole business if I want to. It's my responsibility."

"Not yours alone, Frank," she said. "I could run the lab without you, if I had to."

He smiled at her. "Yes, I suppose you could."

"So don't try to carry this whole load on your own shoulders."

"You want your share of it?"

"I've got my share, whether I want it or not."

Carbo looked into her deep dark eyes for a long moment. Finally he said, "Would you share this burden with me even if you didn't have to?"

Amanda cocked her head and grinned at him. "I'll tell you what responsibility I'll share with you . . . willingly."

"What?"

She nodded toward the dining area table. "Cleaning up the dirty dishes."

"Oh." His face fell.

"I never feel comfortable going to bed unless the kitchen's cleaned up first," Amanda said.

"Oh?" Carbo felt his spirits rise.

They lay side by side on Amanda's bed, a thin sheen of perspiration covering their naked bodies, the only light in the room coming from the soft glow of a luminescent abstract painting on the wall above their heads.

Carbo stroked Amanda's shoulder. His hand wandered down across her breast, her stomach, the gentle curve of her hip.

"You know, my skin is almost darker than yours," he whispered.

"Too many white hunters in my family tree," Amanda answered, smiling.

"There were Moors in my family background," Carbo said. "Centuries ago. People from northern Italy still call southerners Africans, Ethiopians. It's a big joke in northern Italy."

"Not in Africa."

He turned toward her and nuzzled the hollow where her throat and shoulder met. Amanda sighed softly.

"We'll start our own religion," he said at last. "The African-Italian Voodoo Catholic Church."

"Voodoo is West Indian, not African," Amanda said.

"Oh. Yes, of course."

She turned toward him and grabbed a fistfull of hair at the back of his head. "But we can call it anything you like, Frank. Just as long as we leave all that petty nonsense behind us. No barriers between us, Frank! Not race, or religion, or nationality. We are two human beings, ninety-five trillion kilometers from Earth; two human beings who love each other."

"It's a long distance from home, isn't it?" In the semi-darkness, his voice had a lost, sad echo in it.

"A long distance from all the hatreds and terrors o. the past," Amanda said.

"And from all the rules, the laws that defined right from wrong."

She was silent for a moment. Then, propping herself on one elbow, she asked, "Do you need those laws, Frank? Can't you make your own rules?"

He gazed at her beautiful, serious face, barely visible in the soft radiance of the painting.

"Amanda," he whispered, "I don't want to have this colonization effort shut down. I think perhaps Jeff is right, and the wolfcats *are* intelligent, but I still want the colonization to proceed."

He couldn't see the expression on her face, whether she was surprised or disappointed or angry. Her voice was calm, though, as she asked:

"Even if it means wiping out all the animals down there?"

He nodded in the darkness. "Yes."

"But why . . . "

"Because I believe the same way that Foy does, damn my soul! I don't want to believe that way, but I do. I realized while we were talking with Peterson this evening. We've got to subdue and dominate that world down there. We have no choice!"

"Frank, I don't understand why . . . "

"Earth is dying, Amanda! You know that, you saw it every day of your life. The whole planet is suffocating under megatonnages of human flesh. We need colonies, we need places to export people, to ease the population pressure on our home world."

"But Altair VI isn't fit for human life. You said so yourself."

"We'll have to make it fit."

"There are other worlds," Amanda said.

"None like Earth. We haven't found a truly Earth-like planet anywhere. Altair VI is as good as any. We've got to transform it. Otherwise, Earth is lost."

Amanda let herself drop back onto her pillows. To the ceiling, she said, "We've subdued and dominated the Earth to the point of destroying it. Now we've got to subdue and dominate new worlds."

"I don't like it any more than you do," he said. "But we have no choice. It's either tame the new worlds or sink into extinction."

"And the living creatures on this world? The wolfcats and all the rest?"

"It's either them or us, Amanda."

"There must be another way."

"There isn't."

Amanda thought hard about it, but she could find no argument to counter his.

So the wolfcats and all the rest will die, she thought. Just as the gorilla and elephant and giraffe were driven into extinction on Earth. Man the exterminator. It's not enough that we slaughter ourselves and the other creatures of our own planet. Now we have to reach out and begin killing the creatures of every world we touch.

She dozed fitfully, unaccustomed to sharing her bed after the long months away from Earth. She dreamed of Africa, of a dark menacing forest that was totally silent and empty of all animals. Not even an insect buzzed to relieve the oppressive, guilty silence. Yet something, someone was pursuing her. Amanda walked slowly through the shadowy woods, barefoot, frightened. She realized, all of a sudden, that she was naked and that this silence was a danger in itself. Something was behind her, coming after her, and she could not hear it approaching.

She began to walk faster. The sun was a distant glowing blur against the clouds that covered the sky, but even so the heat was thick and heavy. Sweat poured from her, she could feel it trickling along her bare flanks, dripping off her chin, blurring her vision with stinging drops of salt. She wanted to stop, to rest, but she could not. Tangled vines and underbrush flailed at her bare legs. Moving forward was more difficult with each step. But she had to keep going. She ran, her lungs burning, knowing that if she stopped even for a moment she would be horribly, horribly killed.

And then she saw someone up ahead. A man! A friend. He beckoned to her. She knew he was calling to her, but she could not hear a word. She struggled through the thick underbrush, battled against the vines that tried to twine themselves around her naked, sweating body. The man was dark-skinned, smiling to her, beckoning to her, showing her the way to safety.

She broke free of the underbrush at last and ran the last dozen steps toward him. He collapsed onto the grass, his body slashed in a dozen gushing, bleeding wounds. She recognized his face. It was her brother.

Amanda sat bolt upright in the bed, both her fists pressed against her mouth to keep herself from screaming. Carbo slept sprawled on his stomach, oblivious.

She cried for a long while, rocking slowly back and forth, silently. When at last no more tears would flow from her eyes, she lay back again and stared at the ceiling. Carbo stirred and flung an arm across her midriff. She turned her head to look at him and smiled sadly at the sleeping man. She lay there, silent, awake, not daring to close her eyes for fear of dreaming again.

CHAPTER 12

Jeff was surprised when Dr. Peterson came up to his table and sat down beside him. It was early in the morning; the cafeteria was nearly empty, as usual. Only the handful of students who had early chores assigned to them were shuffling through the cafeteria's serving line, half asleep.

Peterson put down a tray heaped with everything the cafeteria offered at this hour next to Jeff's meager breakfast of juice and cereal.

"Mind if I have a few words with you?" he asked, pulling out the chair next to Jeff's.

"Sure," Jeff said.

Peterson folded his long legs around the chair, took up a large glass of juice and drank down half of it. "They don't serve coffee here," he said.

"No. We don't drink coffee or tea," Jeff replied.

"Where I come from," Peterson said, a smile on his craggy face, "nobody can start the day without a big mug of steaming hot coffee."

Jeff said nothing.

Peterson's smile faded by degrees. "Dr. Carbo tells me that you think the wolfcats are intelligent."

"That's right."

Cutting into his eggs, Peterson said, "I've looked at your tapes from the past three days. I'll admit that the wolfcats are a lot more complex than we originally thought they were."

"They have definite social customs," Jeff said. "That's a sign of intelligence, isn't it?"

"It's one possible sign," Peterson said. "But it's not the whole story by itself. True intelligence involves tool use, language . . . "

"They have names," Jeff said.

Peterson ate a forkful of eggs and soy-bacon.

"My wolfcat's name is Crown. His family elder's name is Thunder. The females are Brightfur and Tranquil."

"And the cubs?"

Jeff blinked. "They don't have names yet. They're too little."

The anthropologist grinned and swallowed at the same time. "They must weigh five hundred kilos each."

"That's little for a wolfcat."

"You realize, I hope, that the chances are that you invented those names yourself," Peterson said.

"No," Jeff said. "Those names were in Crown's mind, not mine."

"How can you be sure of that?"

Frowning, Jeff said, "I'm sure. I . . . I just know it. The planet has a name, too. The wolfcats call it Windsong."

Peterson said nothing for a while, he just worked away at his breakfast, chewing each bite methodically while Jeff sat there, his appetite gone.

"Let me ask you this," the anthropologist said at last. "How do the wolfcats tell each other their names?"

"They . . . " Jeff began, then hesitated. "They know."

"Yes, but how? Do they speak to each other? Do they hear each other in their minds, like mental telepathy? Do they use sign language? Gestures?" Peterson smiled kindly to show Jeff that he wasn't trying to attack him.

Jeff thought for a few moments. "It must be some form of telepathy. They don't speak or use sign language."

"We'd have a tough time proving that to Foy, wouldn't we? Or anyone else."

Glumly, Jeff nodded agreement.

Peterson finished off most of his breakfast while Jeff sat in silence, barely picking at the meager meal before him.

"Well," the anthropologist said at last, "we're going down there this morning. If there's anything you can do to help the wolfcat show his intelligence to the landing team . . . well, I'll be looking for a sign."

He got to his feet and Jeff stood up too, barely reaching the older man's shoulder.

"Thank you," Jeff said.

"For what?" Peterson looked genuinely surprised.

"For listening to me. For caring enough not to make fun of the idea."

The anthropologist's rugged face grew very serious. "Son, I'm a scientist. Do you understand what that means?"

"It means that you're interested in science."

"Much more. A farmer can be interested in science." Peterson put a hand on Jeff's shoulder. His grip was strong and sure. "To be a scientist is a way of life. It means that when you come across a new idea, you use your five senses to get as much information about the idea as you can. You listen. You watch. You touch and taste and sniff. You test the idea. Only after all that do you start to make up your mind."

Jeff almost smiled. "In the Church they teach that scientists can never make up their minds."

"We're always open to new information. That makes some people very uneasy. They want to be told 'the truth,' the absolute unchanging final word. We don't deal with that kind of dogma. We're always ready to alter our conclusions in the light of new data."

"So you can never know the truth," Jeff said.

"We can get pretty close." Peterson grinned at him. "Closer than anyone else. But we never claim to have the final, absolute truth."

"The Church has the Truth."

"Not the same thing. Not the same at all. Your Church—any church—establishes a set of rules, and then tries to explain everything in the world according to those rules. Scientists try to discover how the world actually works, how things behave. Different approach."

Jeff thought it over briefly, then said, "But you don't deal with *why* things work the way they do."

Peterson's grin spread across his weathered face. "No. We have our hands full trying to figure out *how* they work. We leave the causes to religion and philosophy."

"But then . . ."

Peterson stopped him by looking at his wristwatch. "We'll have to continue this some other time. I'm due at the shuttle port in ten minutes."

Glancing at his own watch, Jeff agreed. "I've got to get to the contact lab."

They left the cafeteria together, then took different tube-corridors toward their different destinations. The last Jeff saw of Peterson, the lanky anthropologist waved to him and said, "See you down there!"

Jeff waved back and watched the scientist jog down the greenpath of the tube and disappear from sight.

Amanda was already in the lab when Jeff arrived, but Dr. Carbo had not shown up yet.

"He'll stagger in soon," she said, smiling, as she started fastening the cuffs on Jeff's ankles and wrists.

"We're going to be working with the landing team today," Jeff said.

"That's right."

Jeff lay back on the couch. His stomach felt queasy, fluttery, and he knew it was not because the scientists were going down to the surface this morning.

He closed his eyes for a moment, worked up his courage, and said, "Amanda?"

"Yes?" She had moved over to the monitoring instruments on the wall next to the couch.

"Would you have dinner with me tonight? To celebrate, I mean?"

"Celebrate?"

"This is the first time we've worked with a landing team," Jeff said.

Her eyebrows rose a centimeter. "That sounds like a good-enough reason to celebrate," Amanda said.

"Then you'll have dinner with me?"

"Yes. I would like to."

Jeff's heart soared, but then he realized, "Uh . . . it'll have to be in the cafeteria in my dorm area. We don't have our own kitchens."

She seemed to think it over for a moment. "That'll be fine, Jeff."

He let out a long happy sigh and felt his body relax against the warm fabric of the couch.

Dr. Carbo came in, his chin darker than usual. But he grinned happily as he strode up to Jeff.

"All set?" he asked.

"Yessir."

Turning to Amanda, "Everything ready?"

Jeff couldn't hear her reply.

"All right, then," Carbo said. "Let's get started."

Crown was already at the crest of the ridge line overlooking the beach, even though Altair had barely nudged its limb over the sea horizon.

Like he knew we're going to need him today.

Or he remembered the thoughts that Jeff had in his mind from yesterday.

Do you think maybe Jeff's right, and they really are intelligent?

I don't know. It's not my field.

Crown sniffed at the sea breeze. It was heavy with the now-familiar scent of the rusting machines. But the wolfcat knew that something else was going to happen today. Something strange and alien. He growled his displeasure.

How did you sleep last night?

Off and on. I had a nightmare . . .

I'm sorry.

It wasn't your fault.

I'm still sorry.

You went out like a light. You didn't move a muscle. I didn't have any nightmares, either.

I'll bet.

It was a morning like any other morning, yet Crown knew that this one would be different. He padded along the crest of the ridge line, watching the sea and the sky, waiting.

And finally it appeared. Far, far up in the clouded sky he saw a tiny speck racing across the heavens, leaving a thin trail of vapor behind it, like a dark line drawn against the gray clouds. The speck began to grow and take shape: triangular wings, a sleek shining body that ended in a raked-back tail surface.

A sonic boom split the air, making Crown jump back toward the safety of the trees. But still he watched the rocketplane as it banked and turned gracefully overhead, came down low, skimmed the waves, and finally landed on the hard-packed sand of the beach, rolling almost up to the abandoned equipment on four sets of oversized wheels.

The rocketplane had made practically no noise after the sonic boom. Crown hunkered down on his belly, still shaded by the trees and screened by the underbrush, and watched the alien craft for long, silent minutes. Its scent was powerful, but much like the odor of the other machines: dead, metallic, harsh.

At last a hatch opened in the rocketplane's side. A strange creature stood uncertainly just inside the hatchway. It stood on two legs. It was gleaming white, almost like the metal of the shuttle craft. Its head was a bulbous gleaming bowl. To Crown it looked somewhat like one of the apes, up on its hind legs. But it was ridiculously small, puny.

A ladder slid out from the side of the ship and planted itself on the sand of the beach. The alien creature slowly walked down the ladder, using its forelegs to hold onto the railing on either side of the steps. It stopped at the bottom, turned around slowly as if surveying the beach, then looked back up toward the hatch and waved a foreleg. Another alien appeared and started down the ladder. Then another, and still another. Crown counted six in all.

He growled, a deep menacing rumble from inside his chest. But he knew that he must go down to the beach and come closer to these strange creatures. Slowly, reluctantly, Crown got up onto all sixes and started down the slope of the hill, head low, ears flattened, lips pulled back in a barely-repressed snarl.

Harvey Peterson stood at the bottom of the ladder, his heart pounding with anxiety. It was like stepping into the darkest night he could imagine, wading into a bowl of ink. Even with the infrared lamp built into his helmet, he could barely see twenty meters ahead. The microwave radar scanner showed that the beach was flat and level, sloping slightly up from the ammonia-frothing sea toward a line of wooded hills that rose steeply, some hundred meters in from the shore.

He turned back toward the ship, where the other volunteers stood clustered around the hatch, waiting.

"All right," he said into his helmet microphone, "come on down." He almost said that the coast was clear, but such a pun would seem too frivolous in this murky, danger-laden world.

The radar display was superimposed on his visor, so that he saw what the microwaves revealed as a glowing, ghostly image superimposed over the dim murky images that his natural vision could make out.

"The equipment is up this way." He pointed, and started plodding up the beach. The other five men followed him.

Soon enough they came upon the abandoned tractors and broken packing cases of equipment.

"Rusted through," said their engineer.

"Cripes, look at this pump. The plastic's been eaten away and the metal's *etched* — like somebody's been pouring high-grade acid over it."

"Looks like the statues on the Acropolis," said one of the scientists. "Eaten through by sulfur dioxide fumes."

"Just make certain you don't tear your suits," Peterson warned. "This atmosphere is laced with enough methane and . . . "

"Omygod, what's that?"

Peterson turned to see a mountainous gray shape gliding slowly toward them. He blinked twice, then realized what he was looking at.

"Stand perfectly still!" he commanded. "Don't panic. It's the wolfcat that Carbo's people have under control."

"You sure it's under control?"

The beast stood taller than any of them at the shoulder. Its six legs ended in paws bigger than a man's head. Peterson saw that its claws were retracted, but he could imagine the size of them. Its head was enormous, with two huge plates of bony-looking material where the eyes would be on an Earth animal. Its mouth was open a slit, and Peterson could see the tips of dagger-sharp teeth.

145

"It's growling."

"It might be a purr."

Someone laughed, halfway between embarrassment and hysteria. "Jesus Christ, I just shit my pants."

"Just stay where you are, everybody," Peterson said, fighting to keep his voice calm, "until it gets accustomed to us."

"What then?"

"Then it has us for brunch."

The wolfcat's huge head moved slowly from side to side, as if inspecting each of the six humans. It took one step toward Peterson, then slowly lay down on the sand and rested its chin on its forepaws.

"Peterson to base," the anthropologist spoke into his radio microphone. "We have made contact with the wolfcat. Instruct Carbo and Holman to have the animal lead us toward the apes. We want to find and tranquilize at least one family of the apes."

Crown lay on the sand and watched the aliens. They stood frozen, like a deer caught out in the open trying to confuse a wolfcat by standing stock-still. These creatures were too small to consider killing for food, unless the wolfcat was starving. But something in Crown's brain told him that even then, they would be no good to eat. They were poisonous, like some of the smaller animals of Windsong; to eat them would mean death.

The apes. These alien creatures wanted to find a family of apes. Crown snorted at the idea. The apes came along this beach, but he had no idea of where their lairs might be. Still, he rose ponderously and turned northward. He took a few steps, then swung his head back to see if the aliens were following.

"It's heading north!"

Peterson nodded inside his cumbersome helmet. "Higgins," he said to the engineer, "you and Scott stay here and do a complete checkout on the machinery . . ."

"I can tell you right now, it's useless junk."

"Dr. Polchek, Lyle and I will follow the wolfcat. It should be leading us to the apes."

"Don't get out of radio contact," Higgins said.

"We won't."

It was like groping through a nightmare. Even with their radar displays, the humans were lost inside a dark, threatening pit of blackness. It was bad enough to be locked into the heavy, clumsy pressure suits. But the eternal night outside, the knowledge that the very air was eating away at the seals and joints of your protective armor, trying to get inside and burn out your lungs—even Peterson began to feel the pangs of claustrophobia.

The wolfcat padded on ahead, imperturbable as a force of nature. Every few minutes it would turn its massive head to make certain that the humans were following. Peterson began to think of old Norse tales of the netherworld, and the giant beasts that guard the approach to hell. Surely nothing the old Vikings could imagine was worse than this.

Dr. Polchek, the zoologist, broke their long silence. "I haven't seen another animal of any kind along this beach, Harvey. Have you?"

"No. Nothing."

"What d'you expect?" Lyle said. He was the medic in the team, the man who would have to insert the neuro probes into the apes' brains if and when they found and tranquilized some apes.

"Well, I know we can't see very well in this atmosphere," Dr. Polchek replied, "but I'm surprised we haven't stumbled across anything at all."

"The other animals are keeping their distance from us," Peterson suggested. "The wolfcat probably helps to scare them away."

"Ah, yes, of course. And the wolfcat is under intelligent control, from back on the ship."

Peterson nodded, but he found himself wondering just how much of the intelligence was native to the wolfcat itself.

They plodded along the long curving beach for more than an hour, the ocean always at their right, the line of hills gradually but perceptibly edging closer to the water from their left. Finally the wolfcat stopped.

"What's the matter?" Polchek asked. "Can you see anything up ahead?"

"Nothing but black soup," Peterson said. "The hills seem steeper here . . . " He reached for the control knobs on his wrist and increased the range of the microwave radar. The image on his visor blurred and shimmied.

"I don't see any apes," Lyle said.

"The hills come right up to the water up ahead," Peterson said. Glancing at the range indication number at the bottom of his visor, "Looks like a dead end, half a kilometer ahead of us."

"You mean we came this way for nothing?"

Peterson wanted to shrug, but the suit was too heavy for it.

"Hey . . . look at the wolfcat!" Lyle called out.

Crown could smell the apes up ahead, but it seemed obvious that the aliens could not. He stopped. They stopped behind him. For a moment or two Crown did not know what to do. He had no way of making these aliens realize what lay ahead. But he knew that he had to communicate with them somehow.

He turned back toward them, and they edged away nervously. One of them stumbled in the sand and nearly fell. Crown paced back and forth, took a few steps away from the aliens, then a few steps back toward them. They milled around, gesturing to each other.

Finally Crown simply bounded away, scampering up the steep hillside toward the trees at the top of the ridge line. He glanced once back over his shoulder. The aliens stood transfixed on the beach. Good.

Crown raced through the trees, heading for the point where the hills steepened into cliffs that dropped straight down into the frothing sea. The apes lived in caves there, he could tell from their powerful scent. He hoped to catch a few out on the beach itself and get between them and their caves.

He was in luck. A half dozen of the apes were out on the beach, clawing at the sand to find shellfish. To Crown they seemed to be two adult males, three females, and one cub. Good enough. He stayed hidden in the trees atop the ridge line until he was between the apes and the caves in the cliffs. Only then did he scamper down the steep hillside, roaring as he leaped from rock to rock.

The apes panicked. Screaming wildly, they lurched up onto their hind legs and ran blindly down the beach, away from their caves, toward the humans.

"What the hell was that?" Lyle shouted.

Peterson winced at the sound of the medic's frightened voice in his helmet earphones.

"Sounded like a cross between a thunderclap and an earthquake," Polchek said. "It must have been the wolfcat."

"But what . . . "

"Listen!" Peterson snapped.

They could hear the wailing screams of the fleeing apes.

"Whatever the hell it is, it's coming this way," Lyle yelled.

Polchek fumbled with the holster on his belt. "Gentlemen, I suggest we check our weapons."

Peterson yanked the gun from his holster. It fired tranquilizer darts, each with a carefully-calculated dose of chemicals. He had thought the darts were loaded with enough tranquilizer to stop a herd of elephants. But after seeing the wolfcat, and now with the hideous screams of the apes bearing down on them, Peterson wondered if they had enough to do the job.

"Look out!" Lyle yelled.

Peterson saw half a dozen huge gray-white shapes streaking out of the enveloping darkness, heading straight for him. He fired at point-blank range, never hearing the guns go off, his vision, his mind, his *being* completely engulfed with the sight of these immensely powerful beasts crashing down on him.

Something slammed him to the ground. His head spun and he tasted blood in his mouth. He couldn't catch his breath and for a wild frightened instant he was afraid his suit had ripped open.

Then he felt hands on his shoulders.

"Are you all right?" Lyle's voice.

"Harvey, are you injured?" Polchek asked.

"I'm okay," Peterson said, gasping for air. "Just . . . just the wind knocked out of me."

He let them pull him up to a kneeling position. He saw six furry gray-white bodies sprawled along the sand.

"That one there bowled into you before it collapsed," Polchek explained.

Peterson took a deep breath, then climbed to his feet. He saw the wolfcat standing a few meters away, its nostrils twitching.

"All right," he said. "Let's get those implants in before they wake up."

Crown watched the aliens at work. They were not eating the apes, they were doing strange things to them. Deep inside his mind, Crown had the vague memory that something like this had been done to him. He growled nervously, and one of the aliens straightened up and looked toward him.

None of the other apes had ventured this far down the beach. When a wolfcat roars, the apes hide in their caves, Crown realized.

His stomach rumbled with hunger, and he hoped that these strangers would finish whatever they were doing and go away soon, leaving this beach and Windsong forever.

One of the apes, the larger of the two males, stirred slightly. The aliens, bent over the other male, did not notice. Crown padded over toward them, slowly. The aliens were too busy to pay him any attention.

Crown gave a low, warning growl. The ape raised its head.

Peterson heard the growl and looked up. The wolfcat loomed over him like a mountain rising out of the sea.

He swallowed once, then muttered, "It seems that our pet cat is curious about us."

Lyle and Polchek straightened up.

"God Almighty, he is *huge*."

"I hope it isn't lunchtime for him."

The wolfcat made a low rumbling noise, like distant thunder, and turned toward the larger of the two male apes.

"Hey, look, it's coming . . ."

Lyle never finished the sentence. The ape leaped to its hindlegs and with a backhand swipe knocked Lyle completely off his feet. Peterson reached for the gun he had left on the sand at his feet as the ape lunged for him.

But a gray blur blotted out his vision of the snarling ape. The wolfcat moved with the speed of lightning and smashed the ape back into the sand.

Peterson's legs gave way under him and he plopped foolishly onto his backside. Polchek, still on his knees, froze immobile beside him.

The wolfcat growled at the dead ape. Its head was crushed, face ripped away. Peterson fought down the acid bile that rose in his throat to half choke him.

"It . . . it saved us," Polchek whispered.

"Lyle," Peterson said. "Is he . . ."

They scrambled to their feet as the wolfcat backed away slightly. Lyle's body lay crumpled a dozen meters away. His helmet was cracked open, his eyes glassy and staring.

"Merciful God," Polchek whimpered. "He's dead."

Peterson looked at the zoologist, although he could not see the man's face through the visor of his helmet. Merciful God, Peterson thought. What a joke. What a cruel, bitter joke.

CHAPTER 13

Jeff awoke slowly. The first thing he became aware of was the faint hum of the electrical equipment that pervaded every part of the Village, every moment of the day and night. How different from the sound of the breeze on Windsong, he thought.

Then he remembered what had just happened. Crown helping the scientists, saving the lives of Peterson and Polchek, even though he had been too late to save Lyle.

He tried to warn them, Jeff said to himself. I tried to show them that the ape was coming to. Why didn't they pay attention?

Amanda entered the room and wordlessly lifted the helmet off his head.

"Is he dead?" Jeff asked.

"Yes. They're on their way back now. Frank's gone down to the shuttle dock to meet them."

"Did they get the implants into the apes?"

Amanda gave him a long stare. "Yes. All of them, except the one that Crown killed."

He sat up slowly, swung his legs over the couch, then slid off it. His legs felt a little rubbery, but he was stronger than he had thought he would be.

"I'm sorry about Dr. Lyle," Jeff said to Amanda. "I tried to help . . ."

"We know. It's not your fault, Jeff." But Amanda's voice was flat, mechanical. She walked away from Jeff, into the control room.

Following her through the open doorway, he said, "Amanda . . . about dinner tonight . . . "

"I don't think I'll feel much like celebrating," Amanda said as she checked the instrument panels.

He nodded. "I know. I don't either."

"Maybe some other time."

"Yeah. Sure."

He left the lab before she could say anything else. It's so unfair! Jeff told himself. They're blaming everything on me. *I* didn't kill Dr. Lyle. If it hadn't been for me, they would all have been killed. They would never have found any of the apes if I hadn't helped them.

Still, he felt the weight of guilt on his shoulders as he walked slowly back toward his own dome.

As he neared the dormitory domes, the greenpaths along the tube-tunnels became more and more crowded with students. Happy, smiling, students, striding purposefully along, sure of themselves and their place in the world. Jeff wished that he could feel as confident as they did. But they had such simple lives, he knew. Do what the Church tells you. Work, study, pray. Eat to stay alive and serve Nirvan's Church. Obey the Elders. They didn't have to be a good Believer one instant and a bloodthirsty wolfcat the next. They didn't have to kill in order to eat, or try to serve alien invaders who were going to destroy their own home world.

The students were streaming toward the Tabernacle, the dome in the midst of the student domes which housed the central house of worship for all the Believers of the Village. Built exactly like the smaller chapels in each of the dormitory domes, the Tabernacle was large enough to hold all the students in one sitting.

"Jeff! Oh, Jeff!"

He turned toward the voice. It was Laura McGrath, pushing her way through the crowd of students hurrying along the greenpath.

"Jeff, you're out of the laboratory early enough for sundown worship!"

Her smile was dazzling, her green eyes sparkled with delight. Jeff wanted to smile back at her, to share in her pleasure in simple acts such as worship or greeting a friend. But he couldn't.

"What's the matter?" Laura said, as she slipped her arms in his. "You look . . . they've been working you too hard, Jeff, haven't they?"

With a shake of his head. "No, it's okay. Come on, I'll go to sundown services with you."

She seemed perfectly happy to be with him. He didn't have the heart to tell her that he had watched one of the Village's medics get killed by a monstrous giant ape.

As they entered the Tabernacle, the choir was already singing hymns and Bishop Foy was sitting in his high-backed chair at the side of the altar, dressed in his splendid regalia of red and green.

Jeff let Laura lead him to her pew. "It's all right for you to sit with me, I'm sure," she whispered. "Nobody will mind."

He slid into the pew beside her and knelt on the padded kneeler. Bending his head over his clenched fists, Jeff thought, Pray! Pray for guidance. Pray for strength. But when he closed his eyes he saw the beach on Windsong, and the terrified looks on the faces of the apes as they fled from Crown and into the guns of the landing team. Poor dumb beasts, Jeff thought. They were harming no one, and now we're going to turn them into slaves and make them destroy their own world.

And Jeff realized, as the choir sang placidly and the old familiar odor of incense filled the air, that the guilt he felt was not over Dr. Lyle's death—he felt guilty over what he was helping the others to do to the apes, to the wolfcats, to a whole beautiful world.

Amanda Kolwezi felt no guilt, but she was saddened by Lyle's death. All the scientists knew how dangerous it could be on the surface of Altair VI; they all volunteered for duty on the landing team. Still, no one expects to be killed. No one expects a team member to die. It was a bad omen to have a death in the first landing to be tried in months. How many more were going to die?

She waited at the laboratory, sitting in the little swivel chair in front of the silent control panels, waiting for Carbo to return.

He'll come here, she said to herself. Not to his own quarters. He'll come here first.

She was right. Eventually the door from the corridor opened and Carbo stepped in, his swarthy face set in a grimly determined expression.

"You're still here?" he said.

"Just finishing up," Amanda replied.

He glanced at his wristwatch. "You were waiting for me."

"Sort of. I thought you might need some moral support."

Carbo walked over to the other chair and sank into it. "Can you run the lab without me? I'll get you an assistant, of course."

Amanda felt her heart constrict. "You're not going down there, Frank. Please say you're not."

"But I am." He smiled sadly. "They need someone who knows how to implant the probes, with Lyle gone."

"You're not a medical . . ."

"I know how to put the probes in," he said. "They're my invention, my responsibility."

"But it . . ."

He reached up and touched her lips with an upraised finger, as softly as a butterfly touching a flower.

"Amanda, please don't let your emotions get in the way of your good judgment. We came here to this world to make it ready for colonization. The only way we can do that is to use the animals down there to work for us. The only way we can accomplish that goal is to send down landing teams to implant the animals with neuro probes."

"But there are others who can do that!" Amanda

insisted. "You're too valuable, too important to . . . "

"To risk my life?" The sad smile returned. "No, I'm not that important. I came here to make a contribution, to help the human race to expand to the stars. It's either that or extinction for us. You realize that, don't you?"

She pressed her hands against her ears, as if trying to blot out his words. "I still don't see why *you* have to throw away your life."

"Amanda, dearest, I came here because my life on Earth was finished. I have made my contribution: the neuro probe. Now I have a chance to do something more, to see that the probe is used in a way that will actually help humanity. Instead of merely pacifying Earth's billions, instead of merely postponing the inevitable collapse, I can help to open a whole new world for the human race! I can't turn my back on that opportunity."

"Even if it kills you."

"What is my life, compared to seventeen billions?"

"Your living is important to me," she said.

"I know it is. I appreciate that. I marvel that someone as intelligent and beautiful as you could feel that way."

"But I'm not as important to you, am I?" Amanda asked.

He looked shocked. "Of course you are!"

"Then why are you prepared to leave me and kill yourself?"

For a long moment Carbo remained silent. Finally he made a little shrug. "It's an old, old question, Amanda. Why does the hunter leave his mate behind and go out into the wilds? Why does the explorer turn his back on home and family and go seeking new territory? I've got to do it, Amanda. I've got to do what I can to help make this colonization a success."

"Despite . . ." She stopped. It was useless, she knew. Not even begging him would help.

"I talked it over with Peterson," Carbo said quietly. "We'll organize a much larger team; today's group was too small to accomplish much."

"How soon?" Amanda asked.

"The arrangements should take a week or so. In the meantime, we can start to test more of the students with the apes we implanted today."

"I'll need more than one assistant," she said.

"Yes, I know. We'll have to start training students to help you."

"You'll keep Jeff working with Crown, won't you?"

"Yes, of course. But as more students come into the program, we can ease his workload somewhat."

"That sounds sensible."

He looked at her sharply. "Sensible."

"Of course," Amanda said, her voice cold and bleak. "We all have to be sensible, don't we?"

"Yes, but that doesn't mean . . ."

She stopped him with a sigh. "No, Frank, it does mean something very important. It means that we can't stay as close as we have been."

"But why not?"

"I can't make love with you, knowing that you'll be getting up from my bed and going out to kill yourself. I've lost too many loved ones; I can't let myself get so attached to you . . . it would kill me, too."

"But I'm not going to die!" He tried to laugh about it.

Amanda shook her head. "No. Of course not. But I'll die a little, every moment you're down there. Don't put me through that, Frank. Don't ask me to tear my heart out of my body all over again."

He closed his eyes. "I see. I understand."

"I doubt that you do," Amanda said. "But that's the way it has to be. I've got to find the strength to separate myself from you."

"Yes," he said, in a barely-audible whisper. "That will be for the best."

Each of them wanted to cry. But they did not allow themselves that luxury.

CHAPTER 14

If sheer determination could change a world, the scientists and students of the Village would turn Altair VI into a new Eden.

The entire Village was mobilized for the battle against nature. Believers and secularists worked side by side to tame the wilderness of the savage planet below them. After months of studies and preparation, the students leaped into the struggle with wholehearted enthusiasm. The scientists, who had spent those same months actually observing the planet and trying to deal with it, were more cautious.

New landing parties were organized. The rusting,

crumbling equipment from the first camp on the beach was inspected, repaired, refurbished. Many of the pieces were brought back to the orbiting Village to be virtually rebuilt. Many others were simply discarded; the air of Altair VI, rich with methane and sulfur compounds, had ruined the equipment beyond any hope of repair.

As the weeks went by, the landing teams learned that the apes were migrating at this time of the year, heading southward to avoid the coming cold and storms of winter. One of their main migration paths took them directly through the beach on which the humans had established their camp.

"They're being very obliging," Peterson reported to Bishop Foy. "They're coming right to us."

"God's will," the Bishop murmured. "Nirvan is our help and our protection."

The migration was a time of feasting for the wolfcats, who culled the feeble, the sick, the unwary cubs from the families of apes as they trekked southward.

Peterson found that the wolfcats were too successful. "They're in competition with us," he told Carbo. "We want the apes as helpers, but they want them for food."

So Carbo and his hastily-trained teams had to tranquilize wolfcats, too, and implant them with probes. Even when they did, however, few of the students aboard the Village could control a hungry wolfcat. The migrating apes were still being decimated.

The landing teams suffered casualties, too. Like all explorers, they constantly discovered new ways to die.

A biologist made the mistake of stepping on a trigger vine while sampling the flora at the base of the hills that overlooked the beach. The thorny arms of the plant snapped him into their deadly embrace, ripping his suit in a dozen places. His lungs were burned out by the methane-laden air before the vine's poisons could work their way into his bloodstream.

Two zoologists, a husband-wife pair, simply disappeared into the murky darkness one day as they trailed southward to map the apes' migration route. Radio contact was lost in about an hour, and they were never found again.

Dr. Polchek himself was nearly killed when a female ape, frantically defending her already-tranquilized cubs from the terrifying strange aliens, cracked his helmet with a powerful swipe of her paw before he could reload his tranquilizer gun and knock her down. Carbo and another scientist were close enough to get to Polchek in time.

Through it all, Jeff worked with Crown. The big wolfcat helped the humans, despite his growling distaste for them and their machines. He scouted the area for them, warned other wolfcat families away from the migrating apes whenever he could, and protected the frail, puny humans against the wolfcats.

Jeff insisted that Crown's family should not be implanted with neuro probes, despite the plans of the scientists.

He told Amanda, who was now in charge of all the contact work, "We need at least one wolfcat family that behaves normally. If you have all the wolfcats under human control, you might miss all sorts of dangers and warning signs that a free wolfcat would naturally pick up."

Amanda hesitated. "I don't know if . . . "

"And these wolfcats are being controlled by the new

students," Jeff added. "They're not as sure of what they're doing as I am. If their control slips, you could have a band of hungry wild wolfcats right in the middle of the camp. At least, Crown and his family can help keep them under control."

Amanda straddled the question. "Well, we won't implant Crown's family yet. But that doesn't mean that we won't decide to do it later on."

Jeff grinned at her. "You won't need to. Crown can handle them."

Frank Carbo stood by the rocketplane's boarding ladder and surveyed the camp. It was coming along well, despite all their setbacks and problems. The big bubble tent that served as shelter for the team was finally repaired and pumped full of good, breathable air. Several team members had lived in it for as long as three days at a time. Carbo himself had spent his first overnight there, and even though he could hardly sleep because of the roarings and screechings of the animals up in the hills, now they had an almost permanent foothold on this godforsaken strip of beach.

Huge arrays of infrared lamps, specially designed to penetrate the eternal darkness of Altair VI, lit up the beach. Carbo could see a full half-kilometer in either direction, as long as he wore the infrared goggles under his helmet visor.

The machinery was getting organized, too. Instead of haphazard piles of crates and abandoned building equipment scattered across the beach, the earthmovers and other tracked vehicles were parked in a neat row now. The air conversion factory was halfway finished, and a firm landing strip had been cemented over so that the shuttle planes could land and take off easily.

His ideas were succeeding. The apes, implanted ith neuro probes, were not exactly *willing* workers, but as he stood by the shuttle plane Carbo could count four dozen of the big shambling creatures lifting heavy crates and slowly, awkwardly fitting together the prefabricated pieces of a power receiving unit. It looked like a maze of slim pipes spreading across the northern end of the beach; Carbo knew that once it was finished, it would receive energy beamed from a solar power satellite that the Villagers had deployed in orbit around Altair VI. Once the receiving unit began to function, there would be more than enough electrical energy to power the air conversion factory. Then the task of removing the methane and other impurities from the planet's atmosphere could begin.

With a satisfied nod, Carbo clambered up the ladder and through the airlock of the shuttle. Once safely inside, he pulled off his pressure suit helmet and lifted the heavy goggles from his eyes. Rubbing at the bridge of his nose, he found a seat and began to quietly dictate his daily report into the recorder he carried on the belt of his suit.

He was leaner and tougher than he had ever been, even when he was a street urchin back so many years ago in Rome. The physical demands of working on the surface of Altair VI had boiled all the slothful fat out of his body and his mind, as well. He was doing a damnably difficult job, and it was finally starting to show signs of success. Even the wolfcats seemed to be under control.

The shuttle filled up with the rest of his team members. They were all going back to the Village, back to the blessed security of good air and a comfortable bed. A new team was already on the way down, aboard the other shuttle craft. Carbo finished dictating his report, leaned his head back against the seat as the shuttle began its take-off roll along the runway, and was asleep before the wheels left the ground.

By the time he entered his apartment, he was feeling physically tired but mentally, emotionally fresh. Still clumping about in the pressure suit and heavy insulated boots, he tossed his bulbous helmet onto the living room couch and made his way into the bedroom. As he peeled off the pressure suit and its undergarments, he thought about phoning Amanda.

"No," he said softly to himself. "You shouldn't. You know you shouldn't. It wouldn't be fair to her."

He stripped to the skin and stepped into his shower. The water was hot and clean and good against his skin.

"If you call her and she refuses to see you, you'll feel terrible," he told himself aloud, over the delicious rush of the water.

"But," he argued back, "you'll feel just as terrible sitting here alone all night, without a friend, without a love to share your life with."

He stepped out of the shower and the water automatically turned off. Towelling himself, he continued his debate.

"So you call her, and she comes to you, and you spend the night making passionate love. And then tomorrow you go back to the surface and you're killed. What then, eh?"

He looked at his new lean, hard body in the steamy full-length mirror and shrugged.

"If you're killed it won't be until tomorrow. Your immediate problem is tonight."

Wrapping the towel around his middle, he went to the phone next to his bed.

It buzzed before he could command the computer chip to call Amanda.

Frowning slightly, Carbo said, "Phone: no visual; answer."

The screen above the microphone grill remained blank, but he heard a student's voice say, "Dr. Carbo? Bishop Foy wishes to speak to you."

Suppressing an irritated sigh, Carbo said, "Very well, put him on."

The student's voice hesitated. "Sir? Bishop Foy wishes to speak to you in person. In his office."

"Now?" Carbo glanced at the digital clock next to the phone. It was time for dinner, for wine, not for conferences in the Bishop's bare little cubicle of an office.

"He says it is very important, sir, and he must see you immediately."

"Immediately?"

"Yessir."

"Very well," Carbo said reluctantly. "Tell the good Bishop that I will present myself at his office in fifteen minutes."

"Thank you, sir." The student sounded very relieved.

It was actually almost a half-hour before Carbo shaved, dressed, and strolled across the Village to Bishop Foy's austere suite of offices.

Does he work twenty-four hours a day? Carbo wondered. The outer office was fully staffed by young students, sitting at their desk consoles, tapping out messages on keyboards or dictating in earnest whispers into recording microphones.

One of the students, a slim but attractive brunette, recognized him immediately and ushered him down the short hallway that ended at the door to the Bishop's private office. She rapped on the door once, lightly, opened it a crack and whispered Dr. Carbo's name.

They all whisper, Carbo realized for the first time. It's as if they were in church all the time.

He heard no reply, but the student turned to him and gestured toward the partially open door. Carbo flashed his best smile for her, and the corners of her mouth twitched slightly in response.

Ragazza fredda Carbo thought as he stepped into the Bishop's office.

Foy sat hunched behind his massive desk, looking smaller and grayer than ever, his bony skull of a face drawn and wan.

"You wanted to see me?" Carbo asked, as cheerfully as he could manage.

Foy nodded and gestured for Carbo to sit in the straight-backed wooden chair in front of the desk.

"I appreciate your coming immediately," the Bishop said, in his rasping wheeze of a voice.

Politeness? Carbo was instantly wary. Something is in the wind.

Tapping a flimsy sheet of paper that rested on the desktop before him, the Bishop said, "I have received a communication from the Mother Church . . . "

"From Earth?" Carbo blurted.

"Yes, from Earth."

Startled, Carbo thought of how much it must have cost to send the message. Radio or laser beams would take seventeen years to traverse the distance between Earth and Altair. The Church had to send a communications ship, an unmanned radio beacon, by gravity warp drive; that must have cost an immense sum.

"Why . . . what does it say?"

"The news is not good," Bishop Foy muttered.

Carbo held his breath. Until this moment he had not realized how much he had felt cut off from Earth. But a message—even a terrible message—suddenly gave him a feeling that Earth still existed, that he could return to his native land someday, if he wished.

Foy went on bleakly, "Famine has struck Asia again. The monsoon rains failed and billions are starving from India all the way along the southeastern crescent to Japan."

Carbo remained silent. Bad news, yes; but what did this have to do with him? Or the Village?

"Riots have broken out all over the area, and spread to parts of Africa and South America. Virtual civil war in some places. The world government has sent in troops. Millions have been tranquilized and await neuro probe implants to control their violent behavior."

"Oh no . . . " Carbo's heart sank. "Not more . . . "

Foy raised a bony finger. "That is not the worst of it. The world government has forced the Church to accept immediate shipment of several hundred thousand colonists to Altair VI."

"Here? They're sending colonists here already?"

"They have to. The Church was given no choice. The colonists will all be officially converted to the Faith of Nirvan and implanted with neuro probes to assure their behavior."

Carbo wanted to scream, but not a sound could force its way out of his throat. He was choking on the Bishop's words.

"This puts increased pressure on you and Dr. Peterson, I realize," Foy said.

"When?" Carbo managed to gasp out. "When will they send these poor wretches?"

Foy's bloodless lips pulled back in what could have

been either a bitter smile or a bitterer grimace.

"They are already on the way," he said tonelessly. "They were packed aboard several vessels and sent out weeks ago, according to this message. The pris . . . I mean, colonists, are being implanted with neuro probes in transit. The first ship should arrive here within three months."

CHAPTER 15

The news of the colonists' approach spread through the Village like a cold whispering wind.

Bishop Foy ordered a mass convocation in the Tabernacle; every student was required to attend. They all renewed their vows, under the Bishop's stern eye, promising themselves and each other and their God to work even harder than before, to tame the planet they had sworn to redeem for the Church, to prepare Altair VI as a fit home world for the thousands of newly-converted Faithful who were on their way.

Carbo and the scientists held their own meeting, crammed into the conference room in the dome that housed the laboratories and medical center. They had to take the long conference table out into the corridor to make room for everyone. Still, there were not enough chairs for them all, even though the scientists sat literally shoulder to shoulder. Almost half of them squatted on the floor or stood along the walls of the long, narrow room.

Carbo paced nervously at the front of the room as he spoke to them. No one had appointed him the leader, yet no one had expected anyone else to assume leadership. He had called the meeting, and they all had come to the conference room. It was that simple.

Now he paced, thinking in the back of his mind that humans and wolfcats shared a few traits in common as he strode nervously, impatiently from where Amanda sat crosslegged on the floor at his left to the spot where one of the young Japanese biologists knelt placidly, sitting on his heels.

" . . . slightly more than thirty-two thousand colonists," Carbo was saying. "Naturally, they are being converted to the Church of Nirvan during their flight here."

"They're scheduled to arrive here in three months?" a voice from the crowd asked.

With a nod, Carbo said, "We should be able to see their ship in four or five weeks, when it warps back into normal space out at the edge of the Altair system."

"That doesn't give us enough time . . . "

"For anything," a woman's voice interjected.

Carbo swallowed hard. "The colonists are being fitted out with neuro probes to ensure their good behavior while they're on their transit ships. The ships will take up orbit around Altair VI, just as we have. I assume there will be enough supplies aboard to take care of them for two or three years—just as we have here."

No one spoke. A few people cleared their throats,

coughed nervously; feet shifted on the carpeting, hands fidgeted. But no one had a word to say.

"I . . . uh . . . I wanted you to know the entire story," Carbo stammered. "I wanted you to understand the magnitude of the task facing us."

"Nothing's changed, really," said Dr. Peterson, who was sitting in the front row of chairs. "We still have the same job of taming the planet."

"Maybe so," said Lana Polchek, the zoologist's wife, "but knowing that thirty-two thousand colonists are already on their way makes it all—well, more urgent. Don't you think?"

A murmur of agreement rippled through the scientists.

"And this is just the *first* batch of colonists," someone else pointed out.

"What'll they do if we can't tame the planet? If we fail?"

"We won't fail," a man's voice replied. "Given time, we can convert the planet to a fully Earth-like ecology."

"How much time? Is three years enough?"

"It should be."

"But if it's not? What happens to these colonists if we haven't succeeded in three years? What happens to *us*?"

Total silence answered that question.

Finally Carbo clapped his hands together sharply, startling them all out of their frightened musings.

"All right," he said. "It is a very large task that we face. But we can do it . . . if we all work our best and hardest."

Amanda unfolded her long slim legs and rose to her feet. "Okay. So why are we sitting around here instead of getting on with it?"

They all laughed, the tension broke, and the scientists began to leave the meeting and head toward their jobs.

Crown awoke feeling stiff with cold. A biting wind was cutting across the beach, driving sand against the buildings and machines of the humans. The sea looked gray and chill, the sky even grayer. Altair was a dim glow just above the ocean horizon.

It had snowed during the night, the first dark brittle snow of winter. Crown climbed slowly to his paws and shook the sooty clinging flakes off his body. He knew that if the flakes stayed on him for very long, they would eat through his fur and burn his skin.

The apes were still sleeping. The grayish flakes covered them lightly. Crown growled at them, and they instantly snapped awake. There were more than a dozen apes in the camp now. They slept in the scant shelter of an old building that had partially collapsed. It had no roof anymore, and its remaining walls leaned precariously.

The biggest of the apes pulled himself up to a sitting position, his legs poking out awkwardly before him. He shivered and patted his body with his forepaws to dust the flakes away. His actions bumped the apes next to him, who also slowly sat up and began cleaning the sooty flakes from their fur. And so on down the line, until all the apes were poking and rubbing themselves. Not one of them tried to help another, though.

The biggest ape snarled at Crown, his lips pulled back to bare his teeth. He got up on all fours, staring at Crown, growling. Then his body twitched, jerked, in a convulsive spasm that rocked him from muzzle to tail like a private earthquake shock. The ape's growl changed to a snuffle, almost a whimper. He shook his head as if trying to escape something that was buzzing inside his skull. Then he turned away from Crown.

The ape was under control now. One by one, the others twitched and whimpered, then docilely rose to all fours and headed off to begin their day's work.

Crown watched them as they slowly gathered themselves together and trundled off to the hillside where there were shrubs and roots and crawling little insects for their morning meal. Even under human control, the apes stayed as far away from the new buildings as possible.

Bright and gleaming, the new buildings throbbed with the energy of the machines inside them. Night and day, the machinery hummed and rumbled and gave off strange, sickening odors. Even though the walls of these buildings were warm to the touch, and the nights were getting constantly colder along the beach, neither the apes nor Crown and the other wolfcats would go near the buildings unless they were forced to by their human controllers. They all slept as far from the grumbling machines as their controllers would allow.

Crown knew that since the apes were under control, the other wolfcat families up in the hills would be, also. His own tiny family—Thunder, Brightfur, Tranquil and the cubs—were still normal, still untainted by the invading aliens. Crown was grateful for that, even though he rarely saw his family anymore. He stayed down here on the beach almost all the time now. He even slept within a few bounding leaps of the nervous, frightened apes. He got up into the forested hills only to hunt.

He started his morning's trek up the hillside, past

the peacefully-munching apes—who shied away from him instinctively—to find his family and share in the hunting. Halfway up the hill he paused and looked back for a moment at the camp along the beach.

The apes had finished eating and were starting in to work. Standing uncertainly on their hindlegs, slow and hesitant because of the fear that no amount of human control could fully overcome, they were marching off to the crates that had been left next to the new buildings and their humming machinery. Carefully, reluctantly, they reached into the crates and pulled out strange shapes of gleaming metal. Awkwardly, they began to put the shapes together, one piece fitting into another. Crown had watched them build the new machines that way. How many more machines would the apes build? he wondered.

Crown snarled at the scene. These strange things of the aliens were not alive, yet they seemed to breathe and grow like living animals. Far more frightening, though, was the fact that it was becoming difficult, even dangerous, to stay near the machines once they began to hum and vibrate. A few days ago one of the worker apes had collapsed and died, for no apparent reason. The other apes panicked and tried to flee from the beach, but Crown and the other controlled wolfcats outraced them and—snarling and roaring—had herded them back to the camp. The dead ape was dragged away by two wolfcats before the sun went down, but still the other apes were obviously terrified to be near the throbbing, pulsating buildings of the aliens.

Crown himself stayed as far from the new buildings as he could. He found that there was something about them that made him feel weak, drowsy, dizzy.

It's the oxygen. The machines are breaking down

the methane and sulfur oxides of the air and pumping out oxygen and nitrogen.

Crown grunted angrily. Even here, up near the crest of the hills, the scent of the machines was strong. It grew stronger each day.

He spent the morning hunting. Thunder greeted him with an affectionate roar, while Brightfur and Tranquil stayed shyly behind their leader, as they should. The cubs scampered playfully around Crown, though, and he learned that they had at last been named: Strong was the cub with the white fur on her forepaws; Dayrise was the friskier and leaner of the two.

For several happy hours Crown was nothing more than a wolfcat, hunting with his family for their day's meal. There were still antelope in the woods, although they were getting fewer as the days grew colder. Thunder and two females trotted off to hide in the underbrush while Crown and the cubs headed in the other direction. Once they spotted a few straggling antelope, they slinked around their flank—the cubs watching Crown intently and imitating his every move. Eventually the deerlike animals would catch the wolfcats' scent and flee, leaping and bounding, for safety. Crown and the cubs gave chase, forcing the antelope to run straight toward the waiting Thunder and his females.

Each day the wolfcats brought down two or three antelope this way. The beasts never seemed to learn. Every day it was the same, and every day they raced straight into the ambush. Crown and his family could have killed as many as they liked, but a couple of fat antelope were enough for the family to gorge themselves.

Crown knew that the other wolfcats in the area, the ones under human control, were also hunting antelope;

not only for themselves, they brought kills back to the beach, for the apes to eat at the end of each day. But every day the number of antelope they saw was smaller. And farther off to the south. The antelope were migrating southward for the winter, just as the apes had been before the humans had gained control of them. Just as the wolfcats would, under normal circumstances. The antelope migration was slow, measured. The animals were in no hurry to quit these wooded hills, as long as there was shrubbery for them to nibble.

Still, they were edging steadily southward, and each day the wolfcats had to drag their kills a little farther to the camp where the apes worked. Despite the food that the wolfcats provided, though, the apes seemed to be wasting away. They got thinner and slower every day.

This day, as Crown reluctantly headed back toward the beach, it snowed before sundown for the first time. The dark sooty flakes sifted through the trees late in the afternoon as Crown was helping a human-controlled wolfcat to carry one of the day's kill through the forest underbrush. Both wolfcats growled at the snow. It would kill the shrubbery of the undergrowth, Crown knew, forcing the antelope to move even further southward. Even now, it took almost the whole day to find the herd, make the kills, and bring the food back to the beach.

As he got to within sight of the camp, panting and growling from the effort of half-carrying, half-dragging the still-warm antelope alongside the other wolfcat, Crown saw that two of the apes were down on the sand. The others were circling crazily around their two dead companions, neither working nor running away, just milling about on their hindlegs, throwing their long arms over their heads as if in fear or despair.

The wolfcats would usually stay close to the woods up at the crest of the ridge line; Crown was the only one who actually slept down on the beach. The apes feared the wolfcats so much that the cats normally left their kills partway down the grassy slope of the hills and then returned to the woods. The apes would scramble up the hillside to get the meat.

But now Crown dropped his kill. So did the other wolfcat. They both stared down at the camp, standing stock-still, the wind ruffling their gray fur. Crown saw that the other wolfcat dug his claws into the dying grass, growling and rumbling to himself as if fighting against something inside his own skull. Crown started down the hillside, heading toward the apes and the strange, evil-smelling human machines. He turned his head and growled at the other wolfcat. Slowly and very reluctantly, the wolfcat followed Crown.

Other wolfcats appeared out of the trees, growling, snarling at the empty air as they hesitantly made their way down the hillsides toward the beach. Their muscles twitched, as if they wanted to go in two different directions at once.

Crown took command of the wolfcats. With grunts and pushes he directed some of them toward each end of the camp, to make certain that the apes could not bolt and run away. Then he pushed two of the younger males toward the dead apes. Even under human control, they did not want to go. Crown led them himself, walking calmly to the dead bodies, sniffing at them for a few moments, and then turning toward the other apes, who had retreated into a frightened shivering mass back toward the ramshackle shelter where they slept.

The dead bodies lay near the new buildings and their rumbling, evil-smelling machines. The air was hard to breathe. Crown's chest began to hurt, as if there was fire inside him. Quickly, he grabbed at one of the dead apes with his teeth and forepaws and started dragging it away. The other two wolfcats watched him, then slowly went for the other body.

Painfully, with little sparkling flashes of light dancing in front of his eyeplates, Crown dragged the dead ape up the slope and away from the hated machines. It was dark before he had pulled the carcass far away enough so that the other apes seemed to settle down for sleep. Crown watched them huddle together in their sagging shelter, whimpering, clinging to each other as closely as they could manage.

Three meters tall, two and a half tons each, and they're whimpering.

They're frightened, Frank. Frightened out of their wits. It's a wonder the kids could control them at all.

Jeff awoke feeling Crown's weariness. And something deeper, something he did not quite understand but which troubled him like the dark edge of an unknown, barely-realized fear.

After Amanda unstrapped his cuffs and helped him up to a sitting position on the couch, she turned to Dr. Carbo.

"Frank, this is too much. Jeff's working too hard. This has got to stop."

Carbo and Jeff snapped at the same instant, "No!"

Standing in the doorway between the contact chamber and the control room, Carbo shook his head adamantly. "We can't stop now. We need Jeff more than ever."

"He's losing weight, his vital signs degrade a little more every day," Amanda insisted. "We've reached the danger point. His health . . . "

"I'm okay," Jeff said, sounding weak even to himself. "I'll be all right."

Carbo went from the doorway to the couch in three swift strides and stared into Jeff's face. "You *do* look tired. Perhaps she's right . . . a few days of rest . . . "

"I rest all day long, on the couch," Jeff said.

Amanda shot him a skeptical look. "You know that's not what we're talking about."

"It's Crown and the other animals," Jeff realized. "They're in trouble."

"Things are getting tough down there," Amanda agreed.

"There's no way around that," said Carbo. "Jeff, you mustn't get too attached to that animal. A certain amount of empathy is fine, it's helpful. But you've got to be able to disconnect yourself emotionally from the wolfcat."

Jeff knew he was right. Yet—"It isn't as easy as breaking the neuro-electronic linkage, Dr. Carbo."

"I know, but . . . "

"They're dying," Jeff said, almost in a whisper. "The apes . . . the wolfcats will too, if we don't stop."

Carbo glanced at Amanda, then back at Jeff. "Of course they're dying. They've got to die. You know that."

"We're killing them."

"We're starting to alter the atmosphere of the planet. We can't breathe methane, and the native life can't breathe oxygen. So as we alter the atmosphere to suit our needs, we kill off the native life forms."

"But do we have to kill all of them?"

181

Carbo made one of his elaborate Mediterranean shrugs. "There are thirty-two thousand colonists on their way here . . ."

"I know that!" Jeff snapped.

"And more to follow. Millions more. What would you have us do with them? They can't go back. Neither your Church nor the world government would pay for their return to Earth."

Jeff hung his head, feeling miserable. "But do we have to kill all the animals? Do we have to kill the wolfcats? Crown?"

"Maybe we could create a reservation for them," Amanda suggested. "One continent where they could roam free . . ."

"Breathing oxygen?" Jeff asked.

Carbo pulled himself up to his full height. His voice became crisper, more authoritative, as he said, "Jeff, we're up against some hard facts here. We *must* convert Altair VI to fully Earth-like conditions. Otherwise those colonists will be stranded here. They will die. It's either the animals or the humans: them or us."

"But that's not fair!" Jeff cried. "It's their world. Windsong belongs to them, not us."

"Windsong belongs to whoever can take it, shape it, and hold it," Carbo said. "Maybe we can keep from annihilating the native life. Maybe we can create a game preserve down on one of the smaller continents— or build a sort of zoo for them up here in orbit, where we can give them their own atmosphere and environment. But that planet belongs to the strongest creatures who want it—whether that's fair or not."

"It's murder," Jeff murmured. "You're committing ecological murder, and I'm helping you to do it."

"You can quit if you want to," Carbo said firmly.

"We have enough students in contact with the animals to handle things without you."

Jeff felt a pang of shock at that. Quit? Leave Crown down there by himself? But what else could he do? Could he stay in contact with Crown, day after day, knowing that he was helping them to kill him?

"I . . ." Jeff had to swallow hard before he could rasp out, "I just didn't realize we'd be killing all the animals. I thought we would set up the colony on one part of the planet and let them live on the rest of it."

"I don't see how," Carbo answered, more gently. "We can't have half the planet with an oxygen atmosphere and the other half with methane. Higgins and his team are working the robot assemblers twenty-four hours a day, building more oxygen factories up here in orbit. They'll start emplacing them in other spots on the planet within a week or two."

Jeff looked up at him. "I know it's not your fault. but . . ." Suddenly he knew that there were no more words to say. It was all useless. Totally and hopelessly useless.

His vision was blurring. Jeff knew that there were tears on his eyes. Without another word he slid off the couch, pushed past Amanda and Dr. Carbo, and strode swiftly out of the laboratory.

Amanda stared at the door after it closed behind him for a few moments. "Poor kid," she muttered.

"It's a moral dilemma for him," Carbo said. "He's become too attached to that damned wolfcat."

"It's more than that," Amanda said. "Deeper. Down at some level of his mind, Jeff *is* that wolfcat. By killing Crown, he's killing some part of himself. We're asking him to commit mental suicide."

"Maybe we'd better pull him off the job altogether."

Amanda saw that Carbo was just as concerned about the boy as she was. "I don't know if that would help or hurt, Frank. I think we need some professional guidance with this."

He nodded. "I'll ask one of the psychologists."

"They can examine him while he sleeps, can't they?"

"That's the way they prefer to do it," Carbo said. "Get the patient while he's relaxed, while his mental guard is down."

Amanda heard herself sigh. "It's a rotten business, isn't it?"

Carbo cocked his head slightly, as if to say, *What can I do about it?*

"I ran away from Earth to get as far as I could from this kind of trouble," Amanda said.

He grinned. "Me too. I guess almost everybody here did. We all wanted to escape from something."

"But we brought the troubles along with us, didn't we?"

"We always do."

Amanda found herself looking into his sad-yet-hopeful brown eyes. "I've missed you, Frank," she admitted.

"I've missed you too. I think I've fallen in love with you."

She clucked at him. "Now don't go using big words like 'love'! Don't say things we'll both be sorry for afterwards."

He pulled her to him, whispering, "Amanda, *cara mia*, perhaps there won't be an afterwards. Perhaps we will love each other forever."

"No, that's too long a time. No one can say . . ."

She never finished the sentence. He covered her mouth with his lips and she kissed him back fiercely, longingly, happily.

CHAPTER 16

Jeff went straight from the contact lab to Bishop Foy's office.

No matter what the hour, the Bishop's suite of offices was always bustling. Students strode up and down the mini-corridors that had been created by the shoulder-high plastic partitions which walled off the Bishop's anteroom area into a series of busy little cubicles. Inside each cubicle, a student sat at a computer keyboard, earnestly tapping out the messages that ran the Village: more trainees needed for making contact with the animals below; electronic spare parts for the next landing team were not yet loaded aboard their shuttle rocket; food supplies for the Village were being consumed at a higher rate than planned, the autocafeterias must be reprogrammed to make smaller portions of all meat and meat-substitute servings; attendance at sunrise services is lower than normal, check the names of the students against those who attend in their various chapels and prepare a list of the truants; the medical staff requests another six students for training as paramedics.

And on and on. When Jeff had first come aboard this complex starship, he had marvelled at how almost everything was automated and run by computers. Now he realized that the computers needed, demanded human guidance, human decision-making. The computers did not allow the human beings of the Village to work less; instead they allowed the humans to work harder, better, more efficiently.

Jeff almost smiled to himself as he watched the organized dither of Bishop Foy's outer office. Even if the computers could do *all* the work, the good Bishop would never allow the students to relax and spend their days in idleness.

It was a quietly intense dither. No one spoke above a whisper. Even the students who practically ran from one cubicle to another did so almost silently, on tiptoe.

"Yes? Can I help you?" asked the female student who sat behind the reception desk.

Jeff pulled his gaze away from the "worker ants" bustling around their tiny cubicles and focussed on the receptionist. She was also a student, judging by her age, but Jeff did not recognize her.

"I've got to see Bishop Foy right away," he said. Without realizing it, he spoke in the same churchwhisper as all the others.

She pursed her lips, then replied, "I'm afraid that

will be impossible. The Bishop is a very busy man."

"This will only take a few minutes."

She smiled, as if to say, *That's what they all claim.*

"It's very important," Jeff said. "Urgent."

"I'll try to set up an appointment for you . . . " She touched her keyboard and looked at the data screen, which was tilted at an angle so that Jeff could not see it. "Next Thursday. I can give you fifteen minutes immediately after sunrise worship services."

"No, I've got to talk to him *now*. This evening."

Her smile stayed fixed on her lips, but she shook her head.

"Is he in his office right now, or is he having dinner?" Jeff asked.

"Bishop Foy seldom has his meals outside his office. He is *very* busy and very dedicated."

"Well, if he's in there, would you please call him and tell him that I want to see him?"

"I'm not supposed to bother him with . . . "

Jeff leaned over her desk, his face inches away from hers. "This is vital!" he insisted. "The future of this whole mission may depend on it."

She backed away from him a bit, her face showing a mixture of disbelief and alarm. She looked over at the other students, and for an instant Jeff thought she was going to ask for help.

"Tell him that Jeffrey Holman wants to speak with him. Tell him it involves tomorrow's work down on the surface. It can't be put off."

"Jeffrey Holman," the receptionist repeated slowly. "You're one of the students who works with the animals down there, aren't you?"

"Yes," Jeff snapped. "And there isn't going to be any work with the animals if I can't speak to Bishop Foy."

Her nostrils flared slightly as she gave a little huff, but she touched a button on her keyboard and picked up her telephone headset.

"I'm sorry to disturb you, Reverend Bishop," Jeff heard her whisper into the pin mike, "but there's a Jeffrey Holman out here at reception and he is most insistent about seeing you right away."

Jeff could not hear the Bishop's reply, but the receptionist stared up at him as she listened.

"Yes, Reverend Bishop. Jeffrey Holman. He says it concerns tomorrow's work with the animals down . . . "

Her eyes widened. "Yes, Reverend Bishop. I will."

She put the headset down on her desktop and said to Jeff, "Bishop Foy is finishing his only meal of the day at the moment. He said that if you would wait about fifteen minutes, he will see you then."

Jeff didn't know what to say. He realized that he hadn't actually expected the Bishop to agree to see him. He felt as if he had worked up all his strength to break down a heavy locked door, only to find that it swung open as soon as he touched it.

His long training in the Church came to the fore. "Thank you," he whispered. "You are very helpful."

The receptionist dipped her head briefly in the time-honored response to a compliment. With a silent gesture she indicated that Jeff could sit in the stiff little plastic chair against the wall. Then she turned her back to him and began to busy herself with moving stacks of papers from one part of her desk to another.

It was more like half an hour, but finally the receptionist walked Jeff down the short corridor that led from the busy anteroom to the silent blank door of the Bishop's private office. She knocked once, opened the door, and gestured Jeff through.

Bishop Foy sat behind his massive desk. Its gleaming surface was almost entirely bare: only the gray box of a computer screen, a keyboard, and a single pen rested on the desktop. On the small table behind the Bishop's desk, Jeff sat a cafeteria tray with the crumbs from a scanty meal scattered over a single plate.

Bishop Foy looked tired. His bloodshot eyes were sunken, there were dark circles under them.

"I'm sorry to burst in on you like this, Reverend Bishop," Jeff began.

"You said it was important," Foy replied, his voice rasping harshly. "Sit down and tell me what the problem is."

"It *is* important," Jeff said. "It involves the work we're doing down on the surface of Windso . . . on Altair VI."

Bishop Foy steepled his fingers, said nothing.

The chair Jeff was sitting on was stiff-backed and uncomfortable. He leaned forward anxiously as he explained:

"If we intend to convert the planet into a world where human colonists can live, then we will have to kill all the life forms on it now."

The Bishop nodded.

"I don't think we have the moral right to do that," Jeff said.

Again the older man nodded. When Jeff remained silent, he prompted, "Go on."

"That . . . that's it," Jeff said. "That's what I've come to say. I don't believe that we have the right to annihilate the living creatures on Altair VI."

"You don't believe . . . " The Bishop's voice trailed off, leaving the office bathed in awkward silence for several moments. Finally he said, "You see this is as a moral problem, an ethical problem."

"Yes, sir, I do."

"Have you prayed for Nirvan's guidance?"

Jeff nodded, realizing that his prayers had been few and far between, but that it was no lie to say that he had prayed.

"And?"

"And I can't help feeling that what we are doing is wrong. It's murder. Genocide."

He had expected the Bishop to rail at him, to thunder and revile him for his effrontery. Instead, the old man sat hunched behind his desk, looking frail and weak and terribly tired.

At last, Foy said, "Nirvan teaches that the beasts of the field were created by God for man's benefit. Isn't that so?"

"Yes, Reverend Bishop," Jeff answered. "But nowhere in the Bible does it say that we are permitted to destroy God's creations—destroy them completely, wipe them out. Isn't that sinful?"

The Bishop's chin sunk to his gaunt chest, and a ghostly sigh breathed out of him.

"There are times, young man, when the difference between sin and virtue is difficult to perceive. Very difficult."

What kind of an answer is that? Jeff asked himself.

But before he could say anything aloud, the Bishop went on, "Turn your chair around, Mr. Holman. I want to show you something. Just turn around and face the wall, that's right."

Feeling slightly bewildered, Jeff turned the stiff little chair until his back was to the Bishop. The wall he faced was blank. Then it began to glow, and Jeff realized that it was an oversized viewing screen.

"When the Mother Church sent me the information

that thirty-two thousand colonists were on their way here," the Bishop said, "they did not waste an entire communications probe merely for such a short message. No. They filled the probe's tape banks with information, news, data and personal messages."

Personal messages? Jeff thought. A tape from my parents? No, that's not likely. They wouldn't know that the Church was going to spend the money to send a communications probe all the way out here.

"Here is one of the news broadcasts that the Mother Church so kindly included in the tape banks," Bishop Foy was saying, his rasping voice sounding weary and bitter to Jeff. "This is just an ordinary news broadcast, from an ordinary day back on Earth."

The screen began to show a picture of a newscaster, sitting behind a curved desk, looking grimly into the camera.

"Take a good look at this," Bishop Foy said. "A very good look."

Jeff sat rigidly on the uncomfortable chair, his head buzzing and his heart thumping inside him, as the picture on the screen changed from the tight-lipped newscaster to a huge, busy, jampacked city. In an instant Jeff felt all the pangs of months of accumulated homesickness. Earth! Home! He realized that even if the communications probe had carried personal messages for the students, Bishop Foy would have been foolish to let the students have those messages. The psychological reaction would be disastrous.

The newscast showed an aerial view of the vast city, but the camera quickly zoomed down to one public square amid the maze of teeming streets. Thousands of people were thronging into the square, pushing, fighting one another with fists and umbrellas and anything they could get their hands on. The voice of the commentator calmly, flatly spoke about the "unrest" in Chicago over an outbreak of tuberculosis. Several thousand people had died already, and public health officials predicted that as many as two million would succumb before vaccines could check the unexpected outbreak of the long-"conquered" disease. The people in the square were fighting to get into one of the medical centers that was giving free immunizing vaccinations. Police helicopters appeared and started spraying the area with tranquilizing gas, but—the commentator reported in a flat, unemotional voice— not before five hundred people had been killed in the rioting and the medical center hoplessly smashed up. The center's supply of vaccine had been destroyed in the fighting; the precious liquid spilled to mix with the blood that ran in the gutters.

The picture changed to show the lush green farmland of New Mexico, and Jeff's heart lurched within his chest at the sight of it. Kilometer after kilometer of precise rows of green vegetables crisscrossed by the great irrigation canals that had turned what was once useless desert into a cornucopia. All this is now in danger of being wiped out, the commentator's voice said, because of the recent earthquake in southern California which destroyed two water desalting plants. It was these plants that provided the fresh water for the Southwestern Desert Irrigation System. In a choice between giving desalted water to the homeless victims of the earthquake or giving the water to the crops that fed millions, the federal authorities had chosen the city people over the farm crops.

An angry, red-faced man appeared on the screen, shouting slogans and pointing to charts that showed that the crops would die without water and thus millions of people—including those in southern California—would go hungry within three months.

The news tape went on. A hockey game where a new scoring record was set. The assassination of an important politician in Japan. A storm that wrecked fishing boats off the coast of Newfoundland, killing at least a hundred fishermen and destroying millions of dollars worth of equipment. The Global Weather Service had predicted the storm, but the fishermen went out anyway, because their catch was necessary if New York and other dying cities of the East Coast were to avoid famine.

Through it all the commentator's voice remained calm and detached, unaffected by death and disaster. All in a day's work. The tape did not even show the quake in California, or the people dying of starvation in the streets of Calcutta, Singapore, Peking; that was old news.

The screen went blank.

Jeff blinked several times, trying to pull himself back to this orbiting starship seventeen lightyears from Earth. He felt the stiffness of the chair against his spine, heard the muted ever-present hum of the electrical equipment that kept them all alive, breathed in the cool dry air of the Village.

"Now what is more sinful?" Bishop Foy asked, in a weary whisper, "To eliminate the dumb brutes of this savage planet below us, or to allow the human race to decay into brutality and war, back on our home planet?"

Jeff had no answer.

The Bishop placed his bony hands on the desktop. Jeff saw that the knuckles were large, swollen. If he didn't know that there were medicines to cure it, Jeff would have guessed that Bishop Foy was troubled by arthritis.

"Now then," Foy said, in his rasping whisper, "let me ask you another question, one that I pray you can answer affirmatively: Do you Believe?"

"Yes, I do Believe." Jeff automatically gave the answer from his childhood catechism.

"Do you Believe strongly enough to keep a secret that I shall impart to you?"

"I . . . " Jeff hesitated. "What do you mean, sir?"

"There is something that I want to tell you, Mr. Holman. A secret I wish to share with you. But with no one else. Do you understand? No one! Do you promise to keep what I am about to tell you a secret between the two of us?"

Jeff nodded slowly. "Yes, I promise."

"You swear, on your Faith?"

"On my Faith," Jeff echoed, realizing that deep within him, he actually did Believe, no matter how many shortcomings he found in the people who administered Nirvan's Church.

The Bishop almost smiled. "Then let me tell you why we have no choice except to continue altering Altair VI, even though it means slaughtering creatures made by God."

"No choice?"

"None whatsoever," Bishop Foy said. "In the same communications tapes that brought news of the colonists' approach, the Church High Council also informed me that the cost of sending these shiploads of colonists will make it impossible for the Church to pay for bringing us back to Earth, should our mission here end in failure."

"Imposs . . . you mean we can't go back home?"

"Only those who can afford to purchase their own fare will be allowed to leave," Foy said. He seemed to shrink, behind his desk, shrivelling perceptibly as Jeff stared at him.

Thunderstruck, Jeff blurted, "But I always thought that it was just a rumor . . . a bad joke . . . "

"That we will succeed here or die?" The Bishop took a deep, painful breath. "I know that the rumor was rife among the students. Well . . . now it's no longer a rumor. We are marooned here. We cannot return."

"But they can't do that!"

"They can and they have," Bishop Foy said. "It's not that they are cruel. Star flights are enormously expensive. The Church has nearly bankrupted itself in its zeal to tame this planet and convert the millions who will eventually colonize it. We are expendable. If we die here, we will be added to the Church's roll of glorious martyrs."

There was no trace of irony or sarcasm in the Bishop's voice, Jeff realized. Perhaps some bitterness. But it was the almost-proud bitterness of a soldier who realizes that he has been ordered to carry out a suicide mission.

"You see why you must keep this news a secret," Bishop Foy said, his voice strengthening a little. "If the others found out—there would be chaos throughout the Village."

"I understand," Jeff mumbled.

"And, I hope that you also understand why we must be ruthless with those animals down on the surface of the planet. We have no choice. No choice at all."

CHAPTER 17

The work went on. Day after day, as the weeks added up and everyone in the village mentally counted the hours until the colonists' ships showed up. Jeff dragged himself out of his sleepless bed each morning, ate by himself in the autocafeteria, and went to the contact lab to work with Crown.

More landing teams went down to the surface. More oxygen-producing machinery was built in orbit, out of the steel and aluminum smelted from Altair's broad ring of metal-rich asteroids. The Village was becoming a manufacturing center as well as home to the five hundred men and women who lived in it.

Jeff lost weight constantly. It was not the physical effort of working with Crown so much as the psychological stress he was under. Amanda—who was in charge of all the contact work most of the time, since Carbo spent more and more of his time with the landing teams—worried about Jeff's weight loss and the dark, sleepless circles under his eyes. She had the medics check him out regularly, but they could find nothing physically wrong with him.

"He's under a strain," Lana Polchek told Amanda, after her third checkup of Jeff in as many days. "But we all are. He's all right physically. How is he behaving?"

Amanda said, "The psychiatrists say he's in a conflict situation but he seems to be handling it all right. He's under considerable tension, of course, but his performance is fine. Reflexes still as good as ever, and he and the wolfcat have the firmest link of all the student-animal contacts. But I still worry about him . . . "

Dr. Polchek nodded sympathetically. "Don't go mothering him too much. He's young and resilient. Actually, all this strain is boiling away his baby fat. Except for the nervous tension, his body is in better condition now than it was when we first arrived here."

Amanda's eyebrows rose two centimeters.

"Of course," the physician added, "nervous strain can cause severe mental or even physical breakdown—eventually."

"Thanks for the advice," Amanda said.

Although Jeff tended to stay to himself at meals, the cafeteria was no longer empty early in the morning when he took his breakfast. There were more than a dozen other students working in the expanded contact lab now, and they all ate together. They even prayed together, briefly, swiftly, their heads bowed around the cafeteria table before they dug into their breakfasts. Jeff stayed away from them. They were all so relentlessly cheerful, so happy to be doing their work, so dedicated to the Church that would sooner let them die than save them, so boundlessly optimistic as they methodically prepared the annihilation of Crown and all the living creatures of Windsong.

But this particular morning, Jeff was not alone for long. Laura McGrath carried her heavily-laden breakfast tray to the table where Jeff sat, and put it down beside his.

"Do you mind if I join you?" she asked, smiling at him.

Jeff looked up at her, and wished with all his heart that he could be as happy and free from worry as she.

"No, I don't mind at all," he said.

Laura sat beside him. "Everybody else says that you're a snob, you know," she said, still smiling to show that she didn't care what they said.

"I guess maybe they're right."

She ignored that. "I tell them that you're more sensitive than the rest of us. That you care more about your wolfcat—you've been in contact with that same animal for months now, haven't you?"

Nodding, Jeff muttered, "Uh-huh."

"You *do* need to relax, Jeff," Laura said, more seriously now. "You can't carry all the burden of two worlds on your shoulders, you know."

"Yeah, I know."

Laura took a couple of spoonfuls of hot cereal, then went on, "I'm having a birthday party Saturday night. Will you come?"

"You . . . what?"

"A party. It's my birthday. Saturday. It won't go very late, we've all got to get up for Sunday worship and then back to the lab . . . "

Jeff pushed his breakfast tray from him. "You spend all day every day killing the animals down there and then you feel like partying?"

Laura looked startled at his suddenly angry tone. "I . . . I thought . . . "

"Here we've got the apes dropping dead on us, the meat herd moving farther away every day, and you're thinking about parties. Wonderful!"

Her face went red. "Well you don't have to act so superior! I mean, when it comes to Holier Than Thou . . . "

"Is that what you think? Just because I'm the only one who gives a damn about what happens down there? The rest of you are too busy figuring out how much time you can get off from the lab and whose parties to go to."

Laura put her spoon down on the table with a trembling hand. "Don't try to pull that on me, Jeff Holman. Everybody knows why you spend so much time in the contact lab."

"Do they?"

"Yes, they do," Laura snapped. "The way you hang around Amanda Kolwezi . . . like a puppydog!"

Jeff felt as if someone had just punched him in the gut. "What?"

"Don't pretend you don't know what I'm talking about," Laura said. "Your tongue hangs out whenever you're near her."

Jeff's answer strangled in his throat. He pushed his chair away from the table, got up and wordlessly strode away from Laura, heading for the greenpath that led to the contact lab.

Crown had been searching all day.

The antelope herd could not be found. Crown and the other controlled wolfcats had started out at sunrise after them, as usual. But they were gone. Their trail led southward, but even well after Altair had crossed the zenith, there were no antelope in sight.

The wolfcats saw easily enough where the antelope had been. The grass was chewed, cropped down close to the ground. Hoofprints and spoor abounded. But instead of moving a kilometer or so to the south overnight, the entire herd had vanished—dashed away to the south.

The cold's getting too much for them.

Or maybe they know something that we don't know.

We should have implanted neuro probes in some of them. That way we could have kept them nearby.

Too late now.

As the late afternoon sun began to disappear behind the trees, Crown stopped on the open grassland that stretched off to the south. The antelope were gone; nowhere in sight. Even if he could find one now, this late in the day, he could never drag it back to feed the apes before night fell. As it was, it would be dark before he himself got back to the camp area.

With a reluctant growl, Crown turned back toward the camp. Why not go on? the wolfcat wondered. He remembered his hilltop and the peaceful life of his earlier days. But he turned northward and headed back for the beach where the apes worked grudgingly on the strange alien machinery.

It was cold. The wind cut through his fur and

chilled him. Great stretches of the grass had been scoured clean by snowfalls; the sooty flakes seemed to burn away anything living that they stayed in contact with for more than a few hours.

But the trees haven't shed their leaves.

Maybe they keep them all year round. They must shake off the snowflakes somehow.

The woods seemed empty of life. Every animal had either migrated southward or burrowed deeply underground for the winter. There were no other wolfcats around to challenge Crown's invasion of their territory, except for the controlled beasts that were chained electronically to the alien camp.

Crown's own family—Thunder, the two females and their cubs—had moved off to the south several days ago. Crown knew where they were heading, and knew that he could find them again when, and if, he ever got away from the humans and their machines.

He could not stay near the beach camp much longer, he knew. With no food, the apes and the other wolfcats would either have to leave—or starve to death. *You won't starve*, Crown heard inside his head. *No matter what happens, I won't let you starve.*

He sensed something moving in the brush, off to his left, among the tall trees. Something alive. Its scent was very strange, very faint. But if it was alive, it meant food.

Creeping slowly, nose to the ground, Crown poked into the underbrush. In the dim rays of the setting sun he saw a snake. A large snake. Its body was about the width of a healthy antelope's leg—perhaps a quarter of the width of Crown's own foreleg. It was difficult to tell how long the snake was because most of its length was coiled around the trunk of a young tree.

Crown snuffled at the snake. He had never seen this kind of serpent before. Some of them were poisonous, he knew. But poisonous or not, the snake was food.

It hissed at him and opened its jaws wide, showing a blood-red mouth armed with long fangs. Fear was meaningless to Crown. But hunger was not. He snatched at the snake with his forepaw.

The snake was quicker. It dodged to the side, then darted at the wolfcat. Crown jumped back, avoiding the snake by a millimeter. He pounced with both forelegs and pinned the snake, writhing, to the ground. With one midpaw he struck it a crushing blow on the head.

But not before the snake buried its fangs in that paw. Crown felt searing pain flame through his midleg. It was white-hot, unbearable. He crashed to the ground on top of the snake's lifeless body.

Disconnect! Get him out of there!

Crown could not move, could not breathe. There was nothing in the universe except blind, maddening agony. He . . .

. . . opened his eyes and saw the panelled ceiling.

"Crown!" Jeff screamed out.

Dr. Carbo grabbed Jeff by the shoulders and held him down on the couch. "*Aspette!* Wait! Take it easy!"

"He's dying! I tried . . . "

"There's nothing you can do! Calm down!"

Amanda's face appeared before him. "It's not your fault, Jeff. There's nothing you can do about it."

"But he'll die!"

They disconnected him from the couch. Amanda made him drink something hot and bitter. Jeff sat on the edge of the couch, feeling slightly dizzy and terribly afraid, as Dr. Carbo went back to the control room.

"Still getting signals from the probe," he called back to them. "He's still alive. . . . Vital signs are very low, though."

"He's dying," Jeff muttered again.

Amanda leaned against the couch's edge beside him and slipped an arm around Jeff's shoulders. "Come on now, he's a tough old cat. He's been through worse than this and survived it."

"Let me get back in contact with him. Maybe I can help him."

Carbo peered at Jeff through the thick window of the control room. His face was a dark, solemn mask. "No," he said flatly. "There's not a thing you can do for him except tear yourself apart emotionally. If the poison kills the beast, it will kill him whether you're linked to him or not. If it doesn't — well, we'll keep monitoring the signals from the probe. If he makes it through the night he'll probably be okay."

Jeff gripped the edge of the couch with both hands as hard as he could, trying to keep his emotions under control.

"We have bigger problems, Jeff," Carbo said, coming around the control panel to the door of the contact chamber. "The food situation down there is starting to look desperate. I'll have to talk with Peterson and the others to see what can be done."

Amanda nodded. "You go find Peterson; I'll take care of Jeff."

Carbo gave the two of them a grim glance, then went to the door that led out to the corridor and left them alone in the lab. Jeff wanted to collapse into Amanda's arms, to let her hold him and comfort him and love him forever.

But she, instead, lifted his chin with her hand and

gazed straight into his eyes. "It's going to be all right, Jeff. Don't worry. Everything will turn out all right."

Jeff started to reply, but his tongue felt strange, numb. His eyelids were very heavy. He could hardly sit up, he was so tired. Vaguely, far in the back of his mind, he realized that whatever she had given him to drink was putting him to sleep.

"It will be all right, Jeff," he heard Amanda's voice crooning softly, as if from a tremendous distance away. "Everything will work out for the best."

When he awoke he didn't know where he was. It wasn't his dorm room, and it wasn't the contact lab. He was in a comfortable bed. The room was dark, except for the faint glow of luminescence from just over his head. He turned slightly in the bed and saw that the glow came from a bank of monitoring instruments set into the wall above him.

The infirmary.

Voices buzzed nearby, whispering urgently.

Amanda must have given me something to make me sleep, and then they brought me here.

"He'll be perfectly all right," someone was whispering, speaking as low as people did in church. Jeff saw in the dimness that his bed was surrounded on three sides by accordian-fold partitions that reached from ceiling to floor.

"He's exhausted, and emotionally drained," another voice muttered. It sounded to Jeff like Dr. Carbo's. "He's tied very closely to that animal. Emotionally, I mean."

"Yes, the tests have shown that," said the first voice.

"We shouldn't have let it go this far." Jeff knew that was Amanda. "We should have separated him from Crown long ago, for his own good."

"Twenty-twenty hindsight," Carbo said.

"Well, he's separated from the animal now and he's going to stay separated," said the third voice, the one that Jeff could not recognize. "This is as good a time as any to cut the cord."

"Aren't you worried about his emotional reaction?" Amanda whispered.

"I'm more worried about his growing identification with that animal down there. We'll keep him here under observation for a few days. Under no circumstances will he be allowed to return to your laboratory."

Jeff wanted to leap out of bed, yank the partitions down, and show them that he was as strong as ever and ready to continue working with Crown. But he couldn't lift his head off the pillow. He couldn't even scream out his rage and frustration at his helplessness. All he could do was lie there silently, knowing that Crown was dying and he was too weak to help.

CHAPTER 18

Amanda and Carbo walked slowly back to the dome that housed the scientific staff. By wordless agreement they went to his quarters.

"Do you really think Jeff will be okay?" Amanda asked him as they sipped wine and stared up at the stars from his recliner chair. It had not been built to hold two people, but neither of them minded the crowding.

"That snake may have done us a big favor," Carbo said.

"You mean by forcing us to separate Jeff from the wolfcat."

He nodded, then took a long draft of the ruby-red wine from his goblet.

"What are we going to do down there?" Amanda asked. "How are we going to feed those apes and keep them working without killing them off?"

"I talked to Peterson about that. We can't shut down the oxygen conversion equipment just because the apes can't take it."

"But they're dying off."

"I know. We'll just have to find replacements. And we'll have to train more of the students to control the animals."

"Even more work for us," Amanda said.

"For you. I'll be spending more and more time down on the surface, implanting probes."

She shifted her body slightly and turned her face toward him. "I hate that. I'm afraid every second you're down there."

With a grin, he answered, "I don't like it much myself. But it's got to be done."

"There must be a better way," Amanda murmured.

"Find it! I'd be overjoyed to learn how we can tame this planet more easily."

She sighed.

"Now we've even got a worse problem," Carbo said. "Food. The game herd's gone."

"So what can you do?"

"Peterson said we'll synthesize food for them."

"Will they eat synthetics?"

"They'll eat it or starve," Carbo said.

"Or run away."

"Not while they're under control."

"Then we'll have to have them under control twenty-four hours a day," Amanda said.

"Which means we'll need still more students."

"They won't be very effective, at first. New trainees

take a while before they learn how to really control their animals."

"It's got to be done," Carbo muttered.

"Can't we move the camp further south, out of this cold weather?" Amanda asked.

Carbo shook his head. "Higgins and the other engineers won't hear of it. They'd have to give up on all the months of work they've already put in here. Besides, this location was picked for its meteorological advantages. The oxygen they produce at this site will get the best possible distribution throughout this entire continent. The site was picked very carefully. It's the best place."

"Not for the animals."

"The animals," Carbo sighed. "They are all going to die, sooner or later. We can't afford to be kind to them."

Amanda leaned her head back onto his shoulder and stared up through the ceiling window at the glowing stars spread across the darkness of infinity.

"Which one is Earth?" she asked.

Carbo breathed in the scent of her hair and murmured, "*Cara mia,* you can't see Earth from here. I'm not even certain which one of those pinpoints is the Sun."

When Jeff woke up again he had no idea of what time it was, except that it was still dark in the infirmary, and that meant it must still be night. He listened carefully, but could no longer hear voices nearby.

Everyone must be asleep, he told himself. Lying on his back, he began to test his body, to see if the effect of the drug that Amanda had given him had worn off. He lifted his right arm off the bedsheet, then his left.

He pulled up both his legs and let them relax again. Everything felt normal, under full control.

Jeff sat up, swung his legs off the bed, and slowly got to his feet. No dizziness, no weakness. In fact, he felt stronger and better-rested than he had in weeks.

His eyes were adjusted to the dimness, and he saw that there was a closet built into the wall on the other side of the bed. He padded over to it and slid its door back. Sure enough, his coveralls and slippers were neatly stowed there. He put them on quickly, leaving his hospital gown on the closet floor.

Turning, he edged the partition around his bed back a crack. He saw three other beds in the infirmary room, all of them empty. Tiptoeing to the door that led to the corridor, he hesitated as he gripped the door's handle. There would be security cameras out there. But would they automatically trip an alarm if they saw a student walking along a corridor at this hour?

What hour is it? he wondered. Patting his coverall pockets, he found his wristwatch and clamped it on. Its glowing numerals told him that it was not quite 4 a.m. No wonder it was so quiet. Everyone should be asleep, except the few people on third shift. But it would be dawn soon on Windsong. Jeff had to be there when Crown awoke.

He cracked open the corridor door and saw that his way was blocked by a monitoring station, where a sleepy-looking young nurse sat reading something on her video screen. Lucky his own bed hadn't been plugged in to the monitoring system, otherwise alarms would have gone off when he got out of bed. Jeff saw that only two of the viewscreens on the nurse's monitoring panel were lit up. That meant that only two patients were under automatic observation.

He grinned to himself with an idea.

Silently, he slithered out of the room, keeping himself pressed flat against the wall of the dimly lit corridor. Just like a wolfcat stalking his prey, Jeff thought. He slipped into the next room. One of the patients under observation was in there, deeply asleep. Above his bed, a solid bank of monitoring instruments glowed with green and yellow lights. Jeff tiptoed to the bed and touched the nurse's call button. Then he dashed to the door and flattened himself against the wall beside it.

Just in time.

The nurse pushed the door open and strode briskly into the room, heading straight for the bed where the call button was glowing red in the darkness. Jeff ducked around the door and sprinted for the infirmary's exit. He barely heard the nurse's puzzled grumble as he left.

Outside, on the greenpath, he forced himself to walk at a normal pace. It would look odd enough to the security computer to see a student moving around at this hour; a running student might set off an alarm. He only hoped that no one had programmed the security computer with an order to keep Jeffrey Holman in the infirmary.

Apparently no one had. Jeff made his way to the contact lab without any trouble. He pushed through the door to the outer office area and made his way straight to the control room of the contact chamber he had used for so many months. Overhead lights flicked on automatically for him as he sat at the control console and tapped the phone's keyboard.

"Amanda Kolwezi, please," he told the phone computer.

Jeff stared impatiently at the blank viewscreen until

the computer printed NO ANSWER in green letters across the screen's face.

"Where could she be at this time of the night?" he asked himself aloud.

Jeff leaned back in the contoured plastic chair, stymied for a moment. Without Amanda I can't . . .

Then a new idea hit him. He shook his head, telling himself it wouldn't work, but after several minutes sitting alone in the control room facing the blank phone screen, he finally gave a resigned shrug and tapped the phone button again.

"Laura McGrath, please."

The screen stayed blank, but this time he heard Laura's groggy, "Hello . . . what is it?"

"Laura, it's me. Jeff."

"Jeff!" Her voice became more alert. "What . . . it's four in the morning!"

"I know. I need your help. Right away."

She sounded puzzled, dumbfounded, but she promised to meet him at the contact lab in fifteen minutes. Jeff paced the length of the control room as he waited for her.

At last Laura showed up, still rubbing at her sleepy eyes. She had hastily dressed in a pair of blue coveralls. Her thick red hair hung loosely around her shoulders.

"What's going on, Jeff?" she asked. "Why are you . . . "

"I've got to get down to the surface; I've got to get back in contact with Crown."

Her eyes widened. "Now?"

"Yes."

"Where's Dr. Carbo? Where's . . . "

Jeff grasped her by the shoulders. "Never mind the others. I've got to get down there right away and you're the only one who can help me."

"I can't do that!"

"Yes you can. I'll show you how."

Over Laura's protests, he showed her the control panel and its instruments. "It's almost entirely automatic," he assured her. "The only reason they use a human operator at all is to keep an eye on the contactor and start the disconnect sequence when they decide it's time to quit."

Laura was shaking her head, but watching and listening.

Finally he walked her into the contact chamber. "And, of course, you'll have to help strap me down on the couch and put the helmet on me."

"Now wait, Jeff," Laura said firmly. "Wait. Does Dr. Carbo know what you're doing?"

"No," he admitted.

"Does Amanda Kolwezi or any of the other staff?"

"Nobody knows except you and me," he said.

"You mean you're . . ."

"Laura, Crown is dying down there! They want to keep me away from him, but I've got to do what I can to help him. You've been in contact with the animals down there, you know what it's like!" His voice was almost pleading.

"But what you want to do is illegal, Jeff. If they find out—if Bishop Foy learns about this . . ."

"I know I'm asking you to take a big risk. But you're the only one I can depend on. I need you, Laura."

For a couple of heartbeats she said nothing. Then, "But I might make a mistake with the controls. I might even kill you."

"You won't. The controls are almost foolproof."

"Jeff, I can't . . ."

"Please, Laura," he begged. "I've never asked you

213

for anything, but I *need* you now. Please!"

Her eyes, green as a forest pool, locked onto Jeff's. He reached out and took both her hands in his and whispered once again, "Please, Laura."

Finally she nodded, slowly. "You're going to get us both excommunicated."

Jeff grinned at her. "Then we'll have to start our own religion."

He hopped up onto the couch and started strapping the cuffs around his ankles. Laura watched him, saw how eagerly he attacked the task, and knew that there was nothing she could do except help him.

When Crown awoke the pain was still there, throbbing in his leg. But it had not spread any farther. He could still see, still breathe. His heart still beat.

He lifted his massive head up from the ground. It had snowed again during the night, and he had to clamber painfully to his paws to shake the stinging, burning flakes from his back. The bitten midleg would not unfold, it was paralyzed.

But he was alive.

Food is the best medicine, his mind seemed to say. He looked down at the dead snake's body, half covered by the night's snowfall. Pushing aside the grayish, gritty flakes with one forepaw, Crown sniffed at the snake's body, wary of its poison.

It's all right. The poison glands are up in its head. Clamping one forepaw over the snake's head, Crown tore into the long, coiled body. It was mostly bone, but there was a lot of it. The snake was more than five meters long.

Feeling slightly better, but still aching from the snakebite, Crown limped back toward the humans' camp.

It was cold. Each day seemed to be colder, grayer, snowier than the last. As he limped slowly along the crest of the ridge line, under the trees where the snow was thinner, Crown could see the ocean through breaks in the dying underbrush. The water looked dead gray and chilling. The sky was grayer still, and even the beach was gray and grimy looking, under the snow. The carbon flakes would dissolve as the day wore on, but each day they seemed to cling to the ground longer before the sun's heat finally evaporated them.

Not a thing stirred in the woods. As far as Crown could tell, he was the only living creature left in the entire forest. Even the trees had curled up their leaves tightly against the cold. The wind ruffled Crown's fur and made him hold his head low as he limped painfully back toward the camp.

It was going to be a long trek, Crown knew. A long, bitter, hungry journey back to the camp, with his bitten leg flaring in agony every time he tried to move it.

Disconnect.

Crown kept limping through the frozen grass, feeling the sooty snow crackle under each step he took.

Disconnect. Power down. The animal's all right and he's supposed to be in the infirmary.

For a moment it all looked alien to Jeff: the lights, the walls, the ceiling, the couch. Then Laura and Amanda came into his field of vision.

"We got caught," Laura said.

They lifted the helmet off his head and unstrapped the cuffs.

"You're lucky it was me who came in here first," Amanda told him, "and not Dr. Carbo."

Sitting up, Jeff asked, "You can report me if you want, but leave Laura out of it."

Amanda glanced at the redhead, then gave her sternest gaze to Jeff. "Do you realize all the things that could have gone wrong with this harebrained stunt of yours?"

"I know."

"Do you?" Amanda snapped. "Do you realize what danger you put yourself in? And what danger you put Laura in? If anything had happened to you, what do you think Foy would have done to her?"

Jeff started to answer, but realized that whatever he said would sound weak and foolish. He shut his mouth.

"I did it voluntarily," Laura said. "He didn't have to twist my arm. I knew what the risks were."

Amanda scowled at her. "You should have your head examined. Just because you're in love with this lunk is no reason to behave so foolishly."

Laura's face flamed red. Jeff felt his insides flip over. Laura's in love with me? Impossible!

A grin broke out on Amanda's face. "All right, Miss McGrath, get yourself back to your quarters, or chapel, or wherever you're supposed to be at this time of the morning. And don't let me catch you messing around with this equipment again."

"No, ma'am," Laura whispered, falling back into her Church-trained humility. She glanced once more at Jeff, blushed again, then quickly turned and left the lab.

"As for you, Jeffrey Holman," Amanda scolded, "for a man who says he cares so much about the moral rights and wrongs, you're awfully damned quick to put your friend in danger."

"I didn't realize . . . "

"You didn't *think*," Amanda said. "Never mind what could happen to her if Foy found out about this escapade. Suppose you had died while she was sitting there in the control room? How do you think that might have hit her?"

Jeff hung his head.

"All you could think about was that big cat down there, wasn't it?"

"I . . . Crown needed me."

"No he didn't," she answered, more softly. "*You* needed *him*. Don't you realize that when you worry about Crown, you're really worrying about yourself?"

He stared at her. "But . . . "

Amanda arched an eyebrow at him. "Think about it. And you're going to get plenty of time to think it over. I'm going to put this lab off-limits to you, until further notice."

"What? You can't do that!"

"Watch me," she said. "The medical staff agrees that you need a rest. So you're going to get a rest, even if I have to put an armed guard at the door to this lab."

"Amanda, please don't."

"You're too close to the problem, Jeff. You're tearing yourself apart. Crown's all right . . . "

"Until he dies of oxygen poisoning."

That stopped her, for a moment. "Yes, you're right. Until they all die . . . until we kill them all."

"Don't lock me out of the lab, Amanda. Please don't."

"I've got to, Jeff. Lana Polchek and the psychologists have put it into the official record. You are not allowed to resume contact work until further notice."

For a long moment neither of them said anything. Then Jeff slid off the couch and headed for the door.

Amanda wanted to call out to him, but knew that she shouldn't, she mustn't.

Jeff stopped at the door and turned back toward

her. "What makes you think that Laura's in love with me?"

Amanda almost laughed, she was so relieved that his mind was moving in that direction.

"Only a blind man would ask such a silly question," she replied.

Jeff's brow knitted in puzzled frustration. Amanda saw clearly that he did not understand. But that didn't matter. At least he had something to look forward to, something vital and important, something that just might keep him from being crushed as they killed off all the native life on Altair VI.

CHAPTER 19

Jeff awoke the next morning, dressed as usual, and was heading down the dormitory corridor toward the autocafeteria when he remembered that he was no longer on duty. He would not be allowed into the contact lab. He had nowhere to go.

For the first time in months, he allowed himself a leisurely breakfast, and surprised himself by downing a large stack of pancakes, a trio of eggs with simulated bacon, and several glasses of synthetic milk. The long rows of tables filled up, gradually at first, but then almost the entire student body arrived within a few minutes, jamming the serving lines, filling up the tables, making the cafeteria echo with their talk and laughter. Jeff had not seen so many lively men and women since his first day at the contact lab.

He knew that he should feel angry with them, or at least deeply disappointed that they could appear so happy and free of worry in spite of all the problems the Village faced. Yet their laughter and youthful high spirits were infectious. Jeff grinned at the students who sat with him at the cafeteria table.

And they clearly respected Jeff with an admiration that came little short of adulation.

"What're you doing here so late, Jeff?"

"Yeah. You giving the wolfcats a rest today?"

He gave them a slight shrug. "I'm on vacation. They've ordered me to take a rest."

"Holy Nirvan! A rest! How did you finagle that?"

"It wasn't my idea."

"Hey, Jeff, will you be able to go to chapel this morning with us?"

"Sure," he said.

"Laura!" one of the women called across the noisy cafeteria. "Over here! Jeff's with us!"

She came to their table and the other students made a place for her beside Jeff. He wondered, Does everybody know about "us" except me?

They talked and joked and laughed until the overhead loudspeakers droned, "SUNRISE WORSHIP. ALL FAITHFUL TO THE TABERNACLE. SUNRISE WORSHIP."

The students cleared their tables and brought their breakfast trays to the disposal slots set into the cafeteria walls. Then they streamed toward the Tabernacle, off in its own dome.

Jeff offered his arm to Laura, who took it with

obvious pleasure, and they walked along the greenpath toward the Tabernacle with happy grins on their faces.

"I really appreciate what you did for me last night," he told her.

"It was nothing."

"No it wasn't. It was very important — to me. If I didn't know that Crown was alive and able to take care of himself, I'd go crazy."

"I'll look after him for you," Laura said. "Amanda and I will make sure he's all right."

"You're the one who's all right," he replied. "You're pretty wonderful, Laura."

Her smile widened and she lowered her eyes for a moment. Then, "I'm sorry they took you off the contact work. I'll ask Amanda to let you back as quickly as she can."

Nodding, he said, "I'm going to talk to Dr. Carbo about it. They can't keep me away for long."

In the Tabernacle, Jeff knelt beside Laura and tried to feel the religious warmth that he knew she did. But it was like his father's lack of feeling, compared to his mother's. Hundreds of heads were bowed in prayer, the Globe of Nirvan glowed brightly above them, yet Jeff felt no Presence, no awe, no deep stirring of his soul.

Then, from somewhere deep in his mind, came a memory of a Sunday School lesson: Faith is a gift, said Nirvan. God grants that gift to many, but withholds it from others, for inscrutable reasons of His own. Yet even a man who has not been granted the gift of Faith may show his devotion to God and Nirvan by his good works.

By my good works, Jeff thought. And all the burdens that had been lifted from his shoulders since he had seen that Crown was still alive, returned with a crushing new heaviness. The snake had not killed Crown, but we humans are killing him, and all the other creatures of Windsong. But if we don't kill them, the colonists coming from Earth will surely die.

By the time sunrise worship ended, Jeff's high spirits had evaporated. The tension, the pain had returned.

He did his best to keep it from Laura as she and the other students headed off for their day's work. They streamed out of the Tabernacle and into the greenpaths that led to the other parts of the Village. In the midst of that chattering, smiling, purposeful crowd, Laura stood up on tiptoes and gave Jeff a peck of a kiss, directly on his lips. Then she quickly turned and headed off, leaving him standing there with the other students swirling around him, grinning at him.

"See?" he heard Laura telling the young woman walking next to her. "He isn't a stuck-up snob at all. The people who've been saying that are just plain jealous of him, that's all."

The Tabernacle emptied quickly and the students strode with determined vigor toward their morning jobs. Within a few minutes, Jeff was left standing all alone outside the Tabernacle's main doors. In the sudden heavy silence, he felt the cold hand of guilt pressing on him. They were all working while he stood idle.

But not for long. Jeff walked swiftly to his dorm room and phoned Dr. Carbo.

"We'll get this thing straightened out right now," he muttered to himself as the phone computer searched for the scientist. "I don't need a rest, I'm as ready for work as I was the first day here."

But the phone screen printed, DR. CARBO UN-AVAILABLE AT PRESENT. PLEASE LEAVE YOUR MESSAGE AND HE WILL CALL BACK.

"Where is he?" Jeff asked aloud.

LOADING DOCK C.

He must be going down to the surface with today's landing team, Jeff realized. That means he won't be able to talk with me until this evening, at the earliest. Maybe he'll be down there for several days. Blast!

"Tell him it's Jeffrey Holman calling. And tell him it's urgent."

The phone screen printed JEFFREY HOLMAN. URGENT. It added the date and time. Jeff pressed the button that okayed the message. The letters faded from the screen, to be entered on Dr. Carbo's message list. There was nothing more that Jeff could do.

All that day, Jeff felt like a prisoner, an exile. He was free to roam anywhere in the Village he wanted to go, except for the contact lab—which was the only place he wanted to be. He hiked along the greenpaths, went up to the Village's observatory and gazed at the luminous blank face of cloud-wrapped Windsong, then pulled himself away and walked aimlessly for hours.

Finally he headed back to his own room, plopped himself on his bunk and started watching history tapes from the Village's library on his video screen. He examined the history of Earth, overcrowded, overpolluted, dangerous, dirty Earth. The teeming cities, the dying rivers and lakes, the oceans covered with algae farms and man-made islands and huge floating platforms that drank in the energy beamed from the Solar Power Satellites up in synchronous orbit.

He saw the human race, spread across the inner reaches of the solar system, and for the first time he realized how enormous was the difference between the rich and the poor, between those who lived in the vast luxurious colonies that floated serenely at the L-4 and L-5 points between the Earth and the Moon, and those squalid billions who lived in unending poverty down on the Earth's surface. He saw other space colonies drifting majestically out among the asteroids, beyond the orbit of Mars, where they mined the rocks and metals of the minor planets, turning those natural resources into enormous wealth.

For themselves. Very little of that wealth reached the hungry masses of Earth. The human race had split into two groups, early in the Twenty-First Century: those who lived in space, and grew richer every year; and those who remained on the home world, and grew constantly poorer.

Jeff remembered a twisted parody of the words of Jesus of Nazareth: The meek shall inherit the Earth; the rest of us are going to the stars.

To the stars.

He breathed out a long, weary sigh of frustration and despair. Here we are at the stars, working our hardest to create a clean new world for the Earth's poorest people. But at what cost?

Jeff spent hours staring at the history tapes. At the violence and hatred and fear and death that marked human existence. Even with the knowledge to end disease, to build artificial worlds in empty space, to tap the energies of the stars themselves, most of the human race still wallowed in murder and war, in poverty and ignorance. A few million lived in splendor in their space colonies. The seventeen billions on Earth lived in the mud.

He asked himself what he could do about it. As the

past five decades of human achievement flickered by his eyes on the viewscreen, Jeff tried to figure out what he should do. He knew that behind the thirty-two thousand approaching colonists, millions more would soon be heading for Altair VI. And no matter how many of them were fitted out with neuro probes, they were all carrying a full cargo of anger and hatred within their minds. Inside of a few years, a few decades at best, they would turn Altair VI into another Earth—full of violence and conflict.

Is this what we're killing Crown for? Jeff asked himself. There must be a better way. But he could think of nothing better.

Nothing.

The matter was out of his hands. He had helped them to use Crown, to start the inevitable death of the world called Windsong. He had been tricked into betraying a whole world.

"No," he muttered to himself. "Don't blame the others. You tricked yourself."

It startled him to hear a knock at his door. Flicking off the history tapes, he got off the bunk and crossed his room in three strides.

It was Laura, smiling at him hopefully.

"I just wanted to let you know," she said, "that I was with Crown today."

"Is he okay?" Jeff asked eagerly.

"Yes. His leg's pretty stiff, but otherwise he's all right."

"What about food?"

Instead of answering, she said, "We're all going to sunset worship. Want to come along?"

"Sure." He stepped out into the busy corridor and closed the door behind him.

As they started toward the Tabernacle, Jeff asked again, "Are the animals getting any food?"

"Well, some of the apes have been going into the ocean surf and digging up shellfish, but the wolfcats won't touch those."

"There's nothing else in the woods to eat," Jeff said.

Laura replied, "Crown went up there this morning and dug up a couple of animals that were down inside burrows. Dr. Peterson thinks they were hibernating for the winter."

"They can't be very big."

"They're not, but they're better than nothing. We'll have all the wolfcats doing that until the first supplies of synthetics are landed on the beach."

Jeff shook his head. "I don't think the wolfcats will eat synthetics."

"We'll see," Laura said. "It will all work out, one way or the other."

"One way or the other," he repeated.

For the next few days Jeff's only source of news was the students. Dr. Carbo never returned his call, and he found that he couldn't even reach Amanda by phone.

"They're busy," Jeff told himself. "And they know that I just want to pester them into taking me back."

More and more of the students clustered around Jeff each day. He ate breakfast and dinner with them, listened to their problems, suggested solutions.

One evening he sat back in his chair, his stomach filled with the tasteless but nourishing food, and let the other students chatter around him. The cafeteria was bustling with noise. All the table were filled. Hundreds of conversations babbled through the big, echoing room; hundreds of aromas drifted through the air.

Crown would go crazy in here, Jeff thought. Then he grinned inwardly at the thought of the wolfcat suddenly appearing among all these students.

Even Petrocelli seemed to have acquired a new-found respect for Jeff. He sat next to Jeff that evening, his usually-smirking face utterly unsmiling, sober. There were hollows in his cheeks that hadn't been there a week earlier, Jeff saw. The contact work was taking its toll on him. On all of them.

"How's it going, Dom?" Jeff asked.

Petrocelli shook his head. "Slow, man. Very slow. The apes are getting sicker every day."

"And the wolfcats?" Jeff wanted to ask specifically about Crown, but he still felt wary of Petrocelli's sarcastic tongue.

"They're in trouble too. They're starving."

"I thought we were shipping synthetic food down to them," Jeff said.

"We are," replied another student, a lanky sandy-haired youth with a surprisingly deep basso voice. "But they aren't eating it."

Laura explained, "The biochemists have produced synthetics that look and taste just like real meat—at least, to me."

"You tasted it?"

She grinned and nodded.

"Raw?" Petrocelli asked, incredulous.

"It's like raw hamburger," Laura said. "What do they call that in restaurants?"

"Steak tartare," said one of the other students.

"But the animals won't eat it?" Jeff got them back on the subject.

Petrocelli made a sour face. "They land these re-entry capsules full of food right down on the beach,

okay? The things come in like a big bomb: *ca-boom!*
The blasted apes jump out of their skins and run in
the other direction. Even the wolfcats get scared. None
of them will go near the capsules, and the stuff rots
away."

Jeff leaned back in his chair. "Why don't they land
the capsules farther down the beach, out of sight?
Then they can send the wolfcats out to get the food
and bring it back to the camp—just like they did with
the antelope."

Laura's eyes lit up. "Why didn't we think of that?"

Because you're not a wolfcat, Jeff thought. No matter how many times you've been in contact with the
beast, you haven't really *been* Crown.

"I'm gonna tell Dr. Peterson about that," Petrocelli
said, an honest smile spreading across his face. "I
think that'll work."

CHAPTER 20

Jeff's exile ended after five days. Amanda simply phoned him that evening, after dinner.

"Are you ready to stop loafing and get back to work?" she asked, a bright smile on her face.

"Yes!" he said eagerly.

"Good. Report to the contact lab at 0600 hours. All is forgiven."

"Okay, Amanda. Thanks."

Her smile shrank. "We need you, Jeff. We need all the help we can get."

It felt strange at first.

Crown was . . . different. Hungry, as always. But

more than that. He was tense, weary, tight-strung.

The camp was bigger than ever, dominated by the large angular shapes of the oxygen conversion factory which hummed and rumbled and poured out noxious fumes. Other buildings and bubble-shaped tents dotted the beach. Out in the sloshing surf, four re-entry capsules sat half-imbedded in the sand; the stench from the rotting synthetics inside them almost overpowered the evil scent of the human machines.

The apes were clearly on the verge of insanity. Every instinct in their makeup was telling them to flee, to head south, get away from this land of cold and strange, killing machines. But they were under the control of the orbiting Village, and under the snarling guardianship of the wolfcats who, like them, were forced to stay at the camp on the beach. Stay and work. Stay and work and freeze and die.

The wolfcats bedded down each night as far from the camp as their human controllers would allow them, far down the beach. They only went close to the alien buildings when there was absolutely no way to avoid it.

That morning Crown trotted away from the other wolfcats — all of them noticeably leaner and edgier than Jeff remembered them — and headed southward.

The food capsule landed okay. All he has to do is find it.

It took less than half an hour. The capsule was resting in shallow high-tide surf, half under water. Fortunately the hatch, which had popped open automatically upon landing, was above the waterline. But the waves were splashing up dangerously close to it, their breaking foam spraying into the hatch and dripping inside.

Crown sloshed through the surf, growling at the cold and wet. The midleg that the snake had bitten was still stiff, but he could use it now, put weight on it. He stretched up on his hindlegs and stuck his massive muzzle into the open hatch. With one forepaw he scooped out a quivering blob of synthetic meat. Crown sniffed at it, licked at it. Hardly any taste, strange odor, no blood or warmth to it.

Awkwardly he carried the oblong chunk of artificial meat in his forepaws and splashed through the surf to the dry sand above the high-water mark. He dropped it on the sand, sniffed at it again, then bit into it. It felt like meat, despite its faint taste. Crown ate it, all of it. It helped to fill his stomach, but that's all it did.

He went back to the capsule, took out another chunk of the stuff, and carried it back in his jaws to the other wolfcats.

They were prowling around the beach on the southward side of the camp like a band of sullen policemen waiting for trouble to start. Crown dropped the artificial food on the sand, then trotted away and stretched out on a rock that was warmed somewhat by the feeble sun. He watched as, one by one, the other wolfcats edged up to the synthetic meat and sniffed at it. The last to approach it was the biggest male, Sharpclaw, who had been the leader of a large family before the humans had drugged him and implanted him with a neuro probe. He growled at the synthetic, pawed it, slashed it once with his claws. Then he settled down to eating it. The other wolfcats stayed a respectful distance away while Sharpclaw devoured the entire chunk of meat.

Then, one by one, the wolfcats approached Crown, grunting and snuffling, as if to ask where he had the food. Without getting up from his comfortable bed, Crown turned his head toward the south and made a long, low rumble deep in his chest. Down there, he was saying. The food came from down the beach.

The wolfcats started down the beach. All but Sharpclaw.

By the time the day had ended, all the wolfcats had eaten and had brought back enough food to allow the apes to eat, as well. The animals seemed to feel much better and more peaceful with their bellies full.

Just like people.

Frank Carbo absently drummed his fingers on the tabletop as Dr. Peterson presented his figures on the rate at which Altair VI's atmosphere was being converted to a breathable oxygen/nitrogen mixture.

Each Monday morning the heads of each scientific department met together to report on progress, identify problems, discuss solutions. The meetings invariably depressed Carbo. No matter how much progress they made, there was always so much more to do.

"The first oxygen conversion plant is now working well," Peterson said, "at long last. The four others have been built here in orbit and tested. Now the crews are disassembling them so that they can be carried to the planet's surface in sections, and then re-assembled on the ground."

Bishop Foy never attended these meetings, although he reviewed the tapes of them. Still, Carbo felt the Bishop's gloomy presence hovering over them.

Peterson pointed to the slide that was projected on the conference room wall.

"Now that we have actual performance figures from

the first plant," the craggy-faced anthropologist was saying, "we can get some idea of how quickly we can convert the planet's atmosphere into breathable air."

Jan Polchek, the zoologist, asked, "Is the abscissa of that graph numbered in months or years?"

"Or centuries?" somebody else joked.

Peterson grinned. "Months, thank God. With all five oxygen plants working at full capacity, we'll have a completely Earthlike atmosphere on Altair VI inside of thirty-six months."

"Three years," Lana Polchek murmured. As head of medical staff, she and her zoologist husband comprised the only married pair at these meetings.

"And the colony ship has already shown up at the edge of this system," said Higgins, of engineering. "They'll be here in another month."

"We're all going to have to live in orbit for at least three more years," Peterson said. "We might as well face that fact."

"Can we do it? Three years?"

"We have enough supplies, providing the recycling systems don't break down."

"I mean, psychologically? Can human beings live in spaceships for years at a time?"

Lana Polchek answered, "In a ship like this Village, yes, there's no reason why we couldn't live here indefinitely. I've seen no evidence of environmentally-induced stress among the students or the staff. Have you?"

"I wasn't thinking about us," Higgins said. "What about those colonists?"

Peterson nodded grimly. "I see. That's another matter, isn't it?"

"Thirty-two thousand of them crammed into a ship no bigger than the Village."

"And millions more to come."

"They've all been fitted with neuro probes, though," Jan Polchek said. "They can be kept pacified for as long as necessary."

Carbo forced himself to stay silent. He wanted to bolt out of his chair and run from the conference room. But he held himself still as he gripped the arms of his chair with white-knuckled fury. Pacify them all, his mind raged silently. And one inevitable day they'll come to insert probes into our brains so that we won't cause them any more trouble, either.

The meeting finally ended and the department heads drifted out of the conference room, back to their tasks. Carbo lingered behind to catch Louisa Ferris by the sleeve of her coverall as she headed for the door.

"Dr. Ferris, a word with you, please."

She turned toward him, a pleasant smile on her cherubic face.

"Why, you didn't have a thing to say all through the meeting, Dr. Carbo," she said.

"Neither did you."

"Well, no ethical questions arose, did they?"

Carbo sat on the edge of the conference table. "I'm not so sure of that. We did spend most of the meeting discussing how long it would take to wipe out all the flora and fauna of an entire world."

Dr. Ferris' dimpled smile faded. "I know. It *is* distressing. But as long as there are no intelligent creatures down there, my hands are tied."

"I'm beginning to believe," Carbo said slowly, carefully, "that the wolfcats are intelligent."

Ferris' plump face looked suddenly distressed. "Oh,

no! Not you too! First it was that student, and then that black woman who works in your department . . . "

"Amanda?" he blurted, surprised. "Amanda Kolwezi?"

Louisa Ferris pulled out a chair and sat in it heavily, as if her problems were too much to bear standing up. "Yes, Kolwezi. She sent me some tapes yesterday from your contact lab. With a note that says she thinks the wolfcats can communicate with each other."

"I saw those tapes," Carbo said. "I agree with her conclusion."

"But don't you understand?" Ferris asked, her voice rising slightly. "The definition of intelligence is *so* difficult, there are so many aspects to consider . . . "

"But that works both ways, doesn't it?"

"What do you mean?"

"Well, if it's difficult to prove that a species is truly intelligent, isn't it equally difficult to say definitely that it isn't intelligent?"

Ferris blinked rapidly, her mouth slightly open, digesting Carbo's statement.

Without waiting for her to sort it all out, he went on, "Someone in your very difficult position can take either of two positions, it seems to me: Either you can say, 'The animals have got to show unmistakable signs of true intelligence,' or you can say, 'If there's any doubt about the matter, my responsibility is to protect those creatures until the question is resolved.' Isn't that right?"

She sat there looking confused.

"I mean," Carbo said, "it's the most difficult and significant task of anyone in the Village. All this responsibility rests on you!"

"Yes," she mumbled. "It does, doesn't it?"

"And I've admired the way you've been handling it

for all these months," Carbo wheedled. "Never once have you cracked under the strain! How marvelously well you have handled this enormous responsibility. The world government chose well when it assigned you to this mission."

"Why . . . thank you, Dr. Carbo."

"I can understand the terrific pressures you must feel, now that the time has finally arrived to make your decision."

She nodded, gazing up into his eyes.

"It's going to be a very difficult decision to make, I know. Balancing the hopes of those colonists against the lives of all the creatures of a whole world . . . "

Louisa Ferris said nothing. She seemed mesmerized.

"Only someone of your tremendous integrity and strength could stand up to Bishop Foy and represent the world government here, so many lightyears away from home. I admire you for that. We all do."

She shuddered, as if snapping herself out of a trance. "I had no idea that you cared about my work so deeply, Dr. Carbo."

"But I do, dear lady. I do. And I want you to know that if you must tell Bishop Foy that the colonization effort must be stopped because the wolfcats are intelligent, I and many of the other scientists will back you to the hilt."

"That . . . that's very flattering, Dr. Carbo. I appreciate the sincerity of your feelings."

Carbo made himself smile at her, while thinking, If purgatory exists, you've just bought a thousand-year visit, Francesco.

Louisa Ferris got to her feet and smiled sweetly back at him.

"When will you speak to Bishop Foy?" Carbo asked.

"Oh, there will be no need for that."

"No?"

"None whatever, Dr. Carbo. Those poor brutes down there are not intelligent, no more so than dogs or horses."

"*Signorina*, I simply cannot agree . . . "

She dimpled again. "*Signora*, Dr. Carbo. Martin Foy and I were secretly married a month ago. Isn't that romantic?"

With a girlish giggle, she went to the door, leaving Carbo sitting on the edge of the conference room table with a dumbfounded expression on his face.

CHAPTER 21

Crown could sense something different was in the air. Something terrifying.

It wasn't anything he could see, or smell, or hear. But it was there. In every gust of the icy wind that blew in from the gray sea, the terror was there. The dull pewter sky, the snow-covered beach, the trees up on the hills with their leaves rolled tight — everything around Crown reeked with dread and danger.

The apes sensed it, and so did the wolfcats. The apes worked clumsily, slowly, fidgeting, milling around whenever their human controllers slackened the electronic reins for a moment. They stared down the beach plaintively, as if silently begging the wolfcat guards to allow them to run away from this dreadful place. The wolfcats themselves prowled the snow-covered sand nervously, tails twitching, growling at nothing.

Whatever it was, it would be awful when it came.

Not that things were not already about as bad as the animals could stand. Winter storms had lashed the beach three times in the past seven days, wrecking some of the equipment with battering waves that smashed ashore far beyond the usual high-water mark. The snowfalls were heavy now, and apes and wolfcats alike had to sleep under shelter or be buried under the nightly snows.

Under their human controllers, the apes had erected special tentlike structures for themselves and others for the wolfcats. They had to put them up again every time a storm blew them down. The apes now spent every morning clearing the snow from the areas where they had to work. It left their handlike forepaws blistered and burned. The wolfcats' paws seemed to be tough enough to walk on the accumulated snowpack without blistering.

Now Crown stood partway up the slope of the hills, looking out across the beach at the slow-moving apes and the nervous wolfcats. The sea washed up on the beach, colder than ice. The apes moved numbly, reluctantly, at their work. The wolfcats growled.

Crown was on his way to locate the latest food capsule, which had landed crashing through the trees up in the hills the day before. But as he stood on the hillside for a moment, surveying the beach and the camp, waiting for the disaster that he knew was coming, he heard the now-familiar thunder of a sonic boom. Looking up, he saw the contrail of an approaching rocket shuttle. He rumbled and growled to himself.

Crown watched the sleek silvery winged craft swoop along the beach and land on the hard-packed snow. Wolfcats sprinted away in all directions as the shuttle skidded to a stop, spraying powdery gray snow from its landing skis.

The hatch opened and a dozen humans came out, small and frail-looking in their armored suits and bulbous helmets. Then the hoisting arm of a crane swung through the open hatch and the humans started lifting apes out of their ship and winching them down to the beach's surface.

The apes were dying faster than ever, especially those forced to work around the big, throbbing building that gave off the noxious fumes. For three straight days now, the humans had landed shuttles at the beach and brought out new apes, beasts they must have captured further south.

The apes were all unconscious, drugged, of course. But gradually they would awaken and begin to work like the rest, under neuro-electronic control.

Crown snarled at the idea. He realized that he was under control, too. Otherwise he would have long ago left this dismal beach and gone south to find his adopted family. But to Crown, it was more like a sharing, an experience that he had never known before, a force within his mind that led him to roam this world of Windsong and explore as no wolfcat had ever explored before.

I'm with you, Crown, a voice seemed to say within his mind. *You and I are one person, one creature.*

Frank Carbo planted his boots on the firm crust of the packed snow and surveyed the camp on the beach, as best he could. Despite the lights they had strung along the camp and on every side of the big oxygen conversion building, the beach was still abysmally dark. Carbo knew that it was mid-morning, but to his Earth-born eyes it looked like blackest midnight.

He shook his head inside the cumbersome helmet of his armored suit. He knew what Peterson and the other scientists claimed; he had gone through the mathematics and physics of it himself: within three years this entire planet would be transformed into an Earthlike world, with clean breathable air and bright blue skies.

He knew it. But he found it hard to believe.

"Watch out below," he heard in his helmet earphones. It was the voice of one of the students, a burly youngster named Petrocelli.

Carbo looked up to see that Petrocelli had one of the drugged apes rigged into the sling and was ready to lower it to the ground. He stepped aside and Petrocelli let the hoist go, with a faint hum of electrical power. The ape, a gray-white mountain of sleeping muscle, came down slowly, its huge thick arms and legs hanging limply out of the reinforced steel mesh sling.

Carbo and three other scientists couldn't lift the inert ape, so Petrocelli and one of the other students rode the sling down to the snow-covered sand to help. Grunting and sweating inside their heavy suits, they dragged the giant animal a dozen meters or so from the ship. Then the medic bent over it and prepared to give it the injection that would neutralize the drug that kept it unconscious.

"Wait for my word," Carbo told the medic. He could not see who it was, inside the fishbowl helmet. The helmet's visor reflected the lights along the beach without allowing him to see through the plastiglass.

Carbo flicked the dial on his wrist to the communications channel that linked him with the contact lab, up in the Village.

"Contact lab," he heard a student's voice say.

"This is Dr. Carbo. Give me Dr. Kolwezi, please."

"I'm here, Frank," Amanda said.

It felt good to hear her voice. He grinned to himself as he said, "We're ready to activate the first of the new animals."

"We have the controllers ready to make link-up," Amanda confirmed.

"Good." Carbo peered through the murky air at the number they had stencilled on the ape's chest. "This is number 4-01."

"Four dash oh one," Amanda repeated.

"Right."

"Okay, just a minute . . . " He heard muffled voices in the background, then Amanda came back with, "We have 4-01 linked up. The controller is ready."

"All right. We will activate the animal." Carbo clicked his communicator dial back to its first channel and told the medic, "Give it the shot—and then stand back."

The medic rammed the hypodermic into the ape's massive shoulder, then stood up and walked rapidly away, toward Carbo. The beast lay there unmoving for several seconds, then shuddered, twitched, and rolled over onto all fours. It swung its head around toward the humans and growled menacingly.

Without realizing what they were doing, both Carbo and the medic took a step backward. Carbo bumped into Petrocelli, who held a power rifle tightly in both gloved hands.

The ape reared to its hind legs. Its lips pulled back in a snarl that revealed its fangs.

"Jesuto," Carbo mumbled.

"God, it's big," Petrocelli said. But he stepped in front of Carbo as he said it, protecting the two scientists with his rifle.

Carbo remembered someone telling him that Petrocelli was a convert to the Church of Nirvan, and still felt that he had to prove himself.

"Wait a second," he told the student. "Don't shoot unless . . . "

The ape jerked spasmodically and almost tottered off its feet. Then it seemed to take a deep breath. The snarl faded from its lips. It dropped back down to all fours and turned away, walking docilely toward the buildings of the camp where the other controlled apes were already working.

Carbo heard Petrocelli blow out a long-held breath. The medic, who had said nothing through the episode, finally spoke up:

"Do we have to come that close to heart failure with every one of these critters?" It was a young woman's voice, but Carbo had no idea to whom it belonged.

"Well," he answered, "there are only eight more of them." *This trip*, he added silently.

Petrocelli broke his rifle into its two separate parts and clamped them to the magnetic grips on the belt of his suit.

"Okay," he said, "let's go get the next one out." There was real enthusiasm in his voice.

Carbo, already feeling weary, followed the youth back toward the ship. Three more years of this, he said to himself. Three more years.

Crown turned his back on the scene at the beach and headed inland, up the slope of the hills and into the gaunt woods, searching for the food capsule that had landed there. The underbrush was bare now, and the trees had curled up their leaves for the winter. The wind was cold and relentless. It was not a good place to stay. Crown wondered how long he and the other wolfcats could stand the winter cold and storms. He knew the apes would flee south as soon as the wolfcats left them alone.

And there was still that feeling, that foreboding, deep inside him. Some inner sense was warning him that something terrible would happen soon. But he did not know what it was.

Back on his couch in the contact lab, Jeff Holman twisted and writhed as if in pain. He mumbled to himself, eyes closed in deep electronically-induced sleep. The student who was monitoring him became alarmed and called Dr. Kolwezi, who was directing the work in another part of the greatly-expanded lab. Amanda hurried to the control room, scanned the monitoring instruments with a worried eye and watched Jeff struggle against himself on the couch. She shook her head and reluctantly told the student to continue without disconnecting Jeff unless his vital signs went into the danger zone.

Crown padded through the dead forest, under the cold gray sky, every sense alert for danger, every nerve on edge. He saw a pair of trees leaning crazily against their neighbors and headed in that direction. Sure enough, there was the food capsule. It had crashed into the forest, smashing dozens of trees and gouging a still-steaming tear in the ground.

The hatch was open; the food was inside. Crown fed

himself, as usual, and then carried a fair-sized chunk of the tasteless stuff back toward the beach. When he got there he would show the other wolfcats where the capsule had landed, just as he did every day.

He stopped in mid-stride.

Something strange was happening. The air crackled, as if a summer storm were hurling lightning bolts through the sky. The chill wind sighed to a stop, yet the trees seemed to be swaying. The ground itself trembled, only slightly, but enough for Crown to feel it. Every instinct in him told Crown to drop the food he carried and run inland, away from the sea.

For a long moment he stood stock-still and did nothing. The ground's trembling ceased. The wind resumed. The electrical charge in the air seemed to subside.

Still, Crown knew that the beach was not a safe place to be. Yet that is precisely where he headed, dropping the load of synthetic meat he held in his jaws as he bounded through the silent forest toward the camp of the humans.

Carbo felt the tremor. They all did. The men and women on the beach, unrecognizable as individuals in their bulky suits and helmets, all stopped what they were doing and stood still for a moment.

"What was that?"

"It felt like a big truck had just rolled by me."

"You felt it too?"

"Could it have been an earthquake?"

"Pretty small one, if it was."

"It was a tremor," Carbo heard one of the scientists say, his voice sounding quite authoritative even over their suit-to-suit radio link.

"Is it a precursor to a bigger shock?" someone asked.

"No, this area is tectonically very stable. That's one of the reasons why we picked it for the base. I don't think we're in any danger."

Carbo heard his words, but wondered why the hairs on the back of his neck seemed to be standing on end. He peered into the darkness and saw, one by one, the rest of the landing team go back to its work.

Thank God this is the last one of the apes, Carbo told himself as they prepared to activate the giant beast. After this one we can pack up and get back to the Village. Until tomorrow.

Crown raced through the woods and halted only when he got to the top of the ridge line, where he could see the beach and the puny humans working alongside their flying craft.

The apes were working as usual. The wolfcats were prowling nervously down at the far end of the beach. Everything seemed normal. Yet Crown knew that it was not.

He roared out a warning.

The humans jerked to a stop and stared up at him. The apes dropped what they were doing and began to cluster together. The other wolfcats roared back at Crown, to tell him that they understood him, even though their human controllers did not and would not let them run to safety.

What is it, Crown? He sensed within his mind the presence of his friend, the shared consciousness of his alien companion. *What's the danger, Crown? How can we warn them?*

The wolfcat's sudden roar nearly froze Carbo's blood.

He turned around so abruptly inside his heavy suit that he wrenched his neck.

"Damn!" he yelped. "What now?"

The other wolfcats began roaring, somewhere out there in the darkness. The landing team came sprinting toward Carbo.

"What's the matter? Why are they roaring?"

"I don't know," Carbo said, irritatedly, as he tried to rub the back of his neck and was thwarted by the plastic helmet. "Something's bothering them."

"The most astute observation of the week."

Out of the murky gloom a huge gray figure took shape, a six-legged mountain of sleek muscle that padded slowly toward the humans.

"God Almighty, it's coming straight for us!"

"Stand back," Petrocelli said, clicking his rifle together.

"No, wait." Carbo put a restraining hand on the student's arm. "I think it's Jeff's wolfcat—Crown."

"How can you tell one from another?"

"I saw him before, the first time I came down here. Besides, the animal doesn't want to harm us."

The wolfcat's claws were sheathed as it walked up to the frightened knot of humans. It stood taller than any of them at the shoulder, frighteningly huge. The animal sniffed at them, seemed to peer at them one at a time, then turned toward the hills that overlooked the beach. It took a few steps toward the hills, then came back to the humans.

"What's it doing?"

"It wants something . . . but what?"

The wolfcat singled out Carbo and stared at him, its head, bigger than Carbo's whole torso, lowered to the human's eye level.

"Whatever it wants," Carbo said, his voice shaking, "I am willing to give it."

As if it understood what the human said, the wolfcat turned back toward the hills again, took a few steps in that direction, then looked back over its shoulder.

"Does it want us to follow it?"

"Where?"

"And why?"

"I don't understand what . . . oh, my God! Look at the ocean!"

Carbo turned and peered into the midnight darkness. The ocean was going away.

CHAPTER 22

Carbo stared, goggle-eyed. The water was sliding back, slipping away from the land, revealing more and more of the beach, brownish-dark, flat, glistening. Like an ebbing tide filmed in stop-motion, the edge of the sea retreated farther and farther from the normal high-water mark, until human eyes could no longer see it in the eternal gloom of Altair VI's murky atmosphere.

He heard the wolfcat growl, as if it was just as terrified of what it saw as the humans were.

Carbo shivered.

No. It was the ground that was shivering.

"Tsunami!" someone shouted.

"Earthquake and tidal wave! We've got to get out of here!"

But Carbo's feet could not move. He was rooted to the ground where he stood.

"Get back to the shuttle!" he heard someone shout. "We don't have a moment to lose!" Then he realized that it was his own voice barking out the command.

He broke his paralysis and began heading toward the shuttle. The other men, running clumsily in their heavy armored suits, all did the same. Carbo peered out into the darkness, wishing he could see what was happening out there in the ocean. All that he could make out was the suddenly-bare beach where the sea had retreated. It frightened him to his core.

Crown could see the ocean clearly. It had slid away from the beach, as if knowing something terrible was approaching.

With a grinding roar, the ground under Crown's paws shook. Trees began cracking and toppling along the crest of the hills. A boulder up there broke loose and tumbled toward the beach to smash into one of the alien buildings and demolish it.

The apes stood frozen at their tasks for endless moments, then, with a single scream of purest terror wailing in unison from their throats, they threw up their hands and ran pell-mell down the beach on their hind legs. The wolfcats roared, raced back and forth, turned in circles—and then they too dashed down the beach, heading away from the camp as fast as they could run.

They're out of control!

Disconnect these kids before they go into shock.

The ground bucked and heaved. Great fissures tore

through the hillsides. Entire hills collapsed like balloons suddenly bursting, spilling thousands of tons of rock and soil down onto the beach.

The humans were clustered at the hatch of their rocket shuttle, clambering up the ladder. But a new tremor opened a fissure alongside the craft. Its left landing gear slipped into the crack in the ground and the wing smashed against the snow-covered sand, crumpling like aluminum foil.

Crown stood frozen, not knowing whether to try to escape along the beach or go up the crest of the hills. The ground was shaking badly now, rattling every bone in his giant body. Through the haze of steam that was seeping out of the newly opened fissures, Crown could see that the beach was going to be a place of death.

Don't disconnect Jeff! He's still in contact. He's holding steady.

Lord, he's the only one.

Far out along the horizon Crown saw a huge wave of water, like the gray wall of a fortress, rear itself against the eternal clouds of the sky. It was moving toward the beach, speeding toward land, growing taller and taller, mounting, looming, dwarfing everything before it as it rushed closer and closer.

In seconds it would hit the beach, Crown knew. And when it did, it would destroy everything there.

The shuttle suddenly lurched, throwing the men on its boarding ladder into a muddled heap on the snow-packed beach.

"What happened?"

"Are you okay? Are you hurt?"

"My arm. Goddammit, I think it's broken."

253

Carbo had been thrown down onto the seat of his pants by the tremor. He sat there, his head spinning, his legs sprawled out ludicrously before him, and saw that the bogey wheels of the spacecraft's landing gear had fallen into the fissure. The wing was bent and dented; fuel was dripping out of a tear in its titanium skin.

It's going to catch fire, Carbo thought. We could all get killed if it explodes.

And then he realized, It doesn't matter. We can't fly out of here now. We're going to be killed when the tidal wave hits.

All of this had taken only a second or two. The other men of the landing party were still muttering, grumbling, sorting themselves out. They didn't seem to realize how badly damaged the shuttle was. Slowly, painfully, Carbo got to his feet. What do I say to them? he asked himself. How can I tell them that we're all dead men?

The others were mostly on their feet now, several of them huddled around one of the men, who seemed to be injured. Carbo couldn't tell who was who, behind the heavily tinted visors of their helmets.

"Ohmygod, look at the shuttle's wing!"

"It's smashed!"

"For God's sake, get inside to the radio, tell them to get the other bird down here quick! We'll be trapped here if they don't!"

"They're not gonna risk the other shuttle."

"But we . . . "

Carbo turned away from them and looked out along the beach. Most of the buildings had withstood the earthquake; it hadn't been such a major tremor—just enough to kill them all.

Then the gray mountain of the wolfcat slinked into his field of view. The huge beast got between Carbo and the other men.

"What do you want, *animale*? A morsel of Earthman before the tidal wave comes and wipes us all out?"

The wolfcat nudged Carbo with its shoulder, nearly knocking him off his feet.

"Hey, now wait." Carbo reached for the stun gun at his hip, fumbled with the holster. "I don't want . . . "

But the wolfcat suddenly grabbed at Carbo with both its forepaws. Its huge fanged mouth opened wide, gaping like the jaws of hell. All Carbo could see was teeth the size of butcher knives.

"Help . . . " he gasped as the wolfcat lifted him off his feet and closed those fangs on his body. Carbo blacked out.

Crown knew that he could not save all the humans, but this one man could be saved—if he could get him to the crest of the hills before the tsunami struck the beach.

There was no time to waste. Crown tried to show the human what he needed to do, but the alien two-legged creature simply stood dumbly, unable to communicate, unable to understand. As gently as he could, Crown seized the human in his forepaws and then clutched him with his teeth, hoping that the human's frail suit would not rip open. Crown needed all six legs to climb the steaming, fissure-rent hillside.

He loped off from the beach, and heard some of the humans shouting faintly behind him. The man in his jaws had gone limp. The ground had stopped shaking, but behind him, Crown knew, the tsunami was approaching with the swift mercilessness of death itself.

He reached the slope of the hills and started up toward the crest. Trees had toppled up there. A crack yawned in front of him, steaming. Crown leaped across it. Rocks and boulders were strewn everywhere and the ground itself seemed new, raw, soft and slippery. The entire hillside was threatening to slide loose, slipping down toward that all-swallowing wall of gray, foaming water.

Crown scrambled and scrabbled, knowing that he could move much faster without the inert weight of the man in his jaws. But he held onto the human and worked desperately to climb higher. Now he could smell the salt tang of the sea air and the terrible low rumbling sound that meant the end of the world. He clawed his way past the rocks and dirt slides and the tumbled boles of broken trees.

He reached the crest of the hill and turned around to look down at the beach. Gently he deposited the human on the warm, raw-looking soil.

Carbo inhaled a deep breath of life-giving oxygen and realized that he was still alive. The beast hadn t devoured him after all. It stood looming over him. They seemed to be off the beach; he could see the trunks of trees leaning at odd angles above them.

Slowly he rolled over onto his belly, wondering if he had the strength to get to his feet. Through his helmet he heard—almost *felt*—a low growling sound, like the wind at the end of the world, like the inexorable grinding of the mill of the gods. He stared down toward the beach, straining his eyes in the inky darkness of this hell-world, and felt his breath stop. A wall of water was blotting out the sky, rushing up onto the beach, straight toward the struggling knot of humans and their crippled rocket shuttle.

And then the world exploded. The sound was overpowering. The fury of the tsunami smashed onto the beach and Carbo felt himself suddenly lifted by some giant's hand and thrown upward, tossed like a leaf in a hurricane. Trees, rocks, strange shapes he'd never seen before; the sky tilted upward, sideways, and then he was slammed flat onto the hard unyielding ground.

It was over.

Carbo lay on the hilltop, a few dozen meters from where he had been seconds ago. Everything was dripping water: the drunkenly-tilted trees, the bare claws of stripped shrubbery, the rocks. The ground itself seemed soaked, soggy as a sponge.

And he was alive. Bruised, frightened so badly that he could hardly control the shaking of his hands, his heart beating wildly . . . but he was alive.

The mountainous shape of the wolfcat loomed over him, gray and dripping wet. It bent its massive head toward him and sniffed at him like a dragon snorting.

Carbo laughed giddily. "You look as miserable as I feel," he said. The animal's mane was plastered with mud. Water flicked from its twitching tail.

Groggy, every part of his body aching, Carbo struggled to his feet and looked out toward the beach. There was nothing he could see in the darkness. He reached for the infrared booster scope in his belt pack and lifted it up to his visor.

Nothing. The camp was gone. There was no sign that human beings had ever been there. The beach was scoured clean of everything: the buildings, the shelters, the equipment, the rocket shuttle, the men and women — Altair VI had scrubbed them all away, cleansed itself of the intruding alien presence.

Carbo sank to his knees. Tears filled his eyes. Higgins, Petrocelli, all the others were dead. He wanted to die too, to collapse right here on this soggy, spongy mass of branches and wet soil, and give up his life. He had surely killed them all.

Instead, he lifted the booster scope again and searched the area carefully. The sea was calm now, quietly lapping up onto the sand as if nothing had ever disturbed its eternal rhythm. The beach itself was cleared of snow; it glistened gold and smooth in the afternoon sunshine. Carbo could see specks of broken machinery, seaweed, boulders, tree branches littering the beach. Something bobbed in the surf that might have been the helmet from a suit.

Turning toward the giant wolfcat, Carbo muttered, "I suppose they'll send the other shuttle down now to pick me up. It might have been better if you had left me on the beach to die with the others."

The wolfcat gazed at him silently, then opened its huge mouth in a gigantic yawn and stretched languidly. It shook its immense body like an oversized cocker spaniel. Carbo was drenched by the spray.

CHAPTER 23

The Village was officially in mourning for fourteen days over the fourteen men and women killed in the tidal wave. No work was done by any of the students. A single mass funeral was held in the Tabernacle, with empty coffins representing the dead.

Jeff found it strange, disconcerting, to eat with his friends in the cafeteria and not see Petrocelli. The burly convert had turned from antagonist to grudging friend, and Jeff missed his sharp-tongued wit at their table.

Was there something I could have done to save him? Jeff asked himself a thousand times. He had no answer.

He had instinctively helped Dr. Carbo. He could not have done more. No matter how hard he thought about it, he saw no way in which he could have saved any of the others.

Still, the dormitory dome was silent and oppressively gloomy. The students had little to do. No work except routine housekeeping and life support functions was being done. But there were special prayer meetings every day, and more worship services each evening. To Jeff, they were almost unbearably morbid.

He found himself at one of the viewing ports, along his favorite greenpath, late one afternoon, staring out at the dazzling brilliance of the planet below them.

"There you are."

He turned and saw Laura picking her way through the flowering shrubbery to join him.

"I thought I'd find you here," she said.

"Hello, Laura."

She looked out at the cloud-covered face of Altair VI. "Thinking about Crown?"

With a half-guilty grin, he admitted. "Yeah. He's been on his own for more than a week. I wonder if he's found his own family."

"You think he's migrated south to look for them?"

"Sure."

"It's a big world down there," she said.

"It's *his* world. He'll find them."

"I hope so." Laura turned to face him. "Jeff, I'm getting to think that you're right. We shouldn't be ruining their world. We shouldn't be killing them off."

He smiled with relieved pleasure. "You've been in contact with those creatures often enough to start feeling for them, haven't you?"

"Yes," she said.

"Well . . . that tidal wave gave them all a reprieve."

"But it's only a reprieve," said Laura. "We'll all be back at work in another few days. The colony ship will take up orbit with us in another two weeks."

"Right."

"What can we do?"

"If I knew, I'd tell you," Jeff said. "I've been racking my brains over this for months now. I don't see any way out of it."

She started to reply, hesitated, and fell silent.

"One thing I do know, though," Jeff went on. "I'd love to get in contact with Crown again, just to see what he's doing, how he's making out."

"The contact lab is closed."

"Officially," he agreed. "But this wouldn't be work, it'd be . . . observation. I wonder if Amanda would let me . . ."

"Us," Laura said firmly. "We'll both ask her."

On the fifteenth day after the tsunami disaster, Bishop Foy called a meeting of all the science department heads.

Frank Carbo lay in his warm, enveloping waterbed that morning, staring up at the viewing port set into his ceiling, looking out at the eternal night of space. He had been picked up by the rocket shuttle a few hours after the earthquake had subsided. The wolfcat had led him back to the beach; then, as the rocket shuttle announced its presence with a sonic boom, the animal had turned away and headed down the beach, southward.

They had kept Carbo in the infirmary for five days while the physicians tended his bruises and the psychologists probed his guilt-ridden mind. He knew what they wanted to hear and told them quite matter-of-factly that he understood that it was not his fault that the others had died. He knew that they examined him while he was asleep, also, and easily found that the guilt was deeply imbedded in him.

"It's something I'll have to live with," he told them. "There's nothing that any of us can do about it."

He waited for them to suggest a neuro-electronic probe that would blank out the guilt feelings, but they had the tact not to mention it.

Now he lay on his waterbed, luxuriating in its physical comfort, on the morning that everyone in the Village was supposed to get back to work.

Work. It was bad enough to be saddled with the responsibility for scouring an entire planet clean of its native life forms. It was something entirely different to send human beings, friends and associates, to their deaths.

Carbo forced himself to sit up, grunting with the effort. "The planet fights back," he muttered to himself. "Maybe we're not so powerful after all. *It* scoured *itself* clean — of us."

Leaning over, he touched the phone button and asked for Amanda Kolwezi. The phone computer answered that she was not in her quarters.

Carbo thought briefly about calling her at the contact lab. There was no contact work going on yet, he knew, but she was probably there checking out the equipment. If it hadn't been for Amanda these past few days, he knew, he would have gone off the deep end. Her love is keeping me sane.

With a shake of his head, Carbo slid off the bed and stood up. Mustn't use Amanda as a crutch, he warned himself. Stand on your own feet, Francesco. Go to the meeting. Face up to Bishop Foy and the others.

He walked himself into the shower and then reluctantly got dressed.

Foy's meeting was already in progress by the time Carbo entered the narrow, bare, cheerless conference room.

"Ah, Dr. Carbo," said the Bishop as Carbo entered and took a chair as far across the round table from Foy as he could find. "I was just about to send an inquiry to see if you were healthy enough to join us."

"I'm sorry to be late," Carbo almost whispered. "Have I missed anything important?"

The Bishop's smile was ghastly. "Only a few minutes of Dr. Roskopf trying to explain to us how a supposedly tectonically stable area was subjected to a devastating earthquake and tidal wave."

Roskopf, the geologist, looked decidedly unhappy. Sweat beaded his upper lip and forehead. He was one of the older men among the scientists, balding and pouchy-faced. He had been a distinguished professor of geology in some Balkan nation, Carbo remembered, but had been forced to leave his post because of his political views.

"The area was and still is tectonically stable," Roskopf insisted, in a piping tenor voice. "The earthquake—and it was a massive one—took place a thousand kilometers out at sea. The camp area merely happened to be on the fringe of the affected area."

"It seemed like a powerful quake to me," Foy snapped.

"It was not," countered Roskopf. "If you review the data tapes, you will see that the temblor did only minor damage to the camp. A few boulders rolled loose from the hills and one of them crashed into a shelter. It was extremely unfortunate that one of the minor fissures that opened up on the beach incapacitated the shuttle rocket. Otherwise the quake did not damage the camp."

No, Carbo thought, it only killed fourteen of us.

"It was the tsunami that did the damage," Roskopf went on, raising an index finger as if lecturing students. "And the tsunami was the result of the temblor itself, which was centered slightly less than eleven hundred kilometers to the eastward, where two tectonic plates converge at the bottom of the ocean."

"But we still lost the camp. Months of work was wiped out."

Roskopf spread his hands. "In my original report I mentioned that the beach area might be subject to tidal waves. The probability was quite low, but it was there in the report. On page four hundred and six, I believe."

Foy blinked his watery eyes and turned away from the geologist.

"Very well," he said. "I see no use in crying over spilt milk. We have buried our dead. Now we must press on."

An uneasy stir went around the table.

Foy's rasping voice rose slightly. "I needn't remind you that unless we convert this planet into a habitable colony, we lose everything. Instead of being landowners, we will be penniless failures. We will be sent back to Earth in disgrace, our careers in ruins, jobless and destitute."

Carbo looked at the faces of his colleagues. He himself had a private fortune to return to—if the government did not confiscate it. But he knew that the others did not. If they could not gain employment at some university or corporation, they would starve just as the wretched orphans of the streets starved. Worse: these men and women of learning had no knowledge of how to survive in the streets. They would not last a year, Carbo knew. Most of them would not last a month.

They had sold their souls to Altair VI. For the promise of wealth, for the dream of becoming shareholders in a whole new world, they had come out to this hellish planet. They were not greedy, Carbo knew. Most of them would not know what to do with immense wealth. But the lure was there. After lifetimes spent in genteel poverty, after years of watching one student after another return to campus richer than the whole faculty, the temptation of turning their science into personal wealth was overpowering.

And Foy was playing on that temptation now.

"We have had a great setback," the Bishop was saying, in his best pulpit style. "The Lord has seen fit to smite us heavily. But God moves in strange ways, and what we now see as a disaster may actually turn out to the good, in God's own time."

Carbo sank back in his chair, his eyes riveted on Foy as the Bishop rose from his seat and raised his hands to heaven.

"God in His wisdom and His mercy will not allow this great work of ours to fail! If He removed our first camp, it was because it was located in the wrong place. Better to have it removed now than six months from now, when hundreds of our brethren would be living at that spot."

Foy's eyes actually took on a glow of almost maniacal devotion. "What we have done so far should be considered an experiment, an experiment that was in many ways more successful than we would have dared to hope for, only a few short months ago.

"We now have solid experience in controlling and using the animals down there. We have built and operated an oxygen conversion system and have data to show that it works as designed. We know that in three years' time we can convert Altair VI's atmosphere to air that people can breathe."

He let his arms drop to his sides, as if suddenly aware that he was doing something foolish. Blinking his eyes several times, Bishop Foy dropped back into his chair.

For a moment, no one spoke.

Then Peterson cleared his throat, leaned forward and folded his big hands on the tabletop.

"Although I wouldn't use quite the same rhetoric as our good Bishop," he made his craggy face grin, "I agree with what Bishop Foy just said. We've lost a battle, but we can still win the war."

"The other oxygen plants are completed and ready to be emplaced on the planet's surface," said Dr. Glasser, the head of the engineering department. "They've all been checked out in orbit and are ready to go."

"Then we will need absolutely safe sites for them," Foy said, casting a baleful eye at Roskopf.

"There's more than tectonics involved in the siting," Peterson said. "The oxygen conversion equipment must be placed in sites that are meteorologically favorable, as well. After all, we want to convert this planet's atmosphere as quickly as possible."

"We'll have to start rounding up the animals we've already implanted," said Jan Polchek. "They must be scattered all over the place by now."

"And implant more of them."

"That means more expeditions to the surface," Peterson said. "Lots more."

"No!"

They all turned to Carbo.

"Enough is enough," Carbo said. "We've killed fourteen people. How many more are we going to slaughter before we realize that we've got to stop?"

Bishop Foy stared at him the way a snake fixes its gaze on a helpless bird.

"What do you mean, we've got to stop?" Peterson asked.

"What we're doing is wrong. It's not only dangerous, it's morally and ethically wrong. Not only are we going to kill hundreds, maybe thousands of our own people down on that planet's surface—we're sitting here around a conference table talking about killing every plant and animal on that world! That's *wrong*. It is nothing less than wrong."

"But they're not intelligent creatures," countered Louisa Ferris, gently. She sat at Foy's right hand.

"Aren't they?" Carbo snapped. "That wolfcat saved my life."

"It was being controlled by one of the students."

"It knew about the approaching tsunami before any of us did. It tried to warn us. It tried to communicate."

Foy said harshly, "Let's not rake up that old chestnut again. The animals are not intelligent. That much has been settled."

"But to wipe out all the living creatures on a whole planet . . ."

"What alternative do we have? Go out to the observatory and take a look at the colony ship. It's close enough to see in a low-powered telescope."

"Send them back," Carbo said.

"We can't do that!"

"Send a message to the world government and tell them that this planet cannot be altered into an Earth-normal habitat. Tell them that they have to bring us and the colonists back to home."

"That's all right for you," Lana Polchek said. "You can live quite comfortably back on Earth. But what about the rest of us? To send us home means you'll be ruining our careers, killing us!"

"And what about the colonists?" her husband asked. "Should we send them back home to starvation?"

Carbo let out an impatient, angry sigh. "If the government spent as much money helping those poor wretches as they do exporting them to miserable hellholes like Altair VI, there would be no poverty on Earth!"

"But there is poverty," Roskopf said, his voice strangely gentle. "Believe me, my friend, I have seen it. I have experienced it. And to expect governments to do what is best for their people . . . " He smiled sadly and left the thought unfinished.

"I can understand your state of mind," Bishop Foy said to Carbo. "But even if we could return to Earth in honor, we still owe it to the colonists and the students of the Village to persevere."

"The students?" Carbo asked. "Why the students? They wouldn't be blamed for our failure if we all returned to Earth."

Foy shook his head sadly. "They would not be returned to Earth any more than the colonists would."

Jan Polchek asked, "You mean the students are . . . stuck here? Permanently?"

"The students signed up for lifetime missions. There is no provision for returning them to Earth. They and the colonists are here permanently—or until the colony they build becomes rich enough to provide the fare back to Earth."

Carbo felt suddenly hollow inside.

"You and I," Foy told the scientists, "can return home. Our careers would be ruined, our livelihoods would be shattered, but we could return to Earth if we chose to do so. The students and the colonists cannot."

"I had no idea . . . "

"If we leave," Foy said, "we leave them here to die."

"So our choice . . . "

"Is what it has always been," the Bishop said firmly. "Either we convert Altair VI—even though it means killing every living creature on the planet—or we kill the colonists and the students."

CHAPTER 24

While the scientists were meeting with Bishop Foy, Laura and Jeff made their way to the contact lab. Amanda was in charge, directing a group of students as they checked out the equipment that had not been used for two weeks.

"No contact work today," she said to Laura and Jeff.

"Uh, yeah, I know," Jeff replied. "But can we speak to you . . . in private?"

Amanda pressed her lips into a tight, nervous line. "There's an awful lot to do here."

"Please?"

"Just for a minute or two," she said. "We've got to review all our procedures. You know that every student lost control of his or her animal down there when the earthquake struck."

"All but one," Laura reminded her.

Amanda gave them a thoughtful look. "That's right. All but one."

She ushered them back into the contact chamber that Jeff knew so well. The control room, the couch and sensors, they all had the feel of home to Jeff. He could almost smell the scents of Windsong.

"Now I know what you want," Amanda said, "and I can't do it. Repeat, can not. You've been after me for a week and the answer is still no."

He grinned at her. "But we're officially back on work schedule, Amanda."

"But we are *not* authorized to resume contact work. You know that."

"You're checking out the equipment, aren't you?"

Amanda nodded.

"Well, how do you know it really works unless you run a test?"

She planted her hands on her hips and glared at him. "Jeffrey Holman, you're in the wrong business. You should have been a lawyer, or a salesman."

"Come on, Amanda, let me make contact with Crown."

"I can't do it!"

"Call it a test run. I just want to see where he is."

"There's too much to do; I can't sit here monitoring you . . ."

"I can do that," Laura said. "I can monitor the controls. I've done it before."

Amanda stared hard at the two of them. "Now look, just because you want to play with your wolfcat again— and just because you want to help him—is no reason for me to let you get yourselves, and me, into trouble with Bishop Foy."

"We won't cause any trouble."

Her scowl softened into the beginnings of a smile. "The hell you won't. Now listen carefully. I cannot allow you to make a contact test. Do you understand? I am very busy, and I am going to return to my official duties right now. I am so busy, in fact, that I won't even get to checking out this particular lab for several hours. Is that clear?"

Laura looked puzzled, but Jeff understood what Amanda was saying.

"Perfectly clear," he said.

"Good." Amanda gave them a single, satisfied nod, turned and left the room, closing the door softly behind her.

Jeff bounded to the door and snapped its lock home.

"What are you doing?" Laura asked.

He reached out and grasped her gently by the shoulders. "Amanda just told us, in so many words, that if we want to use this lab she'll look the other way. But if anything goes wrong, the responsibility is on our heads. Are you game? Will you run the controls for me?"

"And if something does go wrong?"

"I'll take the blame."

"No you won't," Laura said firmly. "We're in this together."

He kissed her. "You're wonderful. Let's get started."

Crown was padding through a forest glade, warm sunshine on his back. He stopped abruptly as he felt an old, familiar presence return to him. With a purring rumble, he realized that he had missed this alien mind, this stranger who was no longer a stranger, this mental brother who had shared so much toil and adventure with him.

Raising his head to the ever-clouded sky, Crown howled out a roar of pure wolfcat joy. Every other sound in the forest ceased. Every animal froze with fear.

If a wolfcat had been capable of laughter, Crown would have laughed. *No, we're not after you. Our belly is full.*

As if the forest creatures understood his unspoken thoughts, the birds and insects and scampering, chittering creatures of the trees resumed their normal activities. The forest came alive again with the sounds of abundant, teeming, vigorous life.

How different this warm forest was from the dreary cold of that beach, far to the north. How easy and unforced it was to exist here.

Crown resumed his trek southward. For days now he had been following the spoor of other wolfcats, certain that Thunder and his family were among the migrating group. Each day he got closer to them, and although he felt no anxiety, no need to hurry, each day his joy mounted as he got closer to them.

The forest closed in around him again, mottled sunlight splashing the sparse undergrowth with pools of cool shade. Something scampered out of his way to Crown's left and dashed up the sturdy trunk of a huge old tree. Once Crown had passed it by, the creature screeched at him angrily.

We're close to them. I can tell we're close to them.

Suddenly the forest was slashed by a deep ravine, its sides too steep even for a wolfcat to negotiate. Far below, Crown saw a swift stream gurgling and splashing as it surged over boulders and spilled even further down in a series of splashing waterfalls. He followed the track of the other wolfcats until he came to a huge tree trunk that had fallen across the ravine to make a natural bridge. Crown trotted across it gracefully, three tons of clawed muscle moving as lightly as a cloud.

On the other side of the ravine the ground sloped gently downward and the forest thinned until, within an hour, Crown found himself at the edge of a broad open grassland. Ideal hunting ground for a wolfcat — or a hundred wolfcats, for that matter. But in such an open, undefined area, Crown knew, marking family territories became difficult. Fights over territory could decimate wolfcat families in regions such as this, unless they united into a large clan, under the leadership of one very senior male.

He scanned the grassland and, sure enough, saw the gray shapes of a dozen wolfcats gliding through the tall fronds. He roared out a greeting to them, and they stopped in their tracks. One wolfcat roared back.

Crown recognized Thunder's voice. Eagerly, he bounded off to join his family.

There were more than a dozen wolfcats in the group; many more. Crown counted twenty-two adults, with another nine cubs cowering warily between the legs of their mothers.

Crown's own family had suffered, he saw. Thunder was limping and scarred from flank to jaw; the wounds were fresh enough to still be red and oozing blood. He stood alone, off at the edge of the wolfcat clan, and alone welcomed Crown with a rumbling purr from deep in his chest. Brightfur and Tranquil stood beside a wolfcat that was almost twice Thunder's size, a huge snarling male who called himself Brutal. And the cubs, Strong and Dayrise, were nowhere to be seen.

Crown took all this in with a single glance. The story was immediately clear to him. Thunder had been beaten, nearly killed, by the head of the clan, Brutal, who had taken Thunder's two females for himself and killed their cubs. It was not unusual; Crown knew that when a small family joined a larger clan, the clan leader often killed the cubs. But one look at Brutal showed Crown that this leader reveled in his name and enjoyed terrorizing the other wolfcats.

For the first time in his life Crown felt anger growling from deep within his guts. And something more, a strange, eerie, alien sense of . . .

Justice, he heard within his mind. *It's called justice.*

Brutal opened his mouth to reveal razor-sharp fangs, then—with a warning grunt to Brightfur and Tranquil—stepped ponderously toward Crown. He was more than twice Crown's size, and even though he was several years older than Crown, he gave no sign of being slowed or weakened by age.

Thunder moved meekly aside, limping slightly and obviously in great pain.

Crown growled inwardly as the clan leader approached him. He knew what his role must be: to raise his head, expose his throat, in a signal of submission to the acknowledged leader of the clan. To do anything less would mean that he would have to fight Brutal.

Yet Crown's anger seethed inside him, and he knew that Brutal and all the other wolfcats could easily sense it. There would be nothing to stop Brutal from slashing Crown's throat out when he made the signal of submission. Crown himself knew that Brutal would be wise to kill him while he had such an easy chance.

So when the mountainous wolfcat stood before him, and all the others backed away, Crown snarled defiantly. Brutal did not seem surprised. He expected the challenge; he even appeared to be delighted by it. The two wolfcats eyed each other, growling, knowing that this would not be merely a ritual battle of obedience. This fight would go to the death.

I'm with you, Crown. I don't know what I can do to help, but I'm with you.

Laura sat in the control room, one eye on Jeff's seemingly unconscious form lying on the contact couch, the other on the instrument readouts displayed before her. Jeff's adrenaline level was soaring, his heartrate was climbing fast.

She bit her lip in indecision. If I call Amanda, she'll disconnect Jeff right away and send us both back to the dorm. Jeff will be furious with me for pulling him away from the wolfcat.

She watched the viewscreen, seeing what Crown saw, staring at the snarling face of the biggest wolfcat she had ever seen.

But if Crown is badly hurt, or killed, what will it do to Jeff? Laura reached for the switch that started the automatic disconnect sequence. Her hand hovered over it uncertainly.

Crown could see that Brutal bore the scars of many fights on his head and shoulders. But the giant wolfcat showed no hesitation about fighting again. He did not circle warily around his younger opponent, he moved straight in on Crown, reared back to free his forelegs, and jabbed one forepaw lightly at Crown's snout.

Crown blocked it and instinctively backed away.

Brutal moved relentlessly forward. This was no argument over food, or even over territory. This was a fight for survival, life or death. A wolfcat clan can have only one leader, they both knew. All other males must either submit or be killed.

All the other wolfcats dropped down onto their haunches or bellies, forming a ring around the combatants as they watched the opening moves of their struggle.

For long moments Crown and Brutal stood facing each other, radiating hatred and fighting pride, snarling, tails twitching, ears flattened back on their skulls. Then, with a sudden bunching of muscles, they leaped at each other.

Six tons of wolfcat collided with an earthshaking thud as they reared on their hind legs and slashed at each other with the claws of their fore- and mid-paws. Crown felt searing pain rake him from chest to abdomen, but he saw that he also slashed Brutal along one shoulder.

Both animals bounced off and backed away for a moment. Crown felt hot blood dripping down his flank. But he had less than a heartbeat to think before Brutal reared again and attacked. Again they jarred the grassland with the concussion of their furious collision. Muscle and bone, strength and anger smashed against each other time and again, without either wolfcat scoring a telling blow. Their mightily fanged jaws played no role in this stage of the fighting: it was claws against claws, for now, a fencing match where the two ponderous beasts stood facing each other, snarling, glaring, tails twitching—then a roar and a leap, claws flashing. Then back on all sixes again, looking for a weak spot, a half-second's delay, a place and a time to press home the killing attack.

Crown was getting the worse of it. He was as fast as the older male, perhaps even a shade faster. But Brutal was more experienced, more sure of himself, deadly accurate with his claws. Crown was bleeding from a dozen long, raking slashes. None of them was dangerous in itself, except that soon enough the loss of blood would wear him down, tire him, slow him to the point where Brutal could finish him off with a final snap of his fanged jaws.

But the part of Crown that was Jeff was learning faster than any wolfcat had ever learned. Jeff felt the pain, but he and Crown together were watching the way the bigger wolfcat moved, the way he tensed his shoulders just before he leaped, the way he lowered his head to keep his throat protected.

Brutal leaped at Crown again, but this time Crown dodged sideways, twisted in midair, suddenly a three-ton acrobat, and landed on the back of his surprised enemy. His jaws closed on Brutal's neck while all six of his paws dug deeply into the doomed wolfcat's flanks.

A single strangled scream of pain and fury, then it was finished. The old leader lay dead, his blood staining the grass. Crown stood over the corpse—panting, bleeding, but victorious.

He lifted his head and roared long and full and joyously. The other wolfcats got to their feet and approached him. Thunder was the first, and Crown nodded and grunted toward Brightfur and Tranquil. They were Thunder's mates, and no other wolfcat would touch them as long as Crown headed the clan.

Jeff opened his eyes, a contented smile on his face.

Laura came into the contact room, bubbling with excitement.

"You did it!" she exulted. "You did it! You beat that horrible bully!"

Jeff smiled at her. "Crown did it . . . although, maybe I helped a little."

"You're marvelous," she said as she unfastened his cuffs.

Jeff lifted the helmet off his head and swung his legs off the couch. Laura clasped her arms around his neck and they clung together in a long, happy kiss.

"Hey there, that isn't the kind of contact work I expected you two to get into."

They broke apart guiltily, then saw Amanda grinning at them.

"I made contact with Crown," Jeff blurted, "and he's . . . "

Amanda stopped him with an upraised hand. "Don't tell me. I don't want to know. I never authorized you to use this equipment. As far as I'm concerned, you left this lab right after I talked to you this morning."

"Oh! Yes, sure."

"So get out of here before somebody spots you and reports back to Foy," Amanda said, trying to sound stern, and failing.

"We're going," Jeff said.

"But be prepared to report for duty tomorrow morning at 0700 hours," Amanda added. "The orders were issued this afternoon; we start back to work with the animals tomorrow."

Jeff's heart sank. "Not again. Not after everything that's happened."

Amanda nodded gravely. "Bishop Foy's orders. We either whip this planet into shape or die trying."

Jeff looked back at the empty contact couch. "It's the animals down there who will die."

Laura whispered, "What can we do?"

"Nothing," said Amanda.

"That's what you think," Jeff snapped.

CHAPTER 25

The Tabernacle was filled for the evening service. Even the scientists and social technicians were there, at Bishop Foy's express command.

After the opening prayers, the hymns of praise, and the special prayers for strength and guidance, the Bishop—in his full regalia of green and gold—paced slowly, wearily to the lectern to begin his sermon.

With an intensity that even Jeff could see, from his pew halfway toward the doors, Bishop Foy's bony, blue-veined hands gripped the lectern. It had been made of wood taken from the original Church of Nirvan, in St. Thomas. The Bishop seemed to gain strength from touching it.

"Tomorrow," he began, in a voice that Jeff could barely hear from his pew, "we return to the work that God has given us, a task that will determine the fate of millions of souls spread over the dark distances between here and Earth, and uncounted billions of souls of the yet-unborn."

He took in a long, weary breath. His body straightened, his voice grew stronger. "Tomorrow, after fourteen days of mourning, we renew our faith and our commitment and take up once again the task to which we have dedicated our lives. Tomorrow, we pay homage to our dead in the way *they* would have wanted us to: by returning to the work for which they sacrificed their lives."

Jeff knew it was an old orator's trick: start out softly and increase the volume as you drive your points home. And it always worked; it never failed to stir an audience. He probably has the amplifiers set on a feedback loop, Jeff thought, so that the louder his voice, the more wattage they pour into the speakers.

The Bishop became eloquent, powerfully stirring up the images of duty and faith that would strike at the students' souls. He spoke of God's infinite wisdom, and of Nirvan's promise of eternal paradise for those who obeyed God's will.

But how does he know God's will? Jeff asked himself silently. How do I know that he isn't confusing his own desires with the wisdom of the Almighty?

"Let each of us renew our vows," the Bishop commanded, in a voice that rang with certainty and power, "to devote every gram of strength and purpose in us toward the goal that these fourteen martyrs gave their lives for: To redeem that planet of Satan below us and transform it into a new Eden! To find the salvation of our souls in preparing a living home world for the colonists that are on their way! To work, and work, and work still more—no matter what the setbacks, no matter the pain or danger, no matter the obstacles in our path."

Raising his eyes toward the brilliantly glowing Globe of Nirvan that hovered over the packed pews of the congregation, the Bishop raised his hands in benediction and murmured, "Let us pray."

Some four hundred students bowed their heads obediently. Many of the scientists and social techs did also. Jeff lowered his chin a few centimeters, but looked sidelong across the crowded pews. His moment was almost here.

"Amen," said the Bishop, the signal for everyone to sit up straight again. Then the ritual dismissal: "Let all voices be as one in the praise of the Lord as we return to God's work."

His palms suddenly slick with sweat, Jeff rose to his feet, feeling his heart fluttering in his chest.

"Reverend Bishop, may I speak my praise?"

It was a ritual phrasing, inserted into the liturgy when the founders of the Church of Nirvan realized that many potential converts expected the right to speak during the worship services, if the Spirit so moved them.

Foy looked startled. He peered at Jeff in a squinting way that made Jeff wonder if the Bishop recognized him at this distance.

"Every member of the Faithful is free to praise the Lord," Bishop Foy answered, unable to hide the impatient scowl on his face.

"Reverend Bishop," said Jeff, forcing himself to speak loudly enough to be heard throughout the circular chamber, "you ask us to dedicate ourselves anew to the task before us. But, sir . . ."

Jeff hesitated. Can I go through with it? Will the others support me?

He swallowed hard, then went on, "Sir, I find that I cannot in good conscience continue to participate in the destruction of the world we call Altair VI."

A sigh went through the Tabernacle, a sort of collective moan that escaped unbidden from more than five hundred throats. Jeff saw Carbo whip around from his seat in a front-row pew. Amanda, sitting beside him, swung her gaze from Jeff to the Bishop.

Foy stared at Jeff. "May I remind you that you swore before God to transform Altair VI. Do you take your vows so lightly?"

Jeff had expected his legs to turn to putty once the Bishop levelled his guns at him. Instead, he answered firmly:

"I do not take my vows lightly, Reverend Bishop. But my conscience will not allow me to participate in killing all the living creatures of an entire world."

The students stirred and buzzed like a single entity awakening from a chrysalis.

Foy glared, knowing that to control them all, he had to control this one outspoken rebel.

"You stand in danger of excommunication," the Bishop warned.

"Nirvan teaches that the individual conscience is the final authority," Jeff countered. "I ask all those whose consciences are troubled to stand with me, and refuse to continue the genocidal work we have been put to doing."

The Tabernacle went absolutely still. Jeff could hear his heart thudding in his eardrums. Foy stood frozen at the lectern, leaning on it as if he would collapse without its support.

Then, from her assigned pew, Laura McGrath got to her feet. Across the main aisle, Petrocelli's best friend rose. Then another student, and another. Jeff turned to see a half-dozen more standing behind him, and when he faced forward again, Carbo, Amanda, and two others among the scientists were on their feet.

So few, he realized. A dozen students. Four scientists. Not very many. But enough. Enough to stop things where they stand.

Foy thundered, "You fools! Don't you understand that you cannot return to Earth! You students will *never* be brought back to Earth! You will either transform this planet or die here aboard the Village!"

None of the students sat down. Two more got to their feet.

"As your spiritual leader and the head of this project I *command* you to sit down," Foy said. He lowered his voice and added, "If you sit down now and return to Nirvan's path of obedience, we will forget all about this incident."

Jeff called out, "Reverend Bishop, you are asking us to put authority above conscience, to obey rather than Believe."

"I am *ordering* you to remember your vows to God and this Church, and to be faithful to them."

"Those vows said nothing about annihilating millions of God's creatures," Jeff replied. "A vow taken in ignorance is meaningless."

The Bishop's mouth opened, then clicked shut. He glared out at the congregation, shot a special frown at

Carbo and the other standing scientists, then snapped, "The service is ended. Go in peace."

With that, he turned abruptly from the lectern and strode to the gothic-arched door at the far side of the altar, radiating frustration and anger.

Jeff stood there, his knees rubbery, cold sweat trickling down his flanks. How much easier to be a wolfcat, he thought in a distant part of his mind, and deal in the simplicities of life and death.

The students stood in their pews for a stunned few moments after the Bishop had fled from the altar. Then hundreds of dazed, hushed conversations burst out.

Laura pushed her way through the milling crowd toward Jeff's side. "You did it," she said glowingly. "You actually stood up to him. I'm so proud of you!"

But the other students kept their distance from Jeff. Even those who had stood with him made their way numbly to the Tabernacle's exits and toward their dormitory rooms.

"I wonder what he's going to do now," Jeff said to Laura, voicing the fear they all felt.

"What can he do, excommunicate us? We could get that reversed as soon as we get a message back home."

"*If* he allows us to send a message back to Earth," Jeff said.

"He couldn't refuse! We have rights . . . "

"If we're excommunicated, what rights do we have?"

Laura looked shocked. "This is a fine time to think of that, Jeff."

"I thought of it this afternoon."

"And you still . . . ?"

He nodded. "I still went ahead and opposed him. I had to. I meant every word that I said, no matter what Bishop Foy does to us."

Laura began to reply, then realized there was nothing she could say. She stood beside Jeff as the students filed out of the Tabernacle until there was no one left in the huge circular chamber except the two of them, standing alone beneath the dully glowering Globe of Nirvan.

Stretched out on the soft warm buoyancy of the waterbed, Frank Carbo and Amanda Kolwezi were also worrying about Bishop Foy's next move.

"Jeff shouldn't have done it," Amanda said, staring through the darkness to the star-filled viewport in the ceiling.

"He had to. *Somebody* had to. He's the only one with the guts to do it."

"But not like that," she said. "Not in front of the whole Village. He's forced Foy to retaliate."

Carbo gave an exasperated grunt. "You've seen how Foy has responded to persuasion and argument. What else could be done except to face him head-on?"

"I don't know," Amanda answered. "But what Jeff did is bad strategy. It's forcing Foy into a corner, giving him no alternative except to lash back as strongly as he can."

Carbo smiled in the darkness. "You talk like an expert in political strategy."

"I am," Amanda said.

"Really?"

"Do you think a princess of a Congo tribe can live to adulthood—even in London—without learning something of politics?"

He chuckled softly. "No, I suppose not. I am impressed. You are a woman of many, many talents."

She turned toward him and grabbed two handfulls

of his hair. "Which of my many, many talents do you like the most?"

"Your mind, of course," Carbo said. "I love you for your mind."

"Oh?"

"Because it directs such a luscious, beautiful, well-coordinated body."

She laughed and then kissed him.

He held her close to him, feeling the cool softness of her body against his bare skin.

"If a man marries a princess," he asked, "does that make him a prince?"

"No. That makes him a princess' consort."

"Consort. H'mph."

"Would that damage your Italian male ego?" Amanda teased. "Would that weaken your *machismo*, or soften your, eh . . . pride?"

"I don't think so. I guess we'll have to get married to find out."

"A psychobiological experiment?"

"I want to marry you, Amanda," he said, suddenly quite grave. "Will you marry me, my love?"

He felt her breath quicken. "Frank—are you serious?"

"I have never been more serious about anything in my life."

"Marriage," Amanda murmured. "That . . . that's a major step, isn't it?"

"Yes."

"We seem very happy together without it."

"I agree. But there is more involved than merely our physical passion—delightful though it may be."

"May be?"

"Be serious, darling. This project is going to end in a disaster, one way or the other. We could be stranded here, or we could be shipped back to Earth."

"I don't want to return to Earth."

"As my wife," he went on, ignoring her statement, "you would share my personal wealth, which is rather considerable. No matter what happens to me, you would be assured of enough money to return to Earth and live quite comfortably for the rest of your years."

"I will not return to Earth!" Amanda sat up on the bed, sending waves undulating through it.

"But why not?"

"I left Earth behind me," Amanda said, almost fiercely. "I will never go back. Never!"

He sighed. "You're painting yourself into a corner."

"I don't care. I will not return to Earth, to the tribal wars and suicidal politics of that old world. Earth is where all my family is buried. I will not go back there."

"But if you stay here . . . "

She looked up at the stars. "I know. If we stay here we must transform the planet or eventually die."

"There must be some other way, some better alternative."

Amanda said nothing. For long moments Carbo could not speak, either.

Finally, "But will you marry me?"

She turned and looked down at him. "Even if we stay here?"

"Yes. I love you. I want you to marry me."

Amanda touched his cheek with her outstretched hand. "You foolish, wonderful man."

"Will you?"

"Of course I will."

They kissed, long and lingering. Then Amanda broke into a giggle. "But do you think Bishop Foy will perform the ceremony for us?"

Carbo laughed too. Soon enough, though, they grew silent as they lay side by side, gazing up at the stars. Carbo quoted softly:

> *"Ah, love, let us be true*
> *To one another! for the world, which seems*
> *To lie before us like a land of dreams,*
> *So various, so beautiful, so new,*
> *Hath really neither joy, nor love, nor light,*
> *Nor certitude, nor peace, nor help for pain . . . "*

CHAPTER 26

When Carbo awoke the next morning, he felt emotionally exhausted, heavy-spirited. Slowly he turned on the undulating waterbed, to find that Amanda was no longer there beside him.

He squeezed his eyes shut for a moment, then pulled himself up to a sitting position as the bed rocked gently beneath him. Then he heard her voice singing, and he let himself breathe again.

"Good morning," Amanda said as she came into the bedroom. She was fully dressed in a loose orange and brown caftan over a pair of dark form-fitting slacks.

"You're damned cheerful," he grumbled.

"Why not? There's no work to do. I got up early and checked with . . . "

The phone buzzed. Carbo leaned across the bed and clicked it on, holding the bedclothes up to his chest with his other hand.

Bishop Foy's face appeared in the tiny screen, white and drawn, his eyes bloodshot with sleeplessness.

The Bishop grimaced with distaste as he saw that Carbo was still in bed. Amanda stayed at the bedroom doorway, out of the phone's line of sight.

"You haven't tried to get into the contact laboratory this morning, I see," said the Bishop.

"I . . . uh, I overslept." Carbo suddenly felt as if he were being confronted by his Jesuit disciplinarian again.

"Well, get down there as fast as you can and see if you can talk some sense into Holman and the rest of those rebels. If you can't, there's going to be real trouble. I promise you that! *Real* trouble!"

The screen went blank.

Carbo blinked his gummy eyes and turned to Amanda.

"I was just about to tell you," she said, a strange smile on her lips. "Jeff and the other students have taken over the contact lab. They won't let anyone else in."

"Jesus, Mary and Joseph," Carbo gasped.

Jeff fought down the temptation for the twentieth time. Sitting in the flimsy wheeled chair in front of the control console, he could see the couch—*his* couch—where he could be in contact with Crown within minutes.

But we've all agreed there will be no more contact work, he told himself. Not even to see how Crown is getting along. Nobody touches any of this equipment. No matter what the Bishop says or does, we stay here and keep them from using this equipment and killing Windsong.

Still, he itched to be linked up to the equipment, to make contact with Crown, to be a wolfcat leading a whole clan down on the surface of that world.

He shook his head, as if to clear it of such temptation. I've done a lot better for Crown than I have for myself, he told himself ruefully.

"Jeff." Laura's voice broke him out of his thoughts.

He swivelled the creaking chair to face her. "Dr. Carbo's here. He'd like to speak with you."

"Good." Jeff got to his feet and went with Laura to the reception area where the offices and the main exit to the outer corridor were.

Amanda was with Carbo, looking more beautiful than ever. The scientist himself seemed dishevelled, as if he had dressed very quickly. His jawline was dark, stubbly.

"It's all right," Jeff said to the four students who were standing guard at the corridor door. "They can come in."

Jeff led Carbo and Amanda to Carbo's own office, an unkempt cubbyhole at the end of the row of offices. Carbo's eyes took in everything: the students lounging at the reception desk, the others posted at the entrance to the lab area.

"You've really taken over the place," he said as Jeff opened the office door.

"We haven't harmed anything," Jeff said. "We just want to make certain that no one uses the equipment."

Carbo gestured Amanda into the office, then stepped in himself. Jeff and Laura followed. The office was cramped and littered with cassettes of data tapes, book spools, recording tablets.

"May I?" Carbo asked, pointing to the padded chair behind the desk.

"It's your office," Jeff said.

He went around the desk and sat down. Amanda took the chair beside the desk. Laura and Jeff squeezed together on the half-sized couch facing it.

"I didn't know if you'd let me in," Carbo said.

"You stood with us last night, didn't you?"

"Yes, but I'm not sure that I agree with this move — taking over my lab."

"I thought about it all night," Jeff said. "It's the only way we can prevent Bishop Foy from forcing the work to continue."

"And it's the only way we can make him listen to us," Laura added.

Amanda said, "You're going to force him to do something drastic."

"That can't be helped," Jeff said. "He can try to starve us out, prevent other students from bringing food to us."

"Or he can use police powers to muscle you out," Carbo said.

"He'd have to have the Elders agree to the use of physical force," Jeff said.

"Since when have the Elders said no to him?"

Jeff admitted, "You're right. But he'd have to recruit the police from among the students. I don't think they'd attack us. And even if they did, we'd destroy this equipment before they were able to overcome us."

Carbo threw his hands up. "*Jesu*, what talk! Destroy the equipment."

Leaning forward, placing his hands on his knees and staring straight into Carbo's eyes, Jeff said, "We

296

are determined to prevent the annihilation of the living creatures of Windsong—Altair VI."

"But there's got to be a better way than blowing up the lab," Carbo argued.

"I wish I knew one."

Glancing up at the ceiling and the curving wall of the office, Amanda said slowly, "You know, if I were Foy, I wouldn't try to use force against you students. I would just evacuate the rest of this dome, leave you here sitting in the lab, and then turn off your air."

For a moment no one spoke; the only sound in the room was the electrical hum of the air blowers.

"Once we realized he'd done that," Jeff said at last, "we would still have time to wreck the equipment."

"Not if he just opened all the vents in this dome," Amanda said, "and let the whole dome decompress. You'd all be dead inside of a few minutes."

Laura shuddered. "He wouldn't do that."

"Maybe," Amanda said.

"Whether he would or not is unimportant," Carbo said impatiently.

"Unimportant?"

"Maybe to you," Jeff said.

Carbo waggled his hand at them. "Listen, my friends. I am here. I will stay here with you. I made that decision last night in the Tabernacle. We are in this together, to the very end."

Jeff felt his breath catch in his chest. "Do you mean that?"

"Of course. We live or die together, and in the long run, whether we live or die is not important."

Amanda made a sour face at him.

"No, hear me out. What *is* important is that world down below us, and those colonists on their way here.

297

We must find some way to save them both. So far, the way we have been going, we can only save one at the expense of the other. How can we save them both?"

Jeff shook his head. "I've been trying to figure that one out for months now."

"Either we destroy Altair VI and turn it into a habitable planet for the colonists," Amanda said, "or we leave the planet alone and let the colonists die in their ship."

"But they can live in that ship for a long time," Laura pointed out. "For years, can't they?"

"Yes," Carbo agreed. "But not indefinitely. The ship's supplies are limited. Its recycling equipment won't last forever."

"We're in the same boat," Jeff muttered.

"This is no time for a pun," said Amanda, grinning. Jeff shot her a puzzled frown.

"But I don't understand," Laura said, "why we can't live in the Village indefinitely. Can't we convert some of the domes into farms and grow our own food? I mean, the colonists must be bringing seed stocks and frozen livestock embryos, aren't they?"

Jeff turned in the couch to look at her. "You might as well talk about building an O'Neill colony."

"Well, why not?" Laura asked brightly.

"Because," Carbo explained, "O'Neill colonies are incredibly expensive to build. Only the very richest corporations on Earth can afford them. And once they're built, only the richest people on Earth—or the corporations' employees—are allowed to live in them."

But Laura would not be deterred. "You say we need an alternative to lay before Bishop Foy. You say we need a solution that will save both Altair VI and the colonists. So why not build an O'Neill colony here in space? It could be big enough to be a habitat for a million people or more, and it could be built to be just like Earth inside: Earth-type air, gravity, temperatures, everything!"

"It would cost hundreds of billions," Carbo insisted. "It would take years to build it."

"But it would take years to transform Altair VI, wouldn't it?"

"And it wouldn't cost hundreds of billions," Jeff said slowly, "because we don't use money here."

Carbo grumbled, "You know what I meant . . . "

"Yes," Jeff said. "You mean that we can't afford to build an O'Neill colony. But why not? What makes you think we're so poor?"

"We . . . " Carbo stopped abruptly, and stroked his chin as if lost in thought over this new idea.

Jeff said, with growing enthusiasm, "We have energy, a constant flood of energy here in orbit from Altair itself. We have raw materials from Altair's asteroid belt—the same raw materials we used to build the oxygen plants. We have a core of trained, dedicated workers right here in the Village."

"We would need thousands more workers," Carbo said.

"They're on their way," Jeff countered. "The colonists."

"But those people aren't engineers or managers. They're the poor scum of a dozen Asian cities, scooped up off the streets."

Amanda reached out and put a hand gently on Carbo's arm. "Frank, *you* were poor scum scooped off the streets, once."

His jaw dropped open. With a visible effort, he regained control of himself.

"Yes, that's right," he said softly. "But it took almost twenty years of discipline and education to turn me into a scientist."

"And you invented a device that telescopes that twenty years into—what, twenty months? Twenty weeks?"

"The neuro probe?"

Amanda nodded. "It could be the greatest educational tool in human history, Frank. If it's used properly."

"The colonists are already implanted with them," Jeff said.

"We could use them to train those people," Laura added. "Educate them. Turn them into . . ."

"No," Carbo snapped. "I won't use the probes to force people into shapes they don't wish to be."

"But what makes you think they want to be poor and ignorant?" Amanda demanded. "They'd jump at the chance to learn, to change their lives."

"Not all of them would."

"Then to hell with those who refuse!" Jeff snapped. "They're the *real* dregs and they'll be nothing but trouble no matter what we or anybody else does for them."

"But most of them will work with us," Amanda insisted. "Most of them will join us and help us to build."

"An O'Neill colony," Laura echoed.

"More than one," Jeff said. "Five of them, twenty, a hundred. Who needs to destroy an existing world when we can build brand-new ones, exactly fit for human habitation?"

For the first time, Carbo smiled. "You're crazy, all of you."

"Yes, of course," Jeff agreed. "But it will work. We can make it work."

Carbo looked at each of their faces in turn: Amanda, Laura, and Jeff. Then he reached across his desk and flicked on the phone. "Bishop Foy, please. Tell him it's urgent . . . and it's good news."

CHAPTER 27

Bishop Foy scowled at them as he sat behind his broad, massive desk.

"But how would we become land holders of an artificial colony built in space?" he demanded. "Our contract with the world government gives us title to the land of Altair VI and nothing else. Certainly we couldn't claim ownership of an O'Neill colony."

"That's right," answered Jeff. He sat in front of the Bishop's desk, with Laura on one side of him, Amanda and Dr. Carbo on the other. It had taken two full days before the Bishop would agree to meet with them. Foy had insisted that the students disband their occupation of the contact lab. They had refused. Reluctantly, Foy had finally allowed them to come to his office for a face-to-face confrontation.

"We won't own the colony," Carbo agreed. "It will belong jointly to all of us—including the colonists."

Foy grimaced. His jaws worked as if he were grinding his teeth, but he said nothing.

"I know what you're thinking," Carbo said, a soft smile lighting his swarthy face. "I am prepared to donate my personal fortune to the project. I burn my bridges behind me, just as you and all the others have been forced to do. We build this colony together and we build it to last for many, many lifetimes."

Amanda reached toward him and put her hand on his. "None of us will become rich," she said.

"Except in God's grace," Laura added.

The Bishop's face twitched. His hands began to tremble. "You . . . " His voice cracked as he visibly struggled to control himself.

"Reverend Bishop," Jeff said, as politely as he could, "we put it to a vote among the students. They have overwhelmingly approved this plan."

Carbo added, "The scientists, too. And the social technicians."

"It is not the students' prerogative," Foy said stiffly, "to decide such matters. Nor that of the scientists and social technicians whom the Church employs. Only the Elders . . . "

"The Elders may vote as you instruct them to," said Jeff. "But the scientists and the students will not continue the attempt to transform Altair VI. If necessary, we will send a message back to the Mother Church to ask for a new Council of Elders and a new Bishop."

"That's unheard of!" Foy snapped.

Jeff shrugged slightly. "So is building a new world."

The Bishop's face grew crafty. "All communications back to Earth must be approved by me."

"You're not saying that you'd interfere . . . " Laura's shocked voice halted in mid-sentence. Her face showed that she understood the Bishop's meaning quite clearly.

Jeff's hands tightened on the arms of his chair. Glaring at the Bishop, he asked softly, "Will you force us to take complete control of the Village? The comm center, all the domes? Must we lock you in your quarters?"

"That's mutiny!"

Carbo got to his feet and spread his arms, as if trying to separate the two of them. "Wait. Wait. Before we begin to say things that we will regret later, let us admit that we are at impasse."

"What good will that do?" Amanda asked.

"The colony ship is due to take up orbit in a few days. Let us agree to a truce until then. No further work on the surface of the planet. The students will go back to their own domes." Eying the Bishop, Carbo went on, "And we will all pray for guidance until we have a chance to meet the colonists and see what condition they are in."

Foy shook his head. "I don't see what good that will do."

"Frankly, neither do I," Carbo admitted cheerfully. "But it's better than fighting. Perhaps the students and the Elders can use the time to meet with each other and discuss the situation."

Understanding dawned in Amanda's dark eyes, Carbo saw. She understands what I am trying to do, he thought to himself. The students can persuade the

Elders to be more flexible than Foy would allow. We can undermine his position, given a few days' time.

But the Bishop was still adamant when the massive colony ship established itself in orbit a precise hundred kilometers behind the Village. They circled Altair VI as if linked by an invisible thread.

Captain Gunnerson and his family had brought the colony ship to Altair, and now he carried Foy, Jeff, and Carbo in a cramped shuttle rocket from the Village to the huge collection of domes that was the colony ship.

"Her name's the *Ghandi*," Gunnerson said, leaning back in his pilot's chair and puffing great clouds of blue smoke from his pipe.

The tobacco smelled awful to Jeff, and he could see that the Bishop's nose wrinkled in undisguised disgust at Gunnerson's filthy habit. Carbo, however, seemed to take some perverse pleasure in every sniff.

The three of them were sitting strapped into contoured chairs, like astronauts of old, because this shuttle used old-fashioned rocket thrusters rather than the gravity drive that propelled the bigger ships among the stars.

Gunnerson deftly docked the tiny shuttle at the *Ghandi*'s airlock, and introduced his three passengers to the world government representative who was waiting for them in the sterile, metal-walled airlock chamber.

He was a tall, fair, light-haired man named Manning. A career world government bureaucrat, he moved his lanky body slowly, his long legs and arms seeming to probe the air around him cautiously, as if afraid of bumping into something unpleasant. His voice was soft, bland, almost hypnotic.

"I can't tell you how glad I am to see you," he said in

an unemotional monotone. "We have been confined to this vehicle for four months now, and I have another four months ahead of me for the return flight. It will be so good to get back to Earth and my own home once again. Words fail me."

Jeff could not suppress a grin. "Don't you want to take a day or two to see the surface of the planet? It's very exciting."

Manning missed the humor. "No, I think not, but thank you all the same. My duty is accomplished once I have transferred the colonists to your care. I wouldn't dream of keeping Captain Gunnerson here one day longer than necessary."

"The colonists are well?" Carbo asked. "Any problems with them?"

"Oh no, none at all. They were happy to leave their wretched villages and cities. The devastation there was very intense." All in the same monotone. "We implanted them with neuro probes along the way. It took more than a month, but since then they have all been as docile as lambs."

Jeff saw Carbo wince, but the scientist said nothing.

"Well," Bishop Foy snapped, "I suppose we should meet their Council of Elders."

"Yes, by all means. Right this way."

Neither Jeff nor the others were prepared for the shock.

Manning led them to the massive inner hatch of the big airlock chamber. He touched the control button set into the gleaming metal wall and the hatch sighed softly, almost reluctantly, then slid aside.

The smell hit them first. The sour, acrid odor of too many people crowded too close together. Jeff had been expecting that the colony ship would be somewhat like the Village in its interior design. But now he saw that they were stepping out onto a metal catwalk that circled the interior of this dome. The dome itself had been partitioned into many levels, so that the maximum number of people could be squeezed into it. A dozen meters below the catwalk, on a bare metal floor that could barely be seen because of the thick throngs of people standing down there, thousands upon thousands of colonists stood, jammed shoulder to shoulder.

Men, women, children, babes in their mothers' arms, they all stood mutely, not making a sound, their big liquid eyes staring up at the catwalk and the airlock hatch, their dark faces turned upward toward Jeff and Carbo and Bishop Foy—but totally without expression, numb, paralyzed by the neuro probes that ruled out hope, erased fear, buried all expectation. Gray. Their coveralls were gray. Nothing but a sea of lifeless gray. Not a touch of color anywhere. Gray uniforms, dark skin, faces without even a spark of life to them.

Jeff could hear them breathing. He could *feel* it, almost like the sighing rhythm of the surf down on Windsong. He knew that every dome in this huge ship was layered with many decks, and each deck held thousands of colonists sandwiched between its steel plates. And all of them were standing, waiting, their minds held in paralysis by the neuro probes. None of them saying a word; just standing there, breathing and looking blankly into nothingness.

Jeff heard a gagging sound beside him and turned to see Bishop Foy's face go white. The Bishop reached out and grasped the steel railing of the catwalk with both his hands. His knees buckled. Jeff grabbed him around his frail shoulders.

"I . . . I . . . " The Bishop tried to gasp out words.

Carbo came up on his other side, his own face as white as the Bishop's, but the expression on it one of fury and self-hate.

"You were right," the Bishop said. "We must do the best we can for them. We must. God would never forgive us for anything less."

Manning seemed to politely ignore the Bishop's infirmity. "Shall I bring their Council of Elders here, do you think, or would you prefer to meet them in their own quarters?" Before anyone could answer, the bureaucrat went on, "Here is better, if you don't mind my suggesting it. Their quarters are, well, rather cramped and uncomfortable. And they all smell bad, you know."

"Are their Elders under neuro control?" Carbo snarled.

Ignoring the venom in the question, Manning answered, "No, of course not. They have been administering the controls, actually. Under my supervision, of course."

"Of course."

"Here," Bishop Foy said. "We'll . . . meet the Elders here."

Manning nodded and turned to the intercom phone set into the wall. Jeff felt the Bishop's body regain some strength. The three of them stood at the railing and stared down into the eyes of those unmoving gray masses of humanity.

"How wrong I've been," Foy muttered. "What a vain, foolish tool of pride I've been. Thank God for that stubborn conscience of yours, Holman. God has chosen you to show me the path to righteousness."

Jeff took a deep breath, his nostrils flaring slightly at the strange, almost sickening odor from the overcrowded colonists. That's as close to praise as I'll ever get from the good Bishop, he knew. And he realized that he was content with that; it was enough.

Six small, dark men clambered up a ladder and walked briskly along the catwalk to where Jeff and the others stood. They stopped a respectful five meters from the Bishop and bowed to him. As Manning introduced them, Jeff saw that each of them was of a slightly different hue, ranging from the coal-black of one of the Indians among them to the almost golden color of the one who was introduced as a Vietnamese. Their coveralls were like everyone else's, gray and devoid of decoration or any kind of insignia. But, this close, Jeff could see that they were clean and carefully pressed, even though threadbare.

"Welcome to our humble ship," said the Indian, in sing-song English. "We are enormously grateful that you have sacrificed so much merely to help us."

"No," said the Bishop, in a heartfelt tone that Jeff had never heard from him before. "It is we who must thank you for the opportunity to help do God's work."

All six of the men smiled and bowed again.

"It may be of some interest to you to know that, although the official name of this ship is the *Ghandi*, we colonists decided to give it an additional name, a more personal name, a name that meant much more to each of us. We voted on such a name—before," his voice lowered a notch, "before we had to insert the neuro probes into our brethren."

"And what name did you choose?" Bishop Foy asked.

"Hope. We call this ship, Hope."

Jeff felt as if he was going to cry. Turning away from the bowing, expectant Council, he saw that Carbo's eyes looked misty, and even Bishop Foy was blinking.

Carbo said, "We share in your hope. But we have many long years of hard work ahead of us."

"Yes, I certainly can understand that," said the Indian.

"The planet . . . " Bishop Foy began. "The planet we have all been sent to is not fit for human habitation." He said it all in a rush, as if afraid that he wouldn't have the strength to finish if he hesitated even for an instant.

The Councilmen's eyes widened. "Not fit! But how can that be?"

"What are we to do?"

"We will build our own colony," the Bishop said. His voice grew stronger, calmer. "We will build a world for ourselves, a completely Earthlike world. With God's help."

They looked at each other uneasily.

"It can be done," Carbo said. "An O'Neill-type colony, big enough to house all of us."

"But—what of children? What of the future?"

"We will build more colonies. Larger ones. It will be difficult, and we will need the help of every person among you."

"It will take an enormous amount of work," Jeff said. "You and your people will have to learn new skills, new abilities. Will you do this? Will you work with us to build a new world?"

The Indian drew himself up to his full height. Although he was a full head shorter than Jeff, he was the equal of any man there.

"Are we not human? Have we not minds and hands and hearts? Can we not be trusted to help build our own future and the future of our children?"

Jeff felt his face ease into a smile. Bishop Foy

stepped up to the six men and took each hand, in turn. "God will help us in this mighty task," he said.

But Carbo had turned to stare down at the sea of blank, dark faces once again.

"Do you really mean it?" he asked. "Do you really want to be trusted with building your own future?"

"Of course we do!"

"Then turn off the damned controls!"

They were surprised by his vehemence, but Bishop Foy explained that this was the famous Dr. Carbo who had invented the neuro-electronic probe.

"And I never meant it to be used to turn human beings into cattle," Carbo growled. "Turn it off! Let them be human beings again!"

Manning began to object. "But if we do . . ."

Carbo cut him short with a murderous glance.

"Well," Manning muttered. "It's your responsibility, isn't it?"

But he picked up the intercom phone again and spoke into it briefly. Carbo gripped the railing and stared into the crowd.

The first sound came from a baby, which cried out a bawling, tearful demand for attention. Then the entire mass of human flesh seemed to stir, to shake itself, like statues coming to life. The very air rippled, as thousands of human beings began murmuring, moving, turning to look at each other and then, one by one, craning their necks to see who was on the catwalk above them.

Carbo released his grip on the railing. Somewhere down in the crowd, someone laughed. Voices spoke, softly at first, but then louder and louder as hundreds of conversations reverberated against the curving metal walls.

And then someone, either a woman or a child, began to sing a simple Nirvan hymn. A child's prayer, set to music; the kind that mothers use for a lullaby, and all converts are taught in their earliest Church lessons.

Another voice took up the hymn, and then another until the entire mass of people were singing their praise of God and their thanks. Jeff sang it, too, although he was so choked with emotion that he could barely get the words out of his throat. Bishop Foy's voice rang out with the rest, slightly off-key but powerful and happy.

I'll have to teach Dr. Carbo the words, Jeff thought. If he'll let me.

CHAPTER 28

The great cluster of domes called the Village slowly began to spiral away from the sixth planet of Altair. A precise hundred kilometers behind it, the even larger conglomeration of domes known to its inhabitants as Hope, spun in the same looping graceful orbit.

As if leading the way, the Village headed out toward a new position in space, equidistant from Altair VI and its parent star. The scientists in the Village called their destination the Lagrangian libration point, where the Village and its accompanying colony ship Hope would take up a stable orbit around blazing Altair. The students in the Village called their destination L-5, and determined to name the first colony they built there *Gerard K. O'Neill*.

In the contact laboratory, Jeff Holman lay stretched on the couch one last time, as Amanda and Laura fastened the cuffs around his wrists and ankles, then positioned the silvery helmet on his head.

From the control room, Jeff heard Carbo saying, "We'll never find out if the wolfcats really are intelligent, if they truly have some form of communication."

"They are," Jeff called to him, "and they do."

"But we won't be able to prove it!"

"Yes we will. Later. After we've finished the first of the colonies and the colonists themselves have a good start on the next two, then we'll have the time to come back and study the wolfcats."

"And all the other creatures of Windsong," Laura added.

He tried to nod at her, but the helmet prevented his head from moving. No matter how many times I get into this rig, he laughed to himself, I always forget that it immobilizes me.

Amanda said, "Everything checks out here, Frank."

"Controls are ready."

"Are you ready, Jeff?" she asked him.

He licked his lips. "Yes."

"Okay. One last time."

"For a while."

Jeff closed his eyes as the delicate machines of silver and silicon hummed to life, sending electrons dancing through him, mating his mind, his whole nervous system with the pulsing electronic circuitry that flashed outward from the Village as it curved through space and reached toward the planet that was drifting farther and farther away from them.

One last time, Jeff thought. Soon we'll be too far from Windsong to reach Crown. One last time . . . for now.

Sitting on a wooded hilltop under the warm southern sun, looking out over the rich grassland and the forests beyond it that fed his clan, Crown felt the breeze ruffle his fur. It was a good wind, clean and strong. The strange place where the frightening pulsing metal machines and the strange alien intruders had been was already fading into the dark caves of his memory. He almost felt sad; his days of adventure and exploration were ended.

Something touched Crown, deep within his mind, and he felt a familiar thrill of inward excitement. He raised his head toward the sky and peered at the brilliant clouds that stretched from horizon to horizon. He looked for something that his eyes could never see.

But he felt the presence, a voice that spoke to him wordlessly, thoughts that went beyond words.

Goodbye, old friend . . . good hunting . . . I'll be with you again some day, but until then . . . goodbye.

The great gray wolfcat lifted his massive head toward the sky and bellowed a roar of sheer exuberance. A roar that echoed in a human mind, thousands of kilometers away.

—THE END—

POUL ANDERSON
Winner of 7 Hugos and 3 Nebulas

☐	53088-8	CONFLICT	$2.95
	53089-6	Canada	$3.50
☐	48527-1	COLD VICTORY	$2.75
☐	48517-4	EXPLORATIONS.	$2.50
☐	48515-8	FANTASY	$2.50
☐	48550-6	THE GODS LAUGHED	$2.95
☐	48579-4	GUARDIANS OF TIME	$2.95
☐	53567-7	HOKA! (with Gordon R. Dickson)	$2.75
	53568-5	Canada	$3.25
☐	48582-4	LONG NIGHT	$2.95
☐	53079-9	A MIDSUMMER TEMPEST	$2.95
	53080-2	Canada	$3.50
☐	48553-0	NEW AMERICA	$2.95
☐	48596-4	PSYCHOTECHNIC LEAGUE	$2.95
☐	48533-6	STARSHIP	$2.75
☐	53073-X	TALES OF THE FLYING MOUNTAINS	$2.95
	53074-8	Canada	$3.50
☐	53076-4	TIME PATROLMAN	$2.95
	53077-2	Canada	$3.50
☐	48561-1	TWILIGHT WORLD	$2.75
☐	53085-3	THE UNICORN TRADE	$2.95
	53086-1	Canada	$3.50
☐	53081-0	PAST TIMES	$2.95
	53082-9	Canada	$3.50

Buy them at your local bookstore or use this handy coupon:
Clip and mail this page with your order

TOR BOOKS—Reader Service Dept.
49 W. 24 Street, 9th Floor, New York, NY 10010

Please send me the book(s) I have checked above. I am enclosing
$_____ (please add $1.00 to cover postage and handling).
Send check or money order only—no cash or C.O.D.'s.

Mr./Mrs./Miss _____

Address _____

City _____ State/Zip _____

Please allow six weeks for delivery. Prices subject to change without
notice.

Ben Bova

☐	53200-7	AS ON A DARKLING PLAIN		$2.95
	53201-5		Canada	$3.50
☐	53217-1	THE ASTRAL MIRROR		$2.95
	53218-X		Canada	$3.50
☐	53212-0	ESCAPE PLUS		$2.95
	53213-9		Canada	$3.50
☐	53221-X	GREMLINS GO HOME		$2.75
	53222-8	(with Gordon R. Dickson)	Canada	$3.25
☐	53215-5	ORION		$3.50
	53216-3		Canada	$3.95
☐	53210-4	OUT OF THE SUN		$2.95
	53211-2		Canada	$3.50
☐	53223-6	PRIVATEERS		$3.50
	53224-4		Canada	$4.50
☐	53208-2	TEST OF FIRE		$2.95
	53209-0		Canada	$3.50

Buy them at your local bookstore or use this handy coupon:
Clip and mail this page with your order

TOR BOOKS—Reader Service Dept.
49 W. 24th Street, 9th Floor, New York, NY 10010

Please send me the book(s) I have checked above. I am enclosing
$_____ (please add $1.00 to cover postage and handling).
Send check or money order only—no cash or C.O.D.'s.

Mr./Mrs./Miss _____
Address _____
City _____ State/Zip _____
Please allow six weeks for delivery. Prices subject to change without
notice.